By CINDY DEES

STUD GAMES
Poker Face
Dead Man's Hand
Showdown

Published by DREAMSPINNER PRESS
www.dreamspinnerpress.com

SHOWDOWN

CINDY DEES

Published by
DREAMSPINNER PRESS

5032 Capital Circle SW, Suite 2, PMB# 279, Tallahassee, FL 32305-7886 USA
www.dreamspinnerpress.com

Showdown
© 2020 Cindy Dees

Cover Art
© 2020 L.C. Chase
http://www.lcchase.com
Cover content is for illustrative purposes only and any person depicted on the cover is a model.

Trade Paperback ISBN: 978-1-64405-248-8
Digital ISBN: 978-1-64405-247-1
Library of Congress Control Number: 2020936006
Trade Paperback published October 2020
First Edition
v. 1.0
Previously published by Dreamspinner Press as *All In* by Ava Drake, July 2017.

Printed in the United States of America
∞
This paper meets the requirements of
ANSI/NISO Z39.48-1992 (Permanence of Paper).

CHAPTER ONE

"C'MON, C'MON, c'mon. Spit out my bag." Zane Stryker glared at the luggage carousel as if he could will his suitcase into existence—the suitcase carrying all his hopes and dreams. His last shot at catching the eye of a major fashion house.

He was tired, grimy, sore from sleeping bent in all the wrong ways in a middle seat in coach on a nine-hour flight from Milan to New York. He wanted his luggage, a hot shower, a meal, and about twelve hours of uninterrupted sleep. In that order. Starting now.

The shiny metal flaps of the luggage conveyor belt ground to an uncaring halt, empty but for a single bedraggled black duffel bag that bore no resemblance to his navy blue hard-sided suitcase.

He'd poured every last dollar he had into the wardrobe in that suitcase. The clothes were hip and chic—retro design, fashion forward—sure to impress the shit out of the condescending twelve-year-olds the major fashion houses would assign to hiring runway models for the upcoming season. He needed those clothes, dammit.

Zane spied a troll in an airline uniform clumping toward the abandoned duffel bag. He moved forward to intercept the guy. "Excuse me. My bag either isn't here, or you've managed to make it invisible."

"Talk to the people in the baggage claim office," the troll droned. "Past baggage carousel number eight."

Right. The panic becoming real, he hurried over to the glass-windowed office and the line of pissed-off people bitching randomly at one another about how bad air travel sucked. He bit back an urge to suggest that if they hated flying so much, they could have crossed the Atlantic to New York in a ship like people used to. *May they all get scurvy and their teeth fall out.*

The flat leather portfolio that held his best photos was tucked safely under his arm, at any rate. Hell, he would rather lose his passport than lose those.

After the woman in front of him tried unsuccessfully for *Ten. Fucking. Minutes.* to get the airline to replace a guitar case that had obviously been decrepit well before it boarded the flight to JFK, it was finally his turn.

He handed his bag tag to a clerk, who looked harassed enough that Zane actually felt a frisson of sympathy for her. She typed into her computer. Frowned.

Nonononono. No frowns where his suitcase was concerned. He needed expansive smiles of relief and reassuring words of having found his bag to flow from her ruby lips. *C'mon, sweetheart. Gimme some love, here.*

She typed again. Frowned again.

Shit.

"Would you come with me, sir?" she asked.

"You found my bag?" he asked hopefully.

"Please come with me."

The woman led him down a hallway into the utilitarian, grease-scented guts of the airport and gestured for him to go into a room crammed with what looked like lost and unclaimed luggage.

Cripes. He hadn't packed anything illegal in his bag, had he? A drug-sniffing dog hadn't hit on his suitcase, had it? It had been years since he'd snorted cocaine, and he didn't even take pulls on joints when someone passed him weed anymore. Frantically, he reviewed his possessions. No guns, knives, explosives, aerosols, batteries, or anti-American propaganda. What, then?

Ominously, the luggage clerk of the ruby lips didn't go in with him. He stepped into the storage room, which was crowded with suitcases of every size and shape, standing on the floor in messy rows and shoved onto stacks of tall metal shelves. Two men stood in the room, staring suspiciously at him.

One wore a rumpled khaki airline employee's uniform and had the dull expression of a man with a low-double-digit IQ. The other one, though....

Brioni twill, two-button suit in classic charcoal gray. Size 44, tailored in at the waist. A cool five grand for the jacket alone. Trousers, 34 long, also custom-tailored. Another grand. Custom-made Italian leather oxfords. Three grand-ish, more or less, depending on the maker. The tie, a bold red pattern on silk, had to be Roberto Cavalli. But Zane didn't recognize the pattern, and he'd worked the photo shoot for this season's collection. Custom-designed, then. No telling how much *that* had cost.

He lifted his gaze to the man's face, and swear to God, his heart skipped a beat. *Those eyes.*

There were blue eyes, and then there were *blue* eyes. These were Kodachrome cobalt, so brilliant they would leap off the pages of a magazine. And the face to go with them was arresting.

Square jaw, strong nose, chiseled cheekbones. Brows in need of a little shaping. Skin tanned, in need of a moisturizing facial, but otherwise great. Two, maybe three days' growth of dark whiskers to go with brunet hair so thick and touchable it hurt to look at. He wasn't a pretty man the way high-fashion models were beautiful, but he was so damned compelling, Zane couldn't even think about looking away.

"Are you Mr. Stryker?" Blue Eyes asked.

Fuck me now. That voice. Deep. Rich and raspy. Confident as hell. Commanding. Zane's knees turned to jelly and his gut turned to water. "I am Zane Stryker. And you are?"

"Sebastian Gigoni."

"You got called gigolo a lot as a kid, didn't you?" The words were out of his mouth before he could stop them. Jesus. It was probably a really stupid idea to flirt with a hot-as-shit fed, or whatever kind of law enforcement official he was.

A disgusted look flashed through those bluer-than-blue eyes.

Good job, Zane. Piss off the guy who can toss your ass in jail and throw away the key. Hell, the guy was probably straighter than a highway across a desert. In a bid to keep his ass out of jail, he said with what he hoped didn't come across as forced cheerfulness, "So, I lost my bag. The lady at the counter said it would be in here. How do I go about claiming it? Here's my tag." He held out the narrow strip of waxed paper with its printed barcode.

The airline dude—middle-aged, medium build, with thinning hair, and in every way unremarkable—said, "Can you describe your bag?"

"Large. Navy blue. Four wheels. Hard sides. It has a black leather Valentino luggage strap around it. Oh, and there's a glue stain on the top. I don't know what they use to put on destination stickers in Hong Kong, but I haven't been able to get that stuff off the bag."

Sebastian nodded to the baggage guy, who said, "Come with me."

What the hell? He followed the airline employee to the back of the room and into a small, stuffy office with a glass window looking out on the holding room they'd just left. A plain table stood in the middle, and beside it stood his suitcase.

Thank God. The life savings he'd invested in the clothes in that bag, each piece strategically chosen to hide the signs of his age, came close to ten grand. A matter of weeks away from turning thirty, he desperately needed to work the runways for one last season. And this time he was going to save every damned penny he could and not walk away from this business broke and broken.

"What's inside?" Baggage Dude asked.

"Clothes. Two Italian suits that are going to need steaming, four dress shirts, a half-dozen hand-painted T-shirts. Some polo shirts. A pair of Saint Laurent couture slim-fit jeans." They cost three grand new, but he'd lucked into a pair at a thrift shop in Milan whose owner didn't realize what he had. Zane had picked them up for the equivalent of about forty dollars. *Score.* "Underwear. Socks. Razor. Blow dryer—I can give you a complete inventory if you need it."

"No. That's enough," Luggage Lout replied.

Brioni Suit, who'd followed them into the room, crowding it with his large frame and larger presence, said, "Would you mind opening the bag to show us the contents?"

"No problem."

The airline employee lifted the suitcase onto the table, and Zane unbuckled the strap, unlatched the top, and threw it open—

"What the fuck?" he exclaimed.

Where were his clothes?

He stared down at the mostly empty suitcase. In place of his things—of *all* his things—lay one dark, carefully folded suit with a slim brown leather briefcase strapped down on top of it.

"Is that suit yours?" Sebastian asked.

"Never seen it before in my life. That briefcase isn't mine either. This can't be my bag."

Airline Guy flipped the lid down and compared Zane's luggage claim tag to the one on the bag. "It's yours. Numbers and bar codes match. Your name's on the tag for this bag. It even has the glue stain you described."

"Well, yeah. It's my suitcase. But all my stuff is gone. I've been robbed." A stream of mental cursing, born of desperation, erupted in his brain.

"So you're saying these are not your possessions?" Sebastian asked.

"That's what I said," he answered impatiently. His mind was already racing ahead to how in the hell he was going to get clothes to go on auditions for runway work. The go-sees were already starting and would be done for the season in less than two weeks. He couldn't even get a job and a first paycheck in time to buy a decent suit. Thank God he'd carried his portfolio onto the plane by hand, but this was an unmitigated disaster!

"…leave us alone for a moment, please," Sebastian was saying to the baggage handler.

Zane's attention snapped back to the beautiful stranger as the door clicked shut, closeting the two of them alone in the tiny room with his suitcase between them on the table. Any other day, any other situation but this, and he would definitely be throwing out hints to Tall, Dark, and Dangerous that he was single, ready to mingle, and kinky enough to try pretty much anything the man had in mind.

Instead, he let the panic he was feeling creep into his eyes and prayed this man realized how sincere it was.

"Mr. Stryker, I have reason to believe the contents of your suitcase contain illegal contraband. In the absence of you producing a compelling story for how that briefcase and its contents came into your possession, Customs agents are going to come in here in a few minutes, go through the motions of questioning you, and arrest you. You're headed for federal prison to serve hard time for a significant chunk of the rest of your life."

Zane's mind went blank. Utterly, blue-screen-of-doom blank.

"Do you understand me?" Sebastian asked.

Prison? Him? It would be a death sentence. But he hadn't done anything wrong!

"Do you understand?"

"Yes. Wait, no." Finding his voice at last, he burst out, "No, I don't understand at all! That's my suitcase, but the stuff inside it isn't mine. I've never seen it before! I swear. You have to believe me—"

Sebastian cut him off, speaking low and urgent. "Look. I do believe you."

"Who are you?" Zane blurted.

Without answering Zane's question, Sebastian continued, "I'm here to help you. But I need you to help me first. I've got to get you, your bag, and its contents out of here. I had to pull a lot of strings to get your luggage through border control and put in here without you having to walk it through Customs."

"Whoa. You're not some sort of drug dealer, are you? Did you make me some sort of unwitting mule for your shit? I don't appreciate being used like that, and I'm not letting you ruin my life—"

"It's not drugs," Gigoni interrupted sharply.

"Is the contraband yours?" he demanded.

"No!" Another sharp denial that sounded authentic.

"Lawyer?" he tried.

"God, no. Think of me as a fixer."

"A what? I don't understand—"

"I know you don't. I'll explain everything later. Until then, I need you to trust me long enough to get you and your suitcase out of here. Can you do that?"

"Do I have any choice?"

He shrugged under the perfectly tailored shoulder of the Brioni suit. "Sure. I can hand you over to Customs and you can go to jail… for a long time."

"But I didn't do anything wrong!"

"That's your suitcase. You admitted in front of witnesses that it was yours. And inside it is something that will put you in jail for decades. You're royally screwed, my friend."

"What's in the briefcase?"

"Later. Yes or no. Will you help me help you?"

CHAPTER TWO

SEBASTIAN STUDIED the freaked-out man before him. He'd seen some beautiful human beings in his day, but this guy was in a class of his own. His hair was light brown streaked with honey gold, and his eyes were pale green and intense as hell. The guy's facial structure was a sculptor's wet dream.

Zane Stryker was around five foot ten, lean to the point of being spare, and everything about him—the way he moved his hands, the way he carried himself, even the way he turned his head—was elegant. It was no stretch at all to see the guy as a male model or movie star.

Envy stabbed Sebastian in the gut, shocking him into stillness. This Stryker guy oozed class and breeding from every pore. He was everything Sebastian had aspired to be as a poor kid growing up on the tough streets of East London and couldn't have been further from. God knew he'd thrown a fortune at polishing the pig's ear that he was, but he would never achieve the easy, breezy sophistication of Zane Stryker, no matter how many billions he earned nor how many of those billions he threw at adorning himself in wealth.

Right now, however, he had no time for pondering class divisions. He had to get Stryker and that suitcase out of here before they both fell into the hands of the US government. While Uncle Sam would be delighted to seize the contents of the briefcase, the feds wouldn't have any idea what they really had in their possession.

Now was not the moment to stop everything to explain to the feds what they had. Right now it was more time critical that this op run its course than it was to bring the federal government up to speed and run the gauntlet of bureaucracy and paperwork necessary to sanction an official operation on American soil.

Local authorities would have no idea that the contraband represented bait to catch a shadowy criminal organization his former employer and good friend had been chasing for years. An organization that desperately needed to be stopped. Hell, he'd come out of retirement from the security business to help out.

Compliments of an inside informant who'd risked his life to smuggle out a massive cache of information and bank account numbers, Interpol had just made a huge bust. They'd seized most of the group's cash assets and shut down its Asian operations, nabbing most of its smuggling and drug production assets in the process. The crime ring had taken a major hit both in cash and personnel. But lions were the most dangerous of all when they were wounded. And this lion was bleeding profusely at the moment.

The contents of this suitcase represented the tip of the spear that was going to deliver the killing blow.

He spoke urgently. "Listen, Zane. The baggage guy is going to be back in a minute with airport security cops. We may need to move fast, so keep up with me if I take off. Got it?"

"Umm, yeah, I guess so—"

He hated running roughshod over the guy like this, giving him no time and no information with which to make a decision. But they were out of time. Stryker had to go with him now, or everything he and his colleagues had worked so hard for would be lost.

"Grab the bag," he ordered. "I'll check the hallway."

Sebastian peered around the doorframe into the long hall outside the baggage holding room while Zane closed the bag and rolled it to the door. Sebastian murmured over his shoulder, "We're clear. Let's go."

He moved fast, his legs churning up the linoleum. Zane kept up easily, except of course his stride looked like it came straight off a fashion runway, an aggressive, stalking prowl made to draw attention. If they could just get into a public space with lots of people, maybe they could blend into a crowd. Or at worst, lots of camera phones would be there to record any potential confrontation with anyone who might try to question them as they walked that suitcase out of the baggage holding area.

Of course, the worst-case scenario wasn't the police, or even the bag and its contents being seized by the feds. He was actually more worried that whoever had used Zane's bag to smuggle something into New York would try to reclaim it right here at the airport.

It was the reason Peregrine Cardiffe, one of the founders of Wild Cards, Inc., had called and asked him to meet this young man at JFK and spirit both him and his luggage away from the airport safely. Some years ago, before he'd immigrated to America to start a new life, Sebastian had worked for Wild Cards and could handle himself in a tough situation. Where he came from, kids learned to fight early, and after the SAS had honed his skills, Wild Cards had adapted them into the lethal package of a high-end bodyguard.

Under his breath he muttered, "Pick up the pace."

Thank God. When they burst out into the main baggage claim area, two luggage carousels were rolling and a crowd filled the space. He and Zane wound through the mob, weaving quickly toward the exit. He didn't bother looking back over his shoulder to see if they'd been pursued. He wasn't stopping either way. Sometimes the best defense was to run like hell and hope the other guy wasn't fast enough to catch up....

He fished his phone out of his pocket and speed-dialed his driver. "Have the car in front of the exit by carousel eight and ready to pull out in about thirty seconds. I'll get my own door. You be ready to rock and roll."

They burst out into the muggy heat of a morning promising to age into a sweltering afternoon. The black town car was only a few yards away, and he threw the back door open for Zane. "Get in."

Two cops were just coming out of the terminal. Zane shoved the bag inside, leaped in after it, and Sebastian used his body to block both bag and man from the view of the police. He forced himself to climb in the car calmly. As if he hadn't a care in the world. Hell, as if he owned the world. Mustn't alert the cops to anything unusual.

Yanking the door shut, he ordered Etienne, his driver, "Go. But drive casual."

The town car pulled out smoothly into traffic.

"Are they going to stop us before we leave the airport?" Etienne asked calmly.

Sebastian snorted. He'd like to see the airport cops try to stop Etienne Souvant. The guy was former French Foreign Legion and a trained combat driver. Rumor in Sebastian's SAS unit was that Etienne had been a wheelman for bank robbers. When he finished serving a prison sentence, he'd chosen to join the Foreign Legion to get his life back on track. "Get off of JFK property as fast as you can without getting pulled over for speeding."

"I'll do what I can, Seb, but the traffic's a bitch this morning."

"When isn't it a bitch?" he replied dryly.

Etienne met his gaze in the rearview mirror, and crinkles appeared around his eyes. That was as close to an actual smile as Etienne ever came.

"Do your best, Etienne."

"You got it, boss."

The vehicle changed lanes aggressively.

Dammit, he should have known better than to give Etienne permission to drive like a maniac. The guy had cut his driving teeth in Paris, for fuck's sake... possibly a worse city than New York to drive in.

The limo swerved again, this time throwing Sebastian against Zane. Hard.

He caught himself with one arm against the far door and one on the back of the seat, bracketing Zane in his grasp. For his part, Zane threw up his hands, which landed on each of Sebastian's flexed biceps.

Zane exhaled hard, letting out a breathy "Wow" that he heartily seconded.

Up close, Zane's eyes were the color of new leaves in spring, and every bit as dewy and clear. His eyelashes were long and dark too, which made his eyes look even brighter. And the man's skin was like freaking satin. So smooth—

Okay, since when did he notice complexions? People's names, and details like hair color or height, he remembered. But not their flawless skin.

He realized with a start that his right thigh was resting intimately between both of Zane's and that his crotch was dangerously close to rubbing on the man's upper thigh.

He also noticed that their bodies, so different, fit like yin and yang, light and dark. Their legs tangled as the town car lurched again, knocking him sideways until he literally sprawled on top of Zane, their hips and shoulders rubbing suggestively.

And, oh God, their junk rubbed together too.

His cock leaped to eager awareness. In fact, his entire body did the same, as he was abruptly and vividly aware of the lithe body pressing against his. Zane might run lean, but he was vibrant and warm and vital. It felt as if a bolt of electricity ran through him, originating somewhere in the vicinity of Zane's private parts.

Wild. And intense. And sexy as ever-loving hell.

Sebastian stared down at Zane staring back up at him, wide-eyed. *And aware.*

He wasn't crazy about that electricity thing. Zane felt it too.

And, shockingly, the guy seemed interested in it. In him.

A shudder passed through him. *God.* He was a rough-edged, working-class joe at his core... and here he was, imagining rubbing shoulders with this man? Greed to make an elegant man like this the crowning jewel of all his possessions surged through him. It would announce to the world that he'd made it. That he'd crawled out of the manure pile of his early life and joined the elite, the smart, the suave, the upper crust of society.

And as quickly as the impulse came over him, it passed. *Too much.* It was way too much to hope for. One of the few pieces of advice he retained from his mother was not to reach too high in life. For that way lay disappointment and humiliation. God knew life had taught him the truth of that observation over and over.

He'd learned a long time ago that hope led to disappointment, disappointment led to emotional weakness, and emotional weakness led to failure, loss, and pain.

"Sorry," he muttered. He flexed his biceps and realized Zane's fingers were wrapped around them, measuring their circumference. He pushed off the car's side door and Zane's hands fell away.

Awkwardly, he untangled his leg from over Zane's, yanked his foot out from under the damned suitcase, and dug Zane's shoulder out of his biceps. He registered the loss of the physical contact between them as actual pain. It coursed through his body, a cold ache of loneliness and isolation.

They moved to neutral sides of the back seat, both of their backs pressed up against the side doors as if they were afraid to share the same air, let alone touch each other again. The suitcase sat accusingly on the floor between them, and bolts of electricity shot all over the place like a Van de Graaff generator run amok. Good Lord, the magnetism of the guy's looks—

Stop it. Zane Stryker was a job. Or more accurately, a favor owed. Payback for Peregrine Cardiffe saving his ass a few years back from a would-be blackmailer. He'd gotten careless, and a paparazzo had taken photos of Sebastian out on a date with a man in a Manhattan nightclub. His date had preferred not to come out to his family, so a key to an apartment had been obtained, a quick search ensued, pictures had been deleted from a phone, and the problem had gone away. No drama—that was the unofficial mantra of Wild Cards, Inc. Just do the job and fade quietly into the night.

"Where are we going?" Zane asked, startling Sebastian out of his turbulent thoughts.

"For the moment, we're going away from the airport and the threat of your bag being confiscated and you arrested."

"Why shouldn't I talk to the feds and explain that I've been robbed? I should turn the stuff in my bag over to them, shouldn't I?"

"Under normal circumstances, yes. But these aren't normal circumstances. And before you ask why not, I'll explain when we get to somewhere private where we can take a look at what's in your suitcase."

"Why are you doing this for me?"

"I'm not doing it for you. I owe a friend a favor, and he asked me to extricate you and your bag from Customs and deliver you to the city."

"Is your friend the bastard who stole my clothes and left his contraband in their place?"

"No. It's a wee bit more complicated than that." Not to mention this civilian didn't need to know all the details.

"Who is your friend?" Zane persisted.

"No one you'd know."

"Then why would your friend send you to rescue me?"

"Not you. Your bag."

Expectant silence filled the back of the car. Eventually Zane said, "Well?"

"Well what?"

"Well, what's the big deal with my stupid suitcase? We've already established that I've never even seen the suit and briefcase. Speaking of which, what's inside the briefcase? Is that what all this fuss is about?"

He stared at Zane and said candidly, "I honestly don't know what's in the attaché." He added under his breath, "But I bloody well plan to find out. This could all be a big fat fuss over nothing."

"It's not nothing. Someone stole all my clothes, and I need them! I start go-sees in a few days for the fall season."

"Go-sees?"

"Fashion-industry term. They're job interviews for runway models. You go see the designers, and they put their clothes on you to see how they look."

Sebastian frowned, confused. "Then why would what you wear matter? Aren't you going to put on their clothes anyway?"

"I'm not just selling my body to be a walking mannequin. I'm selling a vibe. A style. I have to be so cool and trendy that if I'm seen wearing a designer's clothes, their line or their name will be cooler and trendier because I endorsed it. The clothes—and me in them—will be seen in public when I make appearances at clubs or restaurants, or even at the designer's storefront."

"Sounds like a lot of work."

"It is. I can't be just a model. I have to be *relevant*. On point at all times. A trendsetter, not just one of the crowd of wannabes who follow along imitating people like me."

"Sounds like a lot of pressure and expectations to put on the models."

"Welcome to the high-fashion industry," Zane replied a shade bitterly.

"Then why do you do it?" He might as well have asked Zane why he bothered to breathe, based on the withering stare of *It's totally obvious, you moron* he got in response to his question.

Whatever. Basing an entire career on how cool one could look escaped him. But then, the whole fascination with social media pretty much passed him right by too. He liked his privacy and, furthermore, didn't give a damn what anyone else thought about him.

Still. Real careers were about making money. Achieving success. Security. Having something to show for his hard work. Like his real estate holdings. They were about to cross the one-billion-dollar valuation milestone he'd been working toward for his entire life. It was the only thing he'd ever wanted. To be rich. Really rich. Worth a billion dollars. That was his magic number.

Zane was speaking. "...don't suppose there's any chance my clothes can be recovered, is there? I spent a lot of time and money curating that collection."

"Not likely on your clothes. Sorry." He paused, then added, "Curating? Isn't that what art collectors do?"

"Same diff. My clothes are my art."

He shook his head. "Crazy. I never thought of fashion as anything other than covering to keep my body warm or not naked in public."

"Then why do you wear expensive designer suits and Italian shoes?"

He shrugged. "The uniform required of my job. Other people expect it of me."

"Darling, give me one day to walk you through the top fashion designs and dress you, really dress you, and explain the nuance of men's fashion, and I'll change your mind... no, I'll change your life."

He could think of a few ways Zane could change his life, but they mostly involved taking clothes off, not putting clothes on.

"How did you know to come meet me, anyway?" Zane demanded.

The guy was chatty when he wasn't scared shitless he was about to be hauled off to jail, apparently. Personally, Sebastian ran more to the taciturn. But then, he also lived alone and did much of his work alone.

He answered evasively, "I got a tip. From a friend." Whom he had no interest in naming. The less this model knew about the crime syndicate, the better.

Possibly Zane himself was involved. Just because the guy protested convincingly that he had no idea what was going on, that didn't make it the truth. Was he working with somebody to act as a courier, perhaps?

Of course, it was possible the actual smuggled goods were in the another suitcase with Zane's achingly cool clothes. This suitcase could be the dummy luggage. But until he knew that for sure, he had to proceed as if this one held something highly illegal.

He had to admit, it was a clever tactic. Had their informant inside Erebus not passed them an urgent message to intercept this particular suitcase, neither Wild Cards nor any federal agency in the States would have had any idea.

His money was on drugs. Maybe some new additive to enhance the high of the usual addictive chemicals. He'd heard rumors of a type of fentanyl that was impervious to Narcan—the usual antidote to an opioid overdose. Users were often furious that the police or medical personnel interrupted their highs by administering doses of Narcan. For hard-core addicts, a Narcan-proof fentanyl would be attractive.

And it would be a nightmare to law enforcement agencies and medical services—

"You still haven't told me where we're going," Zane challenged, interrupting his grim train of thought.

That wasn't a question, so he chose not to respond to it.

As the highway rose out of a concrete canyon and topped a rise next to a sprawling cemetery, the skyline of Manhattan loomed in front of them.

Rather than get quizzed further on their destination, he took control of the conversation. "Where are you staying, Zane?"

Zane shrugged evasively. "I haven't nailed anything down. I'll call a friend, maybe. I know loads of people in town. Lots of them have spare couches."

Wow. Sebastian hadn't sofa surfed since he'd first arrived in New York, a lifetime ago. When he was poor and hungry... and full of dreams, ambitious as hell, and determined to succeed.

If what Pere thought was in this suitcase turned out to be there, Sebastian needed to determine how Zane was involved. If the guy wasn't involved at all, it would be his job to impress upon Zane how critical his silence was to his continued breathing. Or, if he was a knowing accomplice of the bad guys, Sebastian would make the call to the Wild Cards to handle him.

But that was a problem for later. After he'd gained Zane's cooperation for long enough to recover the contents of the bag. Then he would figure out how deeply implicated Zane actually was.

If, in fact, Zane was an innocent in this whole mess, he felt bad for the guy. Whoever had swiped Zane's luggage and replaced his possessions with that briefcase had dragged the guy into a hell of a mess. And if Zane *was* in on it, Sebastian had no qualms about making the man's life a living hell. If the informant was correct, Zane and the suitcase were the only direct links to a dangerous and shadowy criminal empire that spanned the globe. He would break Zane and make the man sing like an opera star before he was done with him.

But until he knew which way Zane Stryker fell in this whole scenario, he would withhold judgment and play him as required to get what he needed from the guy.

To that end, he smiled winningly at the model, huddling miserably across the car, his arms wrapped around his middle as if he was considering puking his guts up.

He said as warmly as he could pitch his gruff voice to sound, "I've got an account with a very private, very upscale hotel downtown. Why don't I grab a room there for us? It's close by, and we can have some privacy to examine the contents of your luggage."

"What the hell are you expecting to find inside?" Zane burst out. "Dynamite?"

Huh. Political dynamite, maybe. If Pere was right about the contents, actual TNT would be a relief.

Etienne pulled the car to a stop in front of a very upscale hotel indeed, and came around to get the passenger door. Sebastian climbed out, and a bellhop leaped forward to take the suitcase Zane handed out.

"No," Sebastian said sharply. "I've got it."

Zane stepped out, and several heads turned his way. Men and women alike stared appreciatively at him. Zane was gracious enough to wait for a few cell phones to whip out and snap photos. But then he donned a pair of dark sunglasses, even though the hotel entrance was in shade. Almost reluctantly, the gawkers resumed their regularly scheduled lives and moved on down the sidewalk.

But as quickly as the first batch of people moved on, a new batch stopped and stared.

Damn. That was some effect he had on folks.

"C'mon, Elvis. Let's get you inside where you won't stop traffic and cause accidents."

"Elvis?" Zane murmured. "As in Elvis Presley? I don't look anything like him. He had that whole rockabilly hick vibe going. And that hair…." He shuddered. "Atrocious by today's standards."

"Okay, in the first place, you're going to hell for daring to criticize the King," Sebastian declared darkly. "In the second place, he was famous for causing huge traffic jams when everyone stopped to stare at him."

Zane sniffed. "Fine. I'm not insulted by that comparison."

If he'd known the man better, he'd have told him not to be such a diva. But as it was, he still needed Zane's cooperation for a little while.

The bell captain personally held the door for Sebastian, who followed Zane into the opulent lobby.

The front desk manager came out from behind his desk. "Welcome back, Mr. Gigoni. Will you and your guest be staying with us tonight?"

They were on his turf now. Zane might stop traffic with his looks, but Sebastian stopped the staff of entire hotels with his checkbook. He supposed it was a fair tradeoff. If he had to choose between good looks and a huge bank account, he would take the latter.

"Hello, Herman," he said warmly. "How are Miranda and the kids?"

"Fine, sir. Thanks for remembering them and asking."

He clasped the front desk manager's elbow warmly. "My guest will, indeed, be spending the night. Is there by any chance a suite available for immediate check-in?"

"We've always got room for you, Mr. Gigoni. Will a presidential suite be acceptable? If you need something larger or one of the penthouses, we can accommodate you in a few hours."

"A presidential will be fine."

"Of course, sir."

One thing people in this town did well was suck up to fat wallets. Secretly, it still gave him immense satisfaction to be perceived as suck-up-to-worthy. He tried damned hard to remember his roots and never become insufferable about his wealth, of course. But getting great service everywhere he went was definitely one of the best perks of success. Money did indeed buy convenience, even if it didn't buy happiness.

Interestingly enough, Zane seemed neither intimidated by his surroundings nor fazed by people staring at him. In a matter of seconds, a suite attendant came around the front desk with plastic room keys in hand and personally led them to the elevators.

The attendant opened the suite's door for them and handed over the keys, then backed out discreetly, closing the door behind him.

Zane stopped in the entry and took in the palatial furnishings. "Holy overkill, Sebastian. I can't afford this place."

"No worries. It's on me."

"A place like this is way classier than I'm accustomed to."

"Really?" Sebastian blurted. "It's the only kind of place I can picture you in."

"Aww, thanks, boo." Zane gifted him with a smile so perfect it was almost too dazzlingly white and even to look at.

Sebastian added dryly, "Think of it as a thank-you in advance for cooperating with me."

"Cooperating with what?"

"Let's open the suitcase and see what's inside. If it becomes necessary, I'll answer that question afterward."

"Let's do it on the table," Zane purred.

Sebastian's gaze snapped to the model's. Smartass was smirking. He'd meant that double entendre. In response, Sebastian rolled his eyes. He never had been any good at casual flirtation, and he wasn't interested in taking it up as a hobby at this late date.

Zane lifted the suitcase onto the antique french dining room table. "Should I open it?"

Sebastian shrugged. "It was already opened at the airport and nothing bad happened. I'd say you're safe to pop the lid again."

Zane hesitated for a moment, exhaled hard, and opened it. He stepped back quickly, gesturing for Sebastian to have at the contents. "Feel free to blow yourself up. As for me, I'm going over here out of the blast zone."

"Technically, this entire suite is within the blast zone if there's a bomb in there," Sebastian corrected absently as he checked carefully for booby traps on the briefcase and spotted nothing. "What you want to be outside of is the kill zone."

"I don't give a crap about dying, man, but I *cannot* afford to disfigure my face."

Sebastian snorted. *Pretty boy.*

"Is there really a bomb in there?" Zane called from the vicinity of the kitchen.

"Nah. This bag has been x-rayed and sniffed by bomb dogs in Milan and at JFK. There's nothing explosive in here."

"You mean nothing that dogs have been trained to detect or that the machines have been programmed to detect."

"Bit of conspiracy theorist, are you?" he called. Although Zane did have a point. Not to mention long habits and an abundance of caution made Sebastian take all the precautions of checking for an explosive device.

He carefully unbuckled the nylon straps holding down the briefcase. All clear. He lifted out the briefcase and set it on the table. Still no nasty surprises. It looked like a regular leather attaché case. Nice one, though. Fine leather, slim design. Very classy. He removed the suit next and held it up.

"Nice suit. Armani couture. Spring season this year," Zane announced from the dining room doorway.

"How in the hell can you tell that?" Sebastian demanded. It was a dark suit. Made of... suit stuff. It had sleeves and lapels. The pants had legs and a zipper. As pants did.

Zane snorted. "I can tell that's Armani the same way you'd tell a Ford from a Chevy. By looking at it. The lapel shape, cut of the body, buttonhole and pocket placements—it's obviously Armani."

"If you say so." Sebastian lifted out a dress shirt made of cotton so fine even he could tell it was a top-end designer shirt. Same with the light gray silk tie. He knew silk because Special Forces types used a lot of it in ropes and fabrics. It was strong stuff. Light. Useful.

He dug in the suitcase's interior side pockets and found black dress socks and a pair of narrow, elegant dress shoes. Mr. Fashionista could probably name who'd made those too. All Sebastian could identify was that they were black and leather. Only thing the wearer of this suit would have to provide was boxers or briefs. Personally, he was a boxer guy. Zane, however, struck him as a leopard-print spandex thong type—

Nope, nope, nope. Not gonna speculate on the possible smuggler's underwear type.

"Are you ever going to look in the damned briefcase, or am I going to have to do it?" Zane demanded.

"Let me. It could be trapped."

"As in rigged to blow up?" Zane squawked. "I thought you said it was all x-rayed and sniffed!"

"A booby trap doesn't have to be that dramatic. But there could be, for example, an acid packet inside. It could be rigged to empty on the contents of the bag, or a small fire could break out that would burn up all the papers inside."

"How in the hell do you know about stuff like that? You're not a cop, are you?"

"I never said anything about who I am."

"Well, who are you, then?"

"I already answered that. Don't like to repeat myself."

"I don't know whether to laugh at you or run screaming," Zane declared, staring at him doubtfully.

"I get that reaction a lot from people."

"Should I stand back while you open the briefcase?"

"That might be a good idea." Not because he seriously thought the thing was going to blow up, but because he didn't necessarily want Zane to see the contents.

Sebastian laid the slim briefcase on its side. The brown glove leather was smooth under his fingertips. Cautiously he snapped open the twin brass latches and lifted the lid a millimeter. Nothing. He opened it another two millimeters and poked in a nickel-size dental mirror on a long handle and had a look around the edges of the case. Still nothing. He opened the case all the way and looked down.

It wasn't empty. Far from it.

He stared down at the contents in a combination of dismay, shock, and awe, and breathed, "Son of a bitch."

CHAPTER THREE

CURIOSITY KILLING him, Zane leaned around the doorjamb to peek into the briefcase. It was filled with a piece of gray foam. A pair of shallow cutouts in the foam cradled two pieces of wood cut in the shape of plaques. "Are you kidding me? Someone stole everything I own to get a pair of wall plaques into the country?"

He stepped forward and looked at the metal plates screwed onto each piece of wood. "Annual sales awards for office products? Are you *fucking* kidding me?"

Sebastian grunted. "Don't believe everything you see."

"What do you mean?"

He watched as Sebastian pulled out a pocket knife and unfolded a small screwdriver head. He went to work unscrewing one of the thin metal plates that did indeed announce an annual sales award from the front of a plaque.

"What are you doing?" Zane asked curiously.

"Seeing if the tip we got from our informant was accurate."

"What tip? What informant? What the hell is going on? Do you mean to tell me I lost all my clothes for this crap?"

No answer. Instead, Sebastian finished unscrewing the first plate and turned it over. He swore under his breath.

"What is it?" Zane demanded. "I have a right to know. It was my bag it got here in. That technically makes whatever it is mine, right? Possession is nine-tenths of the law and all that?"

Sebastian laid the metal plate on the table and went to work on the second plaque.

Zane looked down at the plate. At first, the shallow engraving didn't make any sense. But then he tilted his head a little and saw exactly what was engraved on the plate. It was a reverse image of the front of a twenty-dollar bill.

"What the hell is that?" he blurted. Surely it wasn't what he thought it was.

"Nothing." Sebastian finished releasing the second plate and turned it over as well. When he laid it carefully on the table, Zane saw the back side of a twenty-dollar bill engraved on this plate.

"This is a joke, right?"

"Sure. Let's go with that," Sebastian replied grimly. "It's all a big joke."

"Seriously, man. What are those? Where do they come from?"

"Seriously, if I tell you, I could be putting your life in danger."

Zane frowned. "Given that some asshole chose my suitcase to put those in, I'd say I'm already in danger."

Sebastian scowled at him grumpily. Zane's stomach flip-flopped at this big, intimidating man looking at him like he wanted to bend him over his knee and spank him. Not that Zane was particularly into kink.

Down, boy, he mentally admonished his dick. *No sex for you just yet.* The mystery of the metal plates in his bag had to be solved first. And the level of threat to his life had yet to be determined.

"Okay. So somebody changed out my clothes for those metal things. I bring them into the US, and then what? Somebody picks them up from me? Steals them back? Kills me and takes them?"

"Possibly."

"Possibly to which one? I'm not loving the idea of being murdered, here."

"That's a fair reaction," Sebastian replied.

Not helpful. The dude still hadn't told him which option was the most likely. "Exactly how much danger am I in and from whom?"

"I can't tell you."

"Because you don't know or won't tell me?"

Sebastian's scowl turned into something akin to thunderous frustration. The guy's eyes burned, and his square jaw clenched hard enough to show the muscles beneath the bronze skin. His nostrils flared and his generous mouth tightened into a thin, hard line. Everything about him screamed fury, and yet the tiger was tightly leashed. An urge to provoke Sebastian until he lost control surged through Zane. To be taken by a man like that—so burly and strong, so demanding and in control…. He surreptitiously fanned himself a little.

In his line of work, most of his boyfriends tended to be models like him—beautiful, charming, and a bit flaky. It made for a fun ride, but chaotic. Unpredictable and unreliable. What would it be like to be with a man like Sebastian?

He came across as a bit of a control freak. He would definitely want to call the shots in bed. Although he could be in for a bit of a surprise in that department. Zane was perfectly happy taking control of the sex. He knew what he liked and wasn't afraid to go after it.

"Look. You owe me the truth," Zane tried. "I ran out of JFK at your insistence, and I'm probably already on the no-fly list. My God, there's probably an arrest warrant out on me. I can't go to jail. You understand me? A pretty guy like me?" He shuddered. "I can't even think about it."

"Then don't," Sebastian said matter-of-factly. As if it was no big deal to turn off his imagination, to set aside his fears and anxiety at the flip of a switch. If only.

"I fled a Customs officer for you, and I came along nicely like you asked me to. And that's my suitcase. But whoever put that stuff in it must know who I am, or at least know my name and have some way to find me. I'm telling you. I had nothing to do with putting those… money-printing thingies—"

"Technically, they're electroplated intaglio printing plates," Sebastian inserted.

"Money-printing thingies… I had nothing to do with putting them in my bag. But somebody knows they're in my stuff and is going to come looking for me, right? They're gonna want their printing plates back so they can make counterfeit twenties."

"I would say that's a logical assumption."

"Don't be so goddamned calm about it! We're talking about criminals, here. Coming for me!"

"Freaking out isn't going to help the situation," Sebastian intoned with admirable—and totally infuriating—calm.

"Standing there as if nothing's happened—not doing a damned thing—isn't going to help either!" He heard the screech in his voice and didn't like it, but there wasn't anything he could do to keep himself from squeaking like a doggie chew toy. He was fucking terrified.

"Off the top of your head, do you know anyone who's a smuggler or counterfeiter?" Sebastian asked, breaking the spiral of panic sucking Zane down into the mental abyss.

"Counter—" He broke off. "Holy crap! Those *are* actual plates for printing money!" He'd sincerely hoped they were replicas or something, not real plates.

Sebastian looked supremely annoyed.

Ha. He was right! "It's twenty-dollar bills, yes? American currency?"

"As American as apple pie," Sebastian answered. "Although, technically, pie was first made by ancient Egyptians. The Romans made them, and the word *pye* was in common usage in fourteenth-century England. Although most early pies were meat pies. Fruit-based tarts and pies became popular in Elizabethan England and came to America with early English colonists—"

"Seriously?" Zane interrupted.

Sebastian broke off, looking startled. Whether that was because he was unused to being interrupted when lecturing on the history of pie, for Chrissake, or because he'd actually been lost down the rabbit hole of his own trivia, Zane couldn't tell.

"What?" Sebastian mumbled.

"I'm going to be murdered, and you're telling me about the history of tarts. Focus, my dude. Focus."

Sebastian scowled. But at least he shut up about pies.

Zane turned his attention back to the printing plates. "Damn. Too bad they aren't hundreds, or maybe thousand-dollar bills. Those exist, right?"

"Yes. They exist. But they would draw way too much attention if someone walked into a bank with a suitcase full of them. Even hundreds draw extra scrutiny. But twenties… no one looks twice at them. As an aside, it's also the currency of the drug trade. They do everything in increments of five and twenty. That way the street dealers don't have to do a lot of mental math, and all the deals can be done in five-dollar and twenty-dollar bills—"

"Staahhpp," he complained.

"What?"

"This isn't a Trivial Pursuit game. It's my fucking life."

"Fine." Sebastian momentarily sulked, although to his credit, he got over his pout fast enough and said a bit defensively, "For what it's worth, twenties are the currency of choice for counterfeiters too. A twenty is a small enough bill that people don't look too closely at it, but large enough to have a little buying power."

"Umm, good to know?" Zane replied.

"Criminals these days multitask. They don't just deal drugs, or run guns, or sex traffic. They do it all."

"Including printing their own money?"

"A few of the big outfits do."

"Why bother with the other crimes if you can just make cash for yourself? Seems a lot less dangerous and violent to just set up a printing press."

"In the first place, money's got to get laundered and into the money supply somehow. Any decent counterfeiter also needs a way to launder cash, and a lot of it, quickly and without much risk. Hence the other criminal activities. In the second place, money's not that easy to make. You have to get the right paper and ink, know how to wash it, embed holograms in the paper. It's not easy to create passable fake cash. In the case of the syndicate who stuck those plates in your bag, I have reason to believe they're desperate for money, or else they wouldn't be trying to do it."

A whole criminal syndicate was behind his stolen clothes and smuggled printing plates? Oh, he didn't like the sound of that. A crime organization big enough to print its own money sounded like the kind of gang that would have killers for hire on their speed dials. He stared at his suitcase. Who in the world had done this to him? While he might like to think he was famous, his fame didn't extend beyond a tiny group of fashion insiders who bothered to learn the names of the top runway models. Female models were able to build name recognition and fan bases, but the male models—not so much.

Aloud he asked, "So how is this supposed to work? Whoever stuck those plates in my suitcase will call me and tell me where and when to deliver them? And then I'm just supposed to do it?"

"If all goes well, I would love to see the handoff go that smoothly," Sebastian answered. "But until you get that call, I'm staying with you. I'll go with you to the delivery and try to identify or apprehend the recipient—"

"Whoa, whoa, whoa. I thought you said you're not law enforcement."

Sebastian blinked. "I'm not."

"I'm sorry, but I want the police or the FBI or somebody official in on this. I want bulletproof vests and snipers and radios—all the cool toys—hell, I want a fucking SWAT team. My life is on the line here."

"That's the last thing you should do."

"Why?" he demanded, irate.

"In the first place, it would be way too obvious, and the bad guy would never, ever show up to make the handoff with law enforcement crawling all over the place."

"They can hide—"

"Huge surveillance teams aren't as easy to hide in real life as they are on TV," Sebastian responded.

Well, hell. Zane wanted to disagree with that, but since all of his knowledge of police did come from television shows, he couldn't legitimately argue.

"In the second place," Sebastian continued, "whoever has enough clout to get these plates made and sent to the United States has enough clout to buy cops and feds."

"You're saying no cop or fed can be trusted?" Zane exclaimed.

"It only takes one bad cop or fed vulnerable to blackmail or coercion and assigned in the wrong place for us to be screwed."

Not good. Not good at all. An urge to leave the printing plates with Sebastian and flee the city—maybe flee the whole country—came over him. "You take the plates. I don't want them."

Sebastian threw his hands up. "The plates were given to you. Whoever plans to collect them on this end is going to come looking for you. Not me."

"When they call, I'll tell them I gave the suitcase and everything in it to you."

"And then you'll be expendable. You'll have no use to them anymore, and you'll know about the plates. They'll kill you in a heartbeat."

"You don't know that these smugglers and counterfeiters are violent...." His voice trailed off as it dawned on him how naïve and colossally stupid that sounded. Of course they were violent. With those plates, they could produce literally unlimited quantities of cash. Millions. Billions. Tens of billions.

He didn't like it, but Sebastian made sense. The plates' owner would come to him, and he would have to be the one to hand the damned things over—

"Wait. As soon as I hand over the plates, I'll be in the same exact position. I'll know the plates exist and my usefulness will be over. Won't they kill me then?"

"I expect they'll try."

"Nope. That's it. I want SWAT *and* the FBI."

"Technically, the Secret Service investigates all cases of counterfeiting."

"Even better! If they can keep the president alive, they can keep me alive!"

"Different branches of the Secret Service." He opened his mouth to interrupt Sebastian, who added hastily, "But I take your point, Zane."

"So once you figure out who's receiving the plates, will we turn their names over to law enforcement and back the heck out of this?"

"I'm not kidding. If who we think is importing the plates is the actual organization behind these"—he gestured at the plates—"we actually cannot involve the federal government. We already know they've got informants all over the government, including the Secret Service."

"How about NYPD?" he tried.

"Them too."

"Jeez. You're telling me there's no law enforcement who can help us?"

"That is correct."

He threw up his hands. "So, what's the plan?"

"The plan is for me to stick with you, protect you, and apprehend whoever's supposed to pick those plates up from you."

"Why on earth would you attempt something so dangerous alone?"

"Because it's the right thing to do."

"It's the insane thing to do!"

They stared at each other, clearly at an impasse.

"You said 'we' before. Who are you working with?" Zane asked.

"Can't say."

"What can you say?"

"That I'll do everything in my power to get you out of this alive… and keep your face intact."

Did Zane believe this dark stranger? Did he dare trust the man? Was Sebastian Gigoni himself part of the smuggling gang? How in the hell was Zane supposed to know who to trust? One thing he did know. Until these printing plates were completely out of his life and he was far, far away from this whole mess, his life was, in fact, in grave danger.

He stared at Sebastian, who stared back, obviously waiting, watching, to see which way he jumped. Thing was, no matter which direction he looked, he teetered on the edge of a deadly cliff.

Maybe he should just close up his suitcase, take it out of here, and leave. Would Sebastian even let him go?

More to the point, did he want to go?

Stay or go. Trust this guy or don't trust him. Listen to his gut, which pegged Sebastian as a straight-up dude, or do the sensible thing and go to the police.

Choices, choices. God, he hated making decisions.

He was the original queen of FOMO—fear of missing out—and changed his mind no less than three times for every major decision he ever had to make.

Finally, he asked in all seriousness, "Who are you, Sebastian, and what do you want from me?"

"I already told you who I am—"

"Stop treating me like an idiot. Who *are* you?"

Sebastian studied him, then looked at the briefcase, then back at him. "I used to be in the military. A friend of a friend got a tip about these printing plates, and I was asked, as a favor, to check out the tip. And here we are."

No way was Zane letting him off the hook with any more of his evasive bullshit. "Why you?"

"Because I was a good soldier?"

Zane rolled his eyes. "I'm taking my bag and walking out of here right now if I don't start getting some straight answers. *Capisce?*"

"I'd go after you and haul you back here over my shoulder if I had to."

A tiny thrill zinged through him at the idea of finding himself thrown over that muscular shoulder, one of those big palms planted on his ass, being thrown down onto this man's bed. Stripped naked, loved and used until he couldn't walk....

Sheesh. *Earth to Zane. Come in, moron. There's a crisis right in front of you. This guy is now threatening not to let you go.*

Zane snorted. "You think I don't know how to lose a tail? I've been chased by paparazzi for a decade. And they're bloodhounds. Better than you, I'd wager."

Sebastian snapped, "Don't make that bet. You'd lose."

"Arrogant much?"

Sebastian exhaled hard. "Here's the thing. The people who sent those plates are extremely cautious and suspicious. They have their fingers in far too many law enforcement pies. My friend needs someone who's totally unrelated to law enforcement to follow the plates and see where they end up. Hence, me. Because of my military training, I'm good at tracking people and things. But I'm not on any government agency rosters or on any major crime organization's radar."

"Who do you think the plates are being delivered to?" Zane asked.

"No idea. But whoever stuck them in your bag undoubtedly knows who you are. Given that, they likely won't show themselves at a handoff unless you personally deliver the plates. My orders are to get you to play ball with us and deliver the plates so we can spot the people at this end of the transaction."

"So, I'm bait."

"The plates are the bait."

"So, the plates are the hook. I'm the sacrificial worm wrapped around the fish hook."

"Fair enough."

Zane scowled. "How dangerous is this going to be for me?"

"No idea. But I'm not bad at what I do."

"Are you still a soldier?"

"No. I retired some time ago."

"So, you're wildly rusty," Zane accused.

"I wouldn't characterize myself as wildly out of practice—"

"This is my life we're talking about."

"In my day, I wasn't half-bad. Some knowledge, some skills, don't go away. I'm a hell of a lot better than nothing," Sebastian replied stiffly.

"Were you some sort of Special Forces dude?"

Sebastian's lips pressed together in an irritated expression. "Something like that."

"Were you a Navy SEAL?"

"No."

"Marine?"

"No."

"Army Ranger?"

"No."

Zane threw up his hands. "What, then?"

"British SAS."

"British?" Zane stared. "But you don't have an accent!"

"I worked hard at losing my accent when I immigrated to America."

"Why? British accents are hot."

"Classy British ones may be. My East End burr was not. And besides, I'm trained to blend in. It came naturally to adopt the local accent and vernacular."

Zane tilted his head to study Sebastian. The rigid spine, the constantly moving gaze, the balls-of-the-feet balance. Yup, he could see the soldier now. Why hadn't he noticed all of that before? Was Sebastian that good a chameleon, or was Zane just too freaked-out by the whole situation to notice?

"So, you're going to babysit me and play bodyguard until someone calls me and wants their plates back?"

"More or less."

"How about we make that more rather than less?"

"Okay. Whatever. I'll do everything in my power to keep you alive. Up to and including sacrificing my own life for you."

Whoa. "Really?"

"Really."

"Dude. Hawt."

Sebastian rolled his eyes, irritated enough that it was obvious he'd been serious when he made his declaration.

Wow. Aloud, Zane said, "You admit, then, that it's entirely possible the owner of those plates plans to kill me to take them from me."

Sebastian frowned. "I was hoping you wouldn't make that leap of logic."

"Sorry. I'll try to be a clueless moron next time."

"Thanks," Sebastian replied dryly. "That would be helpful."

Zane fingered the fine wool of the Armani suit that had come with the briefcase. "What do you suppose this is for?"

"Probably an additional way of identifying you to whoever's supposed to pick up the plates."

"Do you suppose there are tracking thingies stitched into the seams?"

"Do you want me to check it for you?" Sebastian asked.

"Maybe after I put it on," he purred.

Sebastian rolled his eyes. "See if it fits you first. Then I'll take a closer look at it."

"What if it doesn't fit me?" Zane asked. Although, at a glance, it looked darned close to exactly his size.

"Then the bad guys I think it came from are losing their touch." He added dryly, "Try it on."

Zane scooped up the pile of clothes and carried them into the first bedroom he saw. The room was decorated in a soft yellow with lots of creams and the occasional floral pop of color. It was all very tasteful and bland. Not his style at all. He closed the door, stripped off his jeans and T-shirt, and efficiently donned the suit. One thing he knew how to do like nobody's business was get into and out of clothes at light speed.

The trousers and shirt fit *perfectly*. As in they could have been custom-tailored for him. How in the hell had that happened? Sure, he was an exact size. It helped in his line of work. But how did whoever put the suit in his bag *know* his exact size?

A chill chattered down his spine. This was not a good sign. At all.

He stared in the full-length mirror leaning against the wall, and a sophisticated man in elegant clothing stared back at him. *Damn.* He modeled stuff like this all the time, but he rarely had the cash lying around to own it himself. Sure, he'd been given sample suits from the big designers over the years. But they lasted a season or two before they had to be replaced with the newest on-trend designs.

Absently, he looped the light gray silk tie in a full Windsor knot and tightened it into place. This getup was one step down from a tuxedo. Clearly meant for a formal occasion. Was the owner of the plates worried that he would dress wrong for the handoff and blow it?

He shrugged into the suit coat and, out of long habit, half turned from side to side, striking poses. He stuck his hands in the coat's slit pockets—

What was that?

He pulled out a slim black cell phone and stared at it. Looked like a cheap burner phone. The kind a person bought at a convenience store and preloaded with minutes. He held down the power button, and a white bar crawled across the screen. The phone came to life. Immediately, it dinged to indicate an incoming text message. Frowning, he touched the envelope icon on the screen.

Tell NOBODY about this if you want to live. I will contact you with when and where to bring me the briefcase. A million dollars for you if you follow my instructions exactly. A bullet in the back of the head for you if you don't.

A million? A *bullet*?

Sweet baby Jesus. What had he gotten himself into?

Fear ripped through him. After he'd gotten off the cocaine and amphetamines three years ago, he'd worked his ass off to stay clean. He didn't do drugs anymore, and he sure as hell didn't deal them. He'd left New York and gone to Europe just to get away from toxic friends, old associations with places where he'd partied and gotten high, and the temptation of his old dealers coaxing him to get back on the roller coaster. He'd been in New York under an hour and someone was already trying to mess with him.

This whole trip home to restart his New York fashion career was a terrible, awful mistake. He should've just stayed in Europe. Gotten a job in a nice designer store selling suits to rich bastards and gradually turning into a bitter old has-been.

He ought to turn right around and get on a plane to Milan. Hell, a plane to Timbuktu would do. Except he didn't have the cash to buy a damned ticket. He'd put everything he had into clothes. And now all he had were the jeans and T-shirt he'd flown here in—and this suit.

He stared at the mirror speculatively. This suit was too formal for typical go-sees, but it certainly was a statement piece. He could probably pull it off. He could tell the fashion assistants who hired runway walkers that in honor of his upcoming thirtieth birthday, he'd decided to rock a grown-up look. He could shorten his hair a smidge. Tighten up the walk a bit. Go more businessman tycoon and less easy-breezy hipster....

The phone's screen went black, and he tapped it to stare down at the text again. A million dollars? To hand a briefcase to someone? Hell, he could do that. Why not do it, in fact? No cops were involved, after all. Sebastian had been adamant that he was outside the legal system. And given the way they'd raced away from the Customs guys at JFK, Zane was inclined to believe him.

A million dollars would finance reinventing himself in some new career. Hell, it would finance a whole new life. It would certainly pay for a degree in fashion design and marketing. For that matter, he could study underwater basket weaving and still have plenty of cash to spare.

More practically, he could buy a place in the city—admittedly not a palace, but a little condo. A place to call home. And he could own it outright. Have a home forever in New York. Then, even if he didn't make a fortune, he could still afford to live, if not in Manhattan, close to it. Oh yeah. This could work.

The text's threat of being shot made sense if he thought about it. The owner of the plates wouldn't want to be double-crossed. But Zane had no reason to double-cross the guy if he was willing to pay Zane a freaking fortune to do a simple job.

Truth be told, the hard part was over. The plates were past Customs and safely in New York. All he had to do now was wait for a message and do what the guy on the other end of this phone said to.

"You okay in there?" Sebastian called.

"Yes. I'm fine," he called back hastily. He hid the cell phone in the pocket of his jeans and strode out of the bedroom. "What do you think?"

Sebastian stared at him in disbelief. "Wow," he breathed.

A smile broke over his face. He was used to the jaded workers in the fashion industry who looked at models like him all day long. They were completely unimpressed with him or anyone else. Sebastian's stare of awe was more than a little gratifying.

"That suit looks like it was made for you," Sebastian said in something akin to awe. But then his brows slammed together. He repeated grimly, "That suit looks like it was made for you."

Damn. Zane knew enough about a designer suit to realize that no suit lay this perfectly on anyone, not even a perfect-sized male model like him, without at least a few alterations. It was why preparation for every fashion show included multiple fittings before the event.

He said lightly, "Lucky guess, huh?"

CHAPTER FOUR

SEBASTIAN'S BLOOD ran cold. That suit looked like it had been painted onto Zane's perfect body. *Fuckfuckfuckfuckfuck.* Was Zane Stryker in on the smuggling operation? How else to explain that spectacularly perfect fit? He had to work for freaking Erebus!

The Erebus Consortium was the nightmare every law enforcement official dreaded—a group of smart, capable businessmen who'd decided to pool their resources and monetize crime into a highly organized, highly secretive corporate structure. They'd been slowly, carefully building their empire for decades and had their hooks into every major law enforcement agency, government, and international corporation on earth. They smuggled arms, started wars, paid for it with drugs and human trafficking, all while keeping their own hands spotlessly clean of course, and also branched out into exotic crimes like diamond smuggling, cybercrime, and rigging elections. Erebus was perhaps the most devastating crime syndicate ever built.

What the hell had Peregrine Cardiffe thrown him into here?

Sebastian smiled automatically and said lamely, "Yeah, man. The suit looks great. Lucky, indeed, that it fits. Guess that's what happens when you're a fashion model. Everything looks good on you, eh?"

Zane chirped, "It totally helps that I'm a perfect size. Have to be, in the modeling biz. Designers don't want to spend much time or money tailoring clothing to fit models. You get one, maybe two, fittings at most before a show, and the clothes have to work on you."

Sebastian tuned out Zane's blathering about clothing and fittings while his mind raced. If Zane was part of the organization and hadn't killed Sebastian already, he was probably only a low-level mule and not one of the group's high-level operatives. He might not have the authority or resources to kill.

Or he might.

Which was to say, as long as Sebastian played dumb to Zane's affiliation with Erebus, Zane might let him live. God. Who'd have guessed a pretty male model would actually be part of such a sinister crime syndicate?

Of course, the most dangerous part of this whole charade would come when it was time to deliver the printing plates. Zane's compatriots would undoubtedly want to eliminate the outsider who knew of the plates' existence. That would be when they killed him. It would be a trap for him all the way.

He eyed Zane. The good news was the guy was an extrovert. He liked to talk. If Sebastian could act dumb enough and put Zane at ease, the guy might let some important detail slip. His gut told him he wasn't in immediate danger of being murdered. He could roll with the plan for now. Pretend to protect Zane, wait for the contact to set up a meeting, stick to Zane like glue, and get Zane to let down his guard.

He could do this.

But Christ, it was risky.

"Obviously, somebody's going to contact you and want you to wear that suit to a rendezvous to hand off the printing plates."

Zane nodded. "Makes sense."

"Any idea how they'll get in touch with you?" he tried casually. Not that he expected Zane to slip up and give that away, of course. If Sebastian didn't miss his guess, the man was a whole lot smarter than he let on.

"Nope," Zane answered lightly.

"Ah well. That's their problem and not ours," Sebastian said equally lightly. "At any rate, when they do contact you, I'll plan to go with you to the meet. Undoubtedly, they'll give you some big line about coming alone and not telling anyone about it. I'll follow you, stay out of sight of the bad guys, and provide cover and protection for you."

"How?" Zane asked.

Well, fuck. Now he was the one on the spot. He certainly didn't want to give away to Zane what he planned to do, in case Zane worked for Erebus and would relay the information to his compatriots. But if he didn't give a plausible answer, Zane wouldn't trust him enough to go through with the handoff.

He shrugged. "You know. Bodyguard stuff. I'll stick close enough to tackle anyone who tries to harm you. If you'd like, I can get a hold of a low-profile bullet-resistant vest for you to wear under that suit."

"I doubt there's enough room under it for anything but me. It's perfectly tailored." Zane turned back and forth, eyeing himself in the big mirror in the front entry.

"The good news is I won't try to take down whoever meets you. All I need to do is follow them. Get an image of a face or an address where they go. I will do my level best not to trap you in the middle of a shootout or anything equally exciting."

"Thank God," Zane said fervently.

"Oh, and one more thing. Don't try to be a hero. Don't tackle the bad guys, don't hit them or in any way try to restrain them or stop them. Just go along with what they want, do what they tell you to, and let me take care of the rest."

"Which won't be violent, right?" Zane clarified.

"Right. I'm not here to stop the handoff. I'm just here to watch it and make sure you walk away from it safely."

"Are you sure you can accomplish all of that by yourself?" Zane asked doubtfully.

"I'll figure it out," he said casually. "Don't worry about the details. We've got time to figure those out. I'll keep you safe."

"Thanks." Zane looked up at him, fear naked in his light green gaze for a moment. But then Zane smiled bravely and tossed his head. The mask of the devil-may-care high-fashion model was back firmly in place.

"You hungry?" Sebastian asked.

"Now that you mention it, I'm famished."

"Let's order room service. They're still serving breakfast."

"Great! I'll have dry granola, almond milk, and a bowl of fruit. Lemme go change out of this suit while we wait for the food to come up. I wouldn't want to ruin it."

Sebastian stared at Zane's retreating form. Dry granola? Who ate that crap? The guy might as well gnaw on a few twigs and eat a handful of dirt. Shaking his head, he ordered a tall stack of pancakes, three eggs, bacon and sausage, a pot of coffee, and fresh orange juice for himself. Distastefully, he added the granola and fruit to the order.

Zane emerged from the bedroom, back in his jeans and T-shirt. But now that Sebastian had seen him dressed to the nines, he didn't see the casual hipster anymore. He kept seeing the elegant, well-turned-out man in the suit. The jeans looked like the costume now. Was the whole man an impostor?

Room service knocked at the door, and Zane hastily moved the briefcase and its damning engraving plates off the table and carried it into the yellow bedroom. The waiter laid out their food on the dining room table, and Sebastian sat down in front of his breakfast.

He was just getting ready to dig in when Zane returned. "Good Lord, man. You're going to eat all that by yourself?"

Sebastian looked up from his forkful of fluffy pancakes dripping with butter and syrup. He answered defensively, "I work out."

Zane slipped into a chair across the table. "I work out too. But I would have to run a marathon every other day to be able to eat all that."

Sebastian shrugged. "High metabolism, I guess."

"Lucky bastard." Zane nibbled on a mouthful of the crunchy cereal. "Do you always eat like a bird?"

"When I hit about twenty-seven, I suddenly couldn't eat everything in sight anymore. If I wanted to keep working, I had to start editing my food choices."

An interesting way to describe dieting.

"What do you do for exercise that lets you eat like a lumberjack?" Zane asked.

Sebastian shrugged. "This and that. I lift weights. Run. Swim. Play handball. Do some yoga."

"Yoga?" Zane exclaimed. "That sounds too zen for you."

He looked up from the sausage he was neatly slicing. "Why don't I strike you as a zen guy?" He actually did meditate on a daily basis for stress management and anger control. He'd grown up in a world where people swung their fists first and stopped to think later. He would be damned if he fell back into those early patterns that had cost him so much. In fact, he took quiet pride in how nonviolently he dealt with life these days. His gut might slow burn from time to time, but he never let on. As far as the entire world knew, he was a totally chill human being.

"I don't know. You strike me as the competitive sports type."

"Like what?"

Zane leaned back, studying him closely. "Something mano a mano. Boxing, maybe."

"Good guess. I do box."

"Why yoga, then?" Zane followed up.

"I need the calm and focus. Plus, studies have shown that keeping muscles supple and flexible prevents injury." He sliced into a sausage and savored the succulent pork fat and sage flavor. "How about you?"

"Me? Yoga? No way," Zane declared.

"Why not?"

"You can't win at yoga."

Sebastian glanced up sharply, reassessing Zane. His initial impression had not been of a hypercompetitive person.

As if sensing the train of his thoughts, Zane shrugged. "Don't kid yourself, buttercup. High-fashion modeling is as cutthroat a sport as there is. It's vicious."

"How so?"

"Every pretty gay boy who's too dim-witted to head for Hollywood heads for the fashion industry."

"You don't strike me as dim-witted." Far from it, in fact. The longer he spent with Zane, the smarter he was starting to think the man was.

"That's why I'm successful. I mean, obviously, it takes sharp fashion sense. When you're getting started, you have to align yourself with the up-and-coming designers and ride their coattails at first. But it also takes professionalism, business savvy, and an ability to read people and give them what they want."

Sebastian jolted. Had Zane been reading and playing him? "How do you read me?"

Zane stared at Sebastian's chest and arms. "On the surface, you want to be taken for a physical guy. The kind who talks with his body first. You wouldn't go to a lot of trouble to build all those muscles if you didn't use them from time to time. When do you use them, Sebastian?"

Sebastian almost missed his mouth with his fork. *Sheesh.* Was that a come-on or an innocent question? He actually couldn't tell.

Most people missed that he was gay. He didn't advertise it, and since he stayed out of the news and the publicity spotlight, and more importantly, rarely had time to date, his sexual orientation wasn't a subject that came up often. Had Zane correctly pegged him? Huh. *Note to self: Zane might be much more perceptive than I've given him credit for.*

Discomfort rumbled in Sebastian's gut. He didn't like being wrong about anyone. Made him worry he'd missed something else important. He studied Zane across the table. What was he missing about this guy?

"What else do you read from me?"

"Well, the whole dumb bodybuilder bit is totally a cover, of course. What you really want to be respected for is your mind. I think you hide behind your looks."

"That's rich, coming from you."

Zane leaned back, smiling a little. "Yes, but I make no secret of hiding behind my looks. I accepted a long time ago that people were going to take one look at me and make all kinds of assumptions about me. It makes my life so much easier not to fight against the stereotype."

Jeez. He'd done that exact thing, himself. He'd taken one look at the glamorous model façade and not looked one inch deeper into the man. He'd not only been played, but played deftly, by Zane. Color him impressed.

"What?" Zane demanded in the silence that had fallen between them.

"I beg your pardon?"

"You're staring at me like you're trying to x-ray my insides."

"Sorry. You must get that a lot, though. People staring at you, I mean."

Zane shrugged. "I guess so. It's more of a hassle than a blessing most of the time."

"Why?"

"Have you ever tried living under a microscope where every move you make is seen and judged? It gets old fast. Especially if you're trying to figure out who you are and grow up. Every mistake you make is magnified a hundred times. I may not be movie star famous, but I still live in enough of a spotlight within my own career field to have the same problems."

"That sounds like it would suck."

"It sucks rocks."

Sebastian leaned back to let the pancakes settle in his stomach before he started in on the eggs. "How old were you when you started modeling?"

"Eighteen."

"Wow. That's young."

"I got out of the house as fast as I could."

"Rough home life?"

Zane toyed with his melon balls and strawberry halves. "Home life was fine until I came out."

Sebastian asked quietly, "How bad was it?"

"They didn't kick me out or harm me. But naïve little me thought my parents would be okay with it. When I told them, I didn't expect them to be ashamed." He added lightly, "Imagine my surprise when they told me to hide it from their friends." He toyed with his cereal for a moment before adding, "And then they suddenly wanted me to go out of state for college, and we skipped the family reunion that year."

"It went a hell of a lot better than it could have."

Zane looked up, his eyes bleak. "People keep telling me that. But it didn't feel that way when they gave me a bus ticket to New York City for my eighteenth birthday. Not subtle, my folks."

"They paid to get rid of you, in other words?"

Another shrug from Zane. "It's okay. They still speak to me. And they're less freaked-out about it now. Turns out most everyone suspected already, so it wasn't a huge shock to their friends, after all, when word got out about me."

"Do you go home to visit? Or do they come to New York for holidays?"

Zane laughed a little. "Don't get carried away, now. They're not *that* enlightened."

Sebastian caught Zane's pained gaze. "I'm sorry."

"How about you? What does your family think about you being gay?"

Sebastian blinked. "How did you know I'm gay?"

Zane snorted. "I'm not blind. I saw how you checked me out in that suit. Hell, I felt how you reacted to me when you landed on top of me in the car." He fiddled with a piece of dry wheat toast and then looked up sharply. "You are out, aren't you?"

"More or less. I don't hide my preferences, but I don't hang a neon sign over my head announcing that I like to fuck men."

"Being gay is about a lot more than that," Zane said seriously. "Particularly in this country."

"Hence my being… circumspect… about it."

"Does your family even know?" Zane demanded.

"My dearly departed old man would've killed me with his bare hands if he knew."

"Ahh," Zane said in sudden understanding.

"Ahh what?"

"Is that why you're so buff? You're subconsciously defending yourself against attack from your late old man?"

He blinked. Stared at Zane. Opened his mouth to tell the guy that was crazy talk. Closed his mouth without saying anything. *Sonofabitch.*

"And your mother? What does she think?"

"She doesn't think. She's dead."

"I'm sorry," Zane said quickly and in what sounded like genuine regret. Empathetic, he was.

"She died a long time ago."

"Long enough that she never saw you become rich and successful?" Zane asked.

"Do you have to keep asking all these insightful questions?"

Zane shrugged over his cup of black coffee. "Just trying to understand what makes you tick."

"Is this how you succeed in the fashion industry?" Sebastian snapped.

Zane's voice held infinite sadness as he answered, "No, man. This is how I stay alive in a world that would otherwise beat the shit out of a pretty boy like me."

They traded a long look of loss and betrayal, a deep understanding that a regular person with a normal life would never get. Zane might be more open about his wounds, but his own scars ran at least as deep as Zane's.

Whereas Zane wore his on his sleeve, Sebastian had built the thickest walls around himself that money could buy. "How do you do it?" he murmured.

"Do what?" Zane responded.

"Stay open to other people?"

Zane looked away then, staring down at his plate. "Some of the hits I've taken—physically, psychologically, emotionally—they weren't worth it. I ran around looking for love everywhere I could. But I eventually figured out that for people like me, the odds are damned low of ever finding my soul mate. Hell, it's hard enough just to find a half-decent guy to date, let alone one who fits me perfectly and forever." He shrugged. "You call it being open. I'd say I'm cynical. I've set the bar so low for so long that my faith in love is shot."

"Wow."

"Don't feel sorry for me," Zane replied, smiling brilliantly. So brilliantly Sebastian almost mistook it for a real smile. "Life's a lot easier this way."

Easier maybe, but it sounded empty. "Are you happy?"

"I'm not in pain."

Sebastian frowned. Those were *not* the same thing.

They ate in silence for a few minutes. Then Zane asked, "What's your story?"

It was not a thing he liked to talk about, that was for damn sure. But having torn open a few of Zane's scars, he reluctantly allowed that he owed the guy an answer. "I grew up in East London. Tough part of town. Dad died when I was thirteen, Mum died when I was fourteen."

"How?" Zane interjected.

"He died of stomach cancer. He should've gone in to get the symptoms treated earlier and the NHS should have treated it more aggressively. Shitty way to die. My mum ODed."

"Jesus. I'm sorry. And you were alone after that?"

Sebastian shrugged.

"How did you survive?"

He chose to misunderstand the question. "I got emancipated by the court, shoplifted cheap stuff, and sold it on the street to make ends meet. I got by. And I learned how to sell to people, which is a skill I monetized into all of this." He waved his fork at the posh suite.

"Did you live, I don't know, on the street?"

"I went to live with my mum's sister, who threw me out of her flat promptly on the morning I turned eighteen. Kind of like your parents did, but not as nicely. Overnight, she'd packed up all my shit and threw it off her balcony. Told me to get the hell out and never darken her doorstep again. Which I haven't."

"Does she know how rich you are now?"

Sebastian's mouth turned up in what could probably be mistaken for a smile but was far less pleasant. "Oh, yes. She came sniffing around not long after I made my first million. Flew to New York to visit me."

"What did you do?"

"I let her stay in my condo overnight, and when she woke up in the morning, all her shit was scattered on Fifth Avenue beneath my balcony."

"Nice."

"It was petty." He did grin then. "But satisfying."

Zane held out his fist for a fist bump, which Sebastian touched lightly with his own knuckles.

"Okay, so bitchy aunt tossed you out at eighteen. How did you get to all of this?"

"I joined the Army. Definitely didn't come out there, but I got my shit together, learned carpentry and plumbing, and figured out what I wanted to do with my life. After the Army I went to work for a private security firm for a while to make real money. Saved my pennies and eventually decided to move to the States. I bought a crappy little apartment building and renovated it myself, unit by unit. And I got lucky. It was in a neighborhood that got sexy to live in, and it doubled in value by the time I was done fixing it up."

Zane snorted skeptically enough that Sebastian stopped his story to lift a questioning brow.

Zane explained, "In my experience, luck doesn't just fall into anyone's lap. You make your own luck. You work hard, prepare, and are ready when the timing lines up and an opportunity comes your way."

"Fair point. I did work damned hard on that building. Day and night for almost two years."

"Then what happened?" Zane asked.

"I bought another building. Rinsed, lathered, and repeated. Now I own more buildings."

"So that's what you do? Flip real estate?"

"Mostly I hire contractors to fix them up now, and managers to live in and run them. I spend most of my time looking for new properties to invest in. I have a knack for spotting neighborhoods that are about to turn around."

"And you work out in your spare time," Zane added.

"And I work out."

"Social life?"

"Not much of one." If Zane was fishing to find out if he was single and looking for love, Sebastian wasn't eager to play ball. The last thing he needed was to complicate this dangerous situation with relationship issues.

Zane tilted his head and studied him far too intently for comfort.

"What?" he finally blurted.

"The staff at the swankiest hotel in town knows you by name, and you didn't bother to ask what this suite was going to cost, which means you've got not only money but buckets of money. That makes you both a rich and good-looking guy. How old are you? Thirty, thirty-one?"

"Thirty-seven."

Zane whistled. "What's your skin care regimen, my dude?"

"Good genes. Healthy lifestyle."

"You fucking bitch." Zane delivered the insult with such good cheer that Sebastian took it for the genuine compliment it no doubt was. Then Zane picked up his previous train of thought. "As I was saying. It's getting late for you to find yourself a trophy husband and settle down."

Sebastian didn't hear a question in there, so he didn't offer up any answers.

"God knows the sharks have to be circling around you hard."

Sebastian snorted. "You have no idea."

"You forget that I work in the fashion industry. I live right in the middle of the scheming socialite shark tank."

Sebastian was saved from responding to that by a cell phone ringing. Zane leaped about a foot in the air. *Wow.* That was quite a startle reflex. He watched Zane fish in his left pants pocket and come up with a red cell phone, look at the surface, and say in oddly profound relief, "It's my agent. I have to take this."

"Be my guest."

Zane spoke into the device. "Hey, Janice. Yes, I made it to New York, more or less in one piece. Airline lost my luggage, though. Pain in the ass." A pause. "This afternoon? Yeah, I'm up for it. I've got ratty jeans or a designer suit—" Another pause. "Right. Jeans it is. Yeah, I know the place. Yes, I'll behave. Don't I always? Don't answer that."

"Job interview?" Sebastian asked.

"Yup."

"Good for you. Where are we going?"

One perfect eyebrow arched. "We?" Zane asked ominously.

CHAPTER FIVE

ZANE STARED across the breakfast table at Sebastian in dismay. "I'm not taking you with me on a go-see."

"Sorry, buddy. I'm velcroed to your side until the handoff happens."

"I neither need nor want a bodyguard. That's not how the fashion business works. I mean seriously. Would you take a chaperone with you on a job interview?"

"No. But that's not the point."

"But it *is* the point. I need this job. I have to let the New York fashion scene know I'm back, and I need to strike fast and land work right away to let them all know I'm still the hottest commodity in town."

"And I wish you luck with that. You'll be doing it with me there with you, however."

Good grief. He truly could not show up at a go-see with a Neanderthal in tow. Granted, a hot Neanderthal, but still. The second they set foot inside the fashion house, the designer would ask why Sebastian was with him, and Zane couldn't very well say that he needed a bodyguard now. No designer on earth would hire him if he brought any threat to a show. And no model with an ounce of professionalism would dream of bringing a boyfriend to work.

Desperation flowed through Zane. He couldn't show up with a frigging babysitter! They would all claim to understand. Of course it was no problem having a big, beefy bodyguard with him. They would be polite and smile... and he wouldn't get a single gig.

"I'm serious, man. You'll ruin my life. Everything depends on me getting work this season. I've only got one good year left in me before I age out of the business. This is it for me. You can't screw it up."

"What if I promise not to get in the way?" Sebastian offered.

"What if you promise not to go in with me?" he snapped back.

Sebastian frowned. "I suppose I can work with that. It's not likely the owner of the plates will call you right away. He'll ascertain that you made it through Customs with the plates first. Then he'll have to arrange for a drop site. Check it out. Get his people in place. Not to mention he'll have to figure out how to get in touch with you. Speaking of which, is your cell phone number public?"

"No," Zane answered. "Too many fans would bug me." More accurately, too many ex-boyfriends, ex–drug dealers, and ex-partiers would try to drag him back down into the world he'd left behind three years ago.

"So. The counterfeiter will have to find your phone number. And give you time to arrange to get to the drop-off. Furthermore, you'll need time to get there without arousing suspicion or being followed…. Nah, it'll be a couple days at least before anyone calls you."

The black cell phone in his right pocket all but burned a hole in his jeans. Of course, the counterfeiter had already taken care of a good chunk of that list and knew exactly how to get in touch with him.

But it worked to his advantage to have Sebastian off guard and thinking no contact had happened yet. The guy would be easier to give the slip when the time came. Given the ultimatum staring him in the face—cooperation and wealth or death—he didn't see how he had any choice except to go along with the counterfeiter. He was going to deliver the briefcase, pocket the money, and then he could walk away from the fashion industry with his head held high.

Of course, he had to seriously consider the idea that there was no million dollars, and that only the lead portion of the ultimatum was real. But why did this shadowy criminal group choose him specifically to be their mule? He was known to be a bit wild, to color outside the lines. He had been a partier, a jetsetter to whom the rules didn't apply. He would be the kind of guy to think it was entertaining to deliver some crazy plaques to someone. They probably assumed he would think those stupid plaques were a big joke. He would go along with the program, not look too closely at what was in the suitcase, not ask questions, and be too dumb and dazzled by the cash to cause any trouble.

Zane's guess was the criminals had chosen him because he would do the job and move on with his life without telling a soul where the windfall of cash had come from. For that matter, a top fashion model could plausibly land a million-dollar contract without raising any suspicion. He was relocating from Europe to the States, so nobody here would likely ask where the sudden cash had come from. His New York contacts would assume he'd appeared in some high-end European magazine or landed a product endorsement deal they hadn't seen.

Nah. The counterfeiters expected to pay him off and then part ways with him, no fuss, no muss. And a million dollars would transform his life.

He took a nap after breakfast to help get rid of the jet-lag-induced bags under his eyes and woke up an hour before he had to leave. He showered and shaved using the toiletries the hotel conveniently supplied, then slipped on the robe hanging on the back of the door. It was fluffy and soft and felt amazing against his naked skin. No doubt about it, he did like his creature comforts.

He rinsed out his only pair of underwear and used the blow dryer on it. After today's go-see, he would have to go shopping. He had about twenty bucks in his pocket. That should get him a toothbrush and a couple of pairs of boxers, at least. He dressed, slipped both cell phones in his pockets, and headed out into the suite's living room.

Any thoughts he'd had of ditching Sebastian before this go-see evaporated when he saw him lounging on the sofa, reading the *Wall Street Journal*, looking every inch the successful businessman. If the guy were in the market for an affair, Zane could totally go for his dark, brooding sizzle. And no lie, the smell of money had always been a turn-on for him.

There was no shame in being a little shallow. His mother had always told him it was as easy to fall in love with a rich girl as a poor girl. Gender notwithstanding, she'd made a good point. Somebody had to love the rich ones.

Sebastian peered over his newspaper, and his gaze slid lazily down Zane's body and back up again, setting Zane's flesh on fire everywhere that dark, smoky gaze landed. Zane had always enjoyed the exhibitionist element of being a model, but for once he felt naked in a vulnerable, overexposed way. Lord, this man threw him off-balance. He flashed an impudent grin and did an end-of-the-runway pose-and-twirl in the middle of the living room before flipping his middle finger at his audience of one.

Sebastian laughed. "Watching you move makes me think of a gazelle. So quick. Graceful. Unpredictable."

A flash of warmth filled his belly. He got complimented all the time, but it counted more coming from Sebastian, who didn't strike him as the type either to lie or to butter up anyone with empty flattery.

"Ready to roll?" Sebastian asked.

"Yup."

"My driver's waiting for us downstairs."

Damn. No chance to jump in a cab and do this go-see alone. Spying the stubborn set of Sebastian's jaw, he thought better of picking a fight over it, though. He couldn't afford to be late. Instead he said lightly, "You're going to spoil me."

A shrug. "What's the point of having money if it doesn't make life more convenient?"

"Truer words were never spoken." It was just that money never managed to stay in his pockets for long. Maintaining his image and lifestyle was not cheap, and he was a naturally generous person. And unfortunately, he tended to have friends who were always broke and needed cash for rent or utility bills or some other emergency.

Zane followed Sebastian from the suite and down to the private exit from the Waldorf Towers. It was a slick arrangement for guests in search of privacy. Sebastian held the door for him, and Zane slid across the back seat while Sebastian piled in behind him.

"Hey, Etienne," Zane said wryly. With the burly driver along, he basically had not one but two bodyguards.

"Mr. Stryker." A nod. "Where are we going today? I hear I'm chauffeuring *you* around town." Zane gave him the address, and Etienne replied, "I'll have you there in fifteen minutes, barring any accidents and the New York City Department of Transportation getting a wild hair to shut down the whole damned island."

Nothing had changed in the years he'd been gone. It seemed like half the streets in Manhattan were always clogged by some sort of building project.

The town car pulled out smoothly into traffic. Zane sat back and closed his eyes to prepare.

Once more into the breach.

He gave himself the pep talk. He was young. Energetic. Hip. Dynamic. He could do this. He could flirt with the girls, laugh at the inane jokes, suck up obsequiously. It was honest work, dammit.

Jamming in his earbuds, he chose some random dance music—loud, fast, and with a pounding beat that jacked up his pulse and his blood pressure. Losing himself in the music, he let his body move to the bass line. Let it fill him. Let it seduce him. He pictured a dance floor. Writhing bodies. Half-naked, sweaty bodies rubbing against his equally bare and slippery body. Oh yeah. Sex, drugs, and rock and roll. The remembered high of a good line of blow coursed through him. He was invincible. He could fucking fly.

"We're here, sir."

His eyes jerked open, and he jolted back into the dark interior of a plush town car. Hot, blue eyes stared at him intensely. A pulse visibly pounded within the open neck of Sebastian's shirt, and Zane noticed a fine sheen of perspiration on Sebastian's upper lip. The guy's legs were crossed. The way a guy might if he was hiding a hard-on. And all of a sudden, the fake high Zane had hyped himself up to was real and thick and sexual, hanging in the air between them.

"Uhh, I'll be going in now," he mumbled.

If possible, Sebastian's eyes burned even brighter. "I'll be waiting here when you're done."

Right. *Day-umm.* His pulse just shot up another dozen points. He actually stumbled a little getting out of the town car. He turned to face the nondescript gray office building holding the House of Kato, one of the hottest designers in town.

"Zane!"

Startled, he half turned to look over his shoulder at the car.

"Your portfolio." Sebastian was holding out his flat leather photo portfolio case.

"Crap. Thanks." Bemused, confused, and half-seduced, he jogged up the front steps and into the building. Conveniently just inside the front door was a full-length mirror. He checked his hair—the perfect amount of tousle for this young, boho-goth design house. No food between his teeth. He slapped his cheeks to put a little more color in them and slapped his ass once for good luck.

He walked up to the second-floor design studio slowly, pausing outside to make sure he wasn't the slightest bit out of breath when he went inside. His whole vibe was easy, breezy, young and fit. He couldn't afford to walk in huffing like some old chain-smoking hooker.

A leggy blond with shaved hair on one side of her head, black under-eye liner, black leather leggings, and sporting a sleeveless V-neck top that enhanced her androgynous look, greeted him with a hug and an air kiss.

"Oh my God, Bryce. You look fabulous!" he gushed.

"You're looking fab yourself, Zane. Italy's been good to you. We've missed you here in the Big Apple. You back for good?"

"That's the plan, boo."

"Still got your moves?" she asked slyly, thumbing through his latest glamour shots.

"Of course I've got my moves, babycakes. Learned some new ones in Milan."

"Glad to hear it. I'll put the word out that you're back in town. Maybe I can send some business your way."

God, he hoped she could hook him up with some decent modeling jobs.

"Hey, Zane, we've got a wacky photo shoot coming up tomorrow. Kato thinks it would be a great idea to hang the models in chains to show off his new line of body-conscious athleisure clothing. I just had a flaky newbie kid cancel out, and I need a pro to step in for him. You game?"

"What does it pay?"

"Two thousand for the shoot, another thousand for each major magazine it gets placement in."

It was a shit job. Runway work paid ten times that. But this house was an up-and-comer, and the photographer Bryce named was top-notch. An actual artist who did edgy, avant-garde work. Good starter job to reestablish his bona fides in the New York fashion scene. And given that he had barely enough dough in his pocket for a cup of coffee, he couldn't afford to be choosy.

He said brightly, "Sign me up."

"Awesome, babe. Don't eat before the shoot. We don't need you puking all over the set. Plus, Kato's clothes are wicked unforgiving. You still a perfect 34?"

"You bet your sweet ass I am."

"Got it." She made a note on a clipboard. "It's mostly Spandex, so we can get away with a last-minute fitting right before the shoot. You're so easy to make look great, boo. Fitting's at 4:00 p.m. tomorrow.

Makeup at six. We'll start shooting when it gets dark. Should take around six hours."

"Thanks for the job, Brycey-baby."

"Anytime for you, Zane. Just like old times, eh?"

God, he hoped not. He nodded, smiling, and managed to mumble something noncommittal.

All but running from the building, he nearly killed himself on the stairs when an unfamiliar ringtone sounded in his pocket, startling the hell out of him. He was almost to the front doors and could see Sebastian's profile in the car outside. Backing up fast into the shadows of the lobby, he dug out the black burner phone, fumbling in his haste.

"Hello?" he said breathlessly.

"Zane Stryker?"

"Yes. That's me. I mean, I'm him."

"Go to the American Ballet tonight. Wear the suit and bring the briefcase."

"It's the season premiere. It has been sold out for weeks. How am I supposed to get a ticket? Not to mention I'm a little short on cash at the moment—"

"A ticket will be waiting for you at the Will Call window. We'll give you further instructions there. Come alone and don't fuck it up."

"You've got it. And I have no intention of messing this up." He added, in keeping with his brainless fashion model persona, "This is fucking exciting. All very James Bond. Can you tell me who you're punking with those plaques?"

The line went dead. But not before he thought he heard a snort of derision.

Good. Wouldn't want the homicidal criminal syndicate to overestimate him.

No telling if the man at the other end of the phone believed his "this is so cool" schtick or not. Now to convince the man in the car outside that a last-minute excursion to the ballet was totally normal and nothing to worry about.

He slid into the back seat of the town car, smiling brightly. Sebastian Gigoni was no fool. He wouldn't be taken in by a fake "everything's fantastic" act.

"Did you get the job?" Sebastian asked without preamble.

"Indeed I did. I got lucky—the shoot supervisor is an old friend of mine, and she had a last-minute cancellation to fill tomorrow." Inspiration struck and he continued, "In fact, she invited me to go with her to the premiere of the American Ballet Company's new production tonight. Had I refused, she would have grilled me about what my other plans were, so I went ahead and accepted her invitation. I figure it's a public place with big crowds, so I'll be safe. Not to mention, I can use the exposure to announce my presence in the Big Apple. God. I wonder if there'll be paparazzi outside. It is a premiere, after all." He tapped a front tooth thoughtfully with his fingernail.

"No way—"

He cut off Sebastian, saying brightly, "It's not like I have any choice but to go. Once word gets out that I'm back in town, it would cause gossip and rumors if I didn't go out and be seen. It's what I do."

Sebastian frowned. "I don't like it. You should cancel."

"Look. This is my work. I'm supposed to mingle with the beautiful people. I *am* the beautiful people. I get jobs that way."

The patented Gigoni scowl deepened. "I still don't like it."

"I'm not crazy about being separated from you either, Mr. Hunky, Delicious, Purr-worthy Bodyguard. But think of it this way. What if the counterfeiter needs me to go out in public so he can find me and contact me? If I hole up in some hotel room indefinitely, he'll never get access to me."

Sebastian was still scowling, but Zane would take it as a good sign that the guy didn't come back with any counterargument to that.

He added, "I don't know about you, but I'm eager to get this over with and get on with my life."

Chapter Six

SEBASTIAN'S INTERNAL lie detector was firing wildly. Even being called delicious and purr-worthy by Zane Stryker wasn't enough to derail it.

Zane definitely wasn't being straight with him. But where was the lie? An invitation to the ballet was damned hard to fake. Particularly since the production had sold out within a few hours of seats going on sale. It wasn't like Zane could just sashay out and buy a ticket to give truth to the lie.

The only logical explanation was that Zane had contacted his superiors at Erebus while he was inside the fashion house. Dammit, Sebastian should have insisted on sticking by Zane's side. It had been a calculated risk to let him go into the audition thing alone. But he had his answer now. Zane was indeed an Erebus operative, or at least working with the consortium.

The ballet tonight, huh? Strange place to exchange the plates. He'd expected someplace quiet, where it could happen in privacy and relative security. Maybe this was just an information exchange and not the actual handoff.

"So. Can I interest you in a spot of early supper?" Zane asked. "I'm starving."

"That's what happens when you eat twigs for breakfast."

"I'm here for go-sees. I can't go in with a food baby hanging over my belt."

Sebastian snorted. "Your gut wouldn't hang over your belt if you ate an entire side of beef. There's no fat on you at all."

"You sound like an Italian granny. 'Eat, eat. Put some meat on those bones, sonny,'" Zane teased.

"I wouldn't know. I never met my Italian granny."

Zane's playfulness evaporated. "I'm sorry. I didn't know."

"How could you? And it's okay. I don't miss what I never had."

"I made you think about sad things, though. Tell you what. To make it up to you, how about you pick where we eat supper."

"Sorry, I don't know any joints in town that serve twigs and leaves."

"I am an occasional carnivore, thank you very much. It takes protein to fuel these stunning muscles."

"Sorry again. I haven't seen you shirtless. Have you got a six-pack under there that I don't know about?"

Zane startled him by sliding off the seat to his knees so he could straighten his torso and whipping up his T-shirt to flash his entire front. Of course the man was perfectly tanned, his chest hair manscaped until it was just a suggestion of hair, and his skin was so smooth and perfect that it almost looked oiled. Not only did the guy flash a nice, tight six-pack, but he also obviously maintained under about six percent body fat, so said six-pack was visible even with a casual flex.

"Well, hello," Sebastian blurted. "Where did you get that?"

Zane answered quickly and matter-of-factly, "I picked it up used at a thrift shop."

Sebastian was startled for a moment, and then a crack of laughter slipped out of him. "Okay, fair. I deserved that. What do you do to work out? I know for a fact abs like that don't materialize out of thin air."

"Hell to the no, they don't," Zane responded indignantly. "I followed a special diet, lifted weights, and did a workout custom designed for me by a body sculptor in Italy."

"Body sculptor?" What the hell was that?

Zane explained. "Instead of shaping marble, he shapes living bodies into artistic forms. Works with a lot of the best bodybuilders in Europe. Also perfect for us model types. For a full year, he measured my body every week and built exercise regimens for me to help build the perfect body."

"Sounds… intrusive." Frankly, it also sounded kind of sexy.

Zane snorted. "You ought to go through a fitting for badly constructed clothes. Talk about intrusive. By the time they fit properly, it feels like the tailor has his hand up your ass. And not in a good way."

"I'll pass, thanks."

"How do you get your suits tailored?" Zane asked curiously.

"I buy off-the-rack, and the tailor at my dry cleaning shop alters them."

Predictably, Zane squawked, "*What*? Sacrilege!"

He shrugged. "I only wear suits when I'm dealing with investors. I prefer to spend my time in work clothes crawling around construction sites. Or in gym gear."

"My dear sir. Wearing off-the-rack clothing of any kind is a travesty we must correct at the first possible moment."

"No, thank you," he declared in a combination of alarm and determination.

Zane's eyes narrowed dangerously. "Challenge accepted. I will get you into a bespoke suit if it's the last thing I do."

"I didn't throw down any challenge."

"Nonetheless. I'm getting you properly clothed."

Their glares clashed, and neither one of them was willing to back down. Only the town car banging through a pothole and practically throwing them both into the front seat broke the stalemate.

Zane pushed himself back onto the seat and buckled in while Sebastian regretted losing the view of those spectacular abs. Of course now every time he looked at Zane, he would envision that body.

As the silence between them threatened to grow awkward, he returned to the original topic of Zane's picky eating habits and where they were dining tonight. "If I pick the restaurant, do I also get to order for both of us? And will you have to eat what I order for you?"

Zane looked startled. All of a sudden, a sexual power dynamic crackled between them. Or was that just him being in lust with the guy? Food could be an incredibly intimate and sensual thing, after all.

Zane mumbled, "Umm, sure. I'm game."

Were they still talking about food, or had the conversation shifted to something altogether different? God, if only Sebastian were better at reading social, particularly sexual, signals.

Still, something hot and possessive blazed in Sebastian's gut. Did Zane mean it? Would he be game for any fantasy Sebastian desired to play out upon his willing body? His gaze raked down Zane's torso and back up where he lounged on the other side of the back seat. God, the things he'd like to do to that body. His breath caught as Zane started to lean forward. Started to reach for him. Started to give himself over to him—

And then pulled back, looking troubled.

Surely he hadn't just seen that. What would a man like Zane find attractive in a man like him? Granted, his checkbook seemed to enthrall a lot of people, but Zane didn't strike him as the type to fall in love with money and not the man. For that matter, he didn't seem like the kind of man to fuck a guy for his money either.

It wasn't that he had no self-esteem. He knew he was a decent-looking man and in great physical shape. Women crawled all over him. And if he bothered to let them know he was gay, he suspected men would crawl all over him too.

But Zane... he didn't run in the regular world. He hung out with movie stars, celebrities, the beautiful people. Jetsetters. Sebastian Gigoni was a poor kid from East London made good. Which was nothing to be ashamed of, but was in no way glamorous.

Sebastian retreated into the far corner of the spacious back seat and stared out the window, fixedly not looking Zane's way. He didn't know whether to scream or whimper in frustration. But one thing he did know for sure: he was hot as hell for Zane... and he wished more than anything that the feeling was mutual.

He watched the traffic go by, not seeing any of it. He should have known Zane would flash him when he asked about his abs. The guy was understandably a bit of an exhibitionist about his body and seemed so... physical... in how he attacked life. He would undoubtedly be totally uninhibited in bed too. God, it was tempting to experience a lover like that. Would it loosen up his own hang-ups a little?

What the hell was he supposed to do about Zane? The guy was supposed to be a job. Nothing more and nothing less. He couldn't afford to let this turn into a personal relationship. Professionalism and all.

Except he didn't technically work for Peregrine Cardiffe and Wild Cards, Inc. anymore. This was a favor for a friend. Did that negate the requirement to maintain boundaries of professional distance from clients? Or was he just looking for a convenient excuse to get inside Zane's shorts?

Of course, it didn't help that Zane seemed prepared to act on the sizzling attraction that crackled between them.

God knew Sebastian wasn't ready to act on it. A little voice in the back of his mind snorted in disbelief. Okay. Fine. He *shouldn't* be ready to act on it. In point of fact, he definitely was.

However, sleeping with Zane might convince the guy that he bought Zane's story about not knowing who had put the plates in his luggage. And maybe it would slow him down a hair when it came time for Zane and his buddies to try to kill him. It would probably be the hottest sex he ever had—

No. Stop right there. Sleeping with Zane is a terrible idea.

And yet his body seemed to think it was the brightest idea since the electric light bulb. He shifted in his seat, his erection painfully hard and unpleasantly contained by his briefs and jeans. On one hand, he was desperate to get to the restaurant and distract himself with food. On the other hand, he would have to unfold his body from the confines of the car and stand upright. Which could prove both embarrassing and uncomfortable.

Zane fell into pensive silence as well, seeming distracted about something. Were Sebastian not wrestling with his own pounding lust so damned hard, he might have inquired about it. Instead, he gritted his teeth and thought about tax audits. Nuns. Anything to get his mind off jumping on top of Zane Stryker and ripping that tight T-shirt and those sexy jeans off him.

"We're here, gentlemen," Etienne announced from the front seat.

Praise the Lord and pass the potatoes. Sebastian all but fell out of the damned car onto the sidewalk in his haste to get away from Zane.

The Italian restaurant, narrow and deep, was empty this early in the afternoon, and they were seated immediately at a booth in the darkest, most private, most romantic back corner of the dining room. Only the glow of a tea candle in a schlocky red glass bubble lit Zane's face as he looked around, grinning. "Really? Italian food? You do realize I just flew in from Milan, right?"

Sebastian shrugged. "What can I say? If I'm going to put some meat on your bones, can you name me a better cuisine to do it?" He added archly, "Besides, I'll bet you didn't eat a single bite of pasta the whole time you were in Italy. Your body sculptor dude probably told you carbs are Satan's great temptation, didn't he?"

Zane made a noncommittal sound he would take as verification that he was correct on all counts.

The bartender put down his towel and came over to wait on them. "Hey, Seb. How've you been? Long time, no see."

"I've been busy. Had to go out of town for a while. But I'm back and dying for one of your specials."

"The usual?"

"Better make it extra large. I'm sharing today."

"You got it. Beer?"

"Two of whatever you've got on tap that's dark and sweet."

Zane took a sharp breath beside him, and Sebastian threw him a sidelong glance as the bartender retreated. "You okay?"

"I haven't had anything alcoholic to drink in over three years."

Sebastian swore. "I'm sorry. I didn't know. I'll have him take the beers back."

"No. It's okay. I was never an alcoholic. Drugs were my poison of choice, and no power on earth could make me mess with those now. It was a long, hard climb back, and I won't go through that again. I stayed away from booze because I didn't want to end up using it as a crutch while I broke my drug habit only to end up an alcoholic instead."

"You're sure you don't just want me to order us a couple of sodas instead?"

"I'm sure. I'm in a much better headspace these days. I can drink a beer without falling off the addiction cliff. I'll always be careful about my alcohol intake, of course. But I'm not hyperventilating, and I don't have butterflies in my stomach. This is good. Very good. Believe me."

The bartender plunked down a pair of frosted mugs, and Sebastian made a point of sipping his. No way in hell was he ordering another round and making Zane feel any more awkward than he already did.

He watched carefully as Zane took an appreciative sip of the brew and set the mug down without needing to guzzle the beer. Thank goodness the guy seemed to be addiction-free.

"So, Sebastian. Tell me about this place."

Their gazes met, and Sebastian actually choked a little on the foam as the simmering attraction between them flared up again. Crap. Even a vaguely intimate look from Zane was now inflating his rubber ducky. He'd barely gotten over his last hard-on, dammit. He mumbled, "Do you have any idea how amazing you look in candlelight?" *Hell.* Where had those words come from?

Zane's thousand-watt smile flashed. "Sweetie, I'm a model. I know exactly how I look in every light and from every angle." A pause. "But thanks. It's nice to hear that from someone outside the business."

"You don't paint a very flattering picture of your job or your life."

Zane toyed with the exterior of his mug, drawing idle designs in the frost on the thick glass. "I was too young for it when I started. The hell of it is that youth pays, though. It's a tough business to grow up in. Too many temptations. Too much flattery. It twists you. Kills all your filters."

"*All* of them?" he blurted. *Jesus.* Sebastian's imagination had just taken flight again. His sex life had been pretty boring to date. It was a walk on the wild side to have sex at all, let alone do all the dirty, fun, experimental things he daydreamed about when his guard was down.

One corner of Zane's mouth turned up. He leaned in close to murmur, "I've done all the things, and more, that you've only imagined in secret, late at night, when you're jerking off in the dark."

Sebastian stared, shocked.

Zane leaned back, his smile widening in triumph.

"Are you telling me the truth—" He broke off. "No. Don't answer that. I don't want to know."

"Yes you do. You want all the messy, X-rated details. You want me to describe it all to you and then do it all with you."

He gulped. Literally gulped. All right, then. So it was possible to blow his wad in response to nothing more than dirty talk. "If you ever get tired of modeling, you could make a fortune at a phone sex gig."

Zane picked up his mug and was still grinning when he tipped the thing to his mouth and took a long swig. He smacked his lips together in satisfaction, and Sebastian's imagination galloped away with him again. What would it be like to have those pouty pink lips wrapped around his cock, that audacious tongue swirling around the head of it, flicking and slurping and teasing—

"For fuck's sake, Zane. Quit messing with me."

An elegant shoulder shrug. "Sorry. You're too uptight, my dude. You need to chill out."

And just like that, Zane turned off the flirting, his tone matter-of-fact.

Fuck. Had all of that been just an act? It had been completely convincing. Sebastian had been ready to get down on bended knee and beg the man to sleep with him. But then, that was what the guy was paid to do, wasn't it? To sell sex. He was supposed to sell the idea of every product, every article of clothing he modeled, as the means to be like him. To be gorgeous and young and the embodiment of a desirable male.

Sebastian exhaled hard, one part relieved and one big part disappointed. He changed the subject, regaling Zane with the early history of this joint as a speakeasy and then a mafia hangout. "The old speakeasy is accessible by a secret stairway in the back office. But there's also a trapdoor in the floor behind the bar that leads to it. That way, if police raided this place, wanted criminals could duck out of sight fast and either hide down below or make their way out the back by way of the stairs."

"That's so cool! Can we take a look at it?" Zane asked eagerly.

Sebastian and the bartender exchanged grins, but it was Sebastian who answered. "Seeing as how I own the place, that might be arranged."

Zane's jaw dropped and that delicious mouth of his formed a round O that made Sebastian think yet again of blowjobs and hot, wet kisses. Although, in the state he was in right now, a hole in a wall would probably make him think dirty thoughts. *Jeez.* He hadn't been this horny since he'd been about fourteen and first figured out he was gay. Before that, he'd tried with all his might to be attracted to girls and had utterly failed, assuming that something was broken with his sex drive.

The bartender brought out a huge deep-dish pizza pie and plunked it down on a wire stand in front of them.

"What all's on this beast?" Zane exclaimed. "It looks like the cook threw everything in the kitchen at it."

Sebastian grinned. "It does have every topping in the store on it, except anchovies and pineapple. I'm sorry, but fish and tropical fruit just don't belong on a proper pizza."

"Speak for yourself, Italian boy. I love me a good Hawaiian… all juicy and meaty. Yum."

Christ. Was the guy doing that intentionally, or was Sebastian just finding double meanings in everything Zane said?

They dug in, and the next several minutes were spent in blissful silence. Not only was the crispy, fluffy-edged crust made from scratch, but the tomato sauce was homemade and the cheese flown in from a dairy in Wisconsin each week. It was a pizza connoisseur's pizza.

Zane leaned back after two slices, and Sebastian raised an eyebrow. "You only said I had to eat what you ordered, not that I had to eat all of it."

Sebastian grunted. "You're not stopping yet, my friend. We've already established that you need some meat on those bones of yours." When Zane looked unmoved, he added, "Live a little. You can't deny yourself the pleasure of fine food *all* the time. It's not good for your mental health."

"You do understand that salads, vegetables, and roughage are healthy for a person, right?" Zane retorted.

"I promise. Nothing but salads and lean proteins tomorrow. But tonight, eat up. Who doesn't love a slice of the finest deep-dish pizza to be had in New York?"

Zane groaned, rolled his eyes, but didn't protest as he took a third slice. For his part, Sebastian didn't count how many slices he ate. He took almost more pleasure in watching Zane savor the gourmet pizza than he did from eating it himself. Zane ate slowly, sensually, enjoying every single mouthful with eyes closed and a beatific look on his face.

Eventually, when Sebastian's stomach ached and his belt felt tight, he leaned back. "Now that's a pizza."

Zane sighed in similar satisfaction. "Thank you. I'd forgotten how amazing an American pizza could be."

Except as their gazes met and the words came out of Zane's mouth, it almost sounded as if he was saying he'd forgotten how good New York could be. Or maybe how good an Italian guy in New York could be.

"Sebastian?"

"Hmm?"

"Are you really gay?"

Sebastian started, the combination of food coma and sensual haze pierced. "Seriously? You have to ask?"

"It's not that I don't believe you. It's just that most men would've made a pass at me by now. Aren't you attracted to me?" He added hastily, "Don't get me wrong. I don't expect to be everyone's cup of tea. And I don't need you to throw yourself at me to bolster my self-esteem. It's just that... am I wrong to feel a... a vibe... between us?"

"No. You're not."

"Thank God. I would hate to think I had completely lost my mojo in the three years I've been out of the Big Apple."

"Your mojo is fine. It's me. I'm the problem. I'm sitting here wrestling with myself over the ethics of getting involved with someone I've promised to protect."

"I don't need your protection. I mean, it's really decent of you to be worried about me. Kind, actually. But I can figure this out by myself, honestly. Sure, Customs could've been a bitch, and I'm grateful you stepped in to make that go more smoothly, but if you want to tap out on this whole thing of the—" He leaned in and whispered, "—you know. The things in my suitcase—" He leaned back. "I'm cool with that."

"Ready to get rid of me, are you?" He asked the question lightly, but it felt like a brick had lodged in his intestines and wouldn't budge.

"Not at all!" Zane exclaimed. "I would like to stay in touch after this is all over. Maybe more than in touch. I just feel weird about foisting off my problem onto you."

"What if I don't mind you foisting yourself on me?" His chagrined gaze snapped up to Zane's. Apparently, it was his turn to make blatant innuendoes. In a lame effort to cover up his cheesy flirtation, Sebastian slid out of the booth, his dick significantly more alert than it should be in public. "Come with me. There's something I'd like to show you."

"Please God, let it come from inside your pants," Zane muttered behind him.

Sebastian laughed. "While I applaud the sentiment, I haven't finished torturing myself yet over the moral dilemma of being attracted to the guy I'm supposed to be protecting."

"Isn't it possible to do both?"

"Don't be all logical with me. Let me torture myself a little longer before you go and let me off the hook with common sense and reason."

Zane grinned. "Got it. Knock yourself out. Just let me know when you've inflicted enough misery on yourself and I can move in on you."

"Will do. This way." Sebastian gestured toward the swinging door to the kitchen. He stepped through, and a round man with a scruffy black five-o'clock shadow shouted a hello in Italian. Sebastian waved back and hustled Zane through. The cook was an inveterate gossip and never, ever shut up once he got going.

He led the way to a tiny back office crammed with a desk, filing cabinets, and a tall built-in bookcase.

"It's a little cramped in here for hanky-panky, big guy," Zane murmured.

"That's why we're going down here." Sebastian tilted out the correct book and heard a click. He pushed the fake bookcase inward to reveal a set of steps leading down into darkness. "The trapdoor has always been only for emergency use. The actual entrance has been here all along."

"That is so cool!"

Sebastian felt his way down the narrow staircase to the light switch at the bottom. He flipped it, and both the staircase and a vintage bar straight out of the 1920s lit up. Jazz music began to play, and the red velvet sofas scattered around a dance floor, in front of a slightly raised stage big enough to hold a band, glowed in the soft light of crystal and tin chandeliers.

"It hasn't been used in a while, so I haven't had it cleaned recently. It's a bit dusty."

"It looks like a time warp down here. Was it in this good a shape when you bought the place?"

Sebastian laughed. "God, no. I had it restored. Took a couple of years for my designer to find all the furniture and fixtures and bring them in. Over here on the wall is a collection of photographs taken down here over the years. We used these to guide the renovation."

Zane moved around the vintage club in wonder, trailing his fingers along the carved mahogany backs of the sofas and chairs, twirling across the oak-paneled dance floor, and laughing as he stepped up to a bulky microphone hanging on a thick wire dangling from the ceiling. "My God. It's perfect."

"Thanks. I'll let Kelsey know. She spent a lot of time on this project."

"You said it hasn't been used in a while. How long?" Zane asked.

"Let's see. I threw a party down here last year."

"Who uses it besides you?"

Sebastian strolled over to his favorite booth directly in front of the stage and band risers, and opened a box of Cuban cigars he kept in a humidor sitting on the table. He inhaled their expensive tobacco scent appreciatively. "Every now and then I let someone else host a party here. But it's on a case-by-case basis, and only for personal friends."

"I know fashion designers and photographers who would *kill* to do a shoot or a fashion show down here."

"I only allow private events."

Zane strolled up to him, doing his best catwalk, and put a playful hand on his chest. "How private, big guy?"

Sebastian scowled. "You do realize we're alone down here and this room is completely soundproofed, right?"

A fine shiver passed across Zane's smooth, bronzed skin, and the smile slipped from his face.

Oops. Tactical mistake to make the Erebus operative nervous. "You're not afraid of me, are you?" Sebastian teased lightly.

"More like I'm afraid of me. Ever since I landed at JFK and you swept in to rescue me, I've felt... out of control. Not myself." Zane stalked pensively around the half-circle banquette.

Sebastian did the same, keeping the booth between them. "Why's that?"

Zane hesitated, then continued circling. "Because you're not like anyone else I know."

"Is that good or bad?"

"Undecided. I don't know what to expect from you. I mean, how many British ex-soldiers would so painstakingly restore something like this?"

"Depends on how many could afford to do it, I suppose."

"That's not my point, and you know it."

Fair. Sebastian stood still, stopping the game of cat and mouse. "What do you want from me, Zane?"

"Undecided." A pause. "Thing is, the crowd I run with doesn't do real relationships. And I get the feeling you don't know how to do anything but real."

Also fair. "I don't have a history of doing relationships at all."

Zane asked quietly, "Do you want to start?"

"With you?"

"Yes." A pause, then quickly, "No." A much longer pause, then, "Maybe."

CHAPTER SEVEN

ZANE'S HEART was doing flip-flops in his chest. This dim, romantic setting, the sexy wail of saxophones in the background, the ghosts of flappers and mobsters swirling around him, the big, dark, handsome man in front of him—his imagination was going wild.

"Here's the thing. I'm worried about this weirdness with my suitcase. I want to take care of it and get my life back to normal before I drag you into anything sketchy or dangerous."

Sebastian's dark gaze flared with what Zane could swear was confusion.

"Don't get me wrong, Sebastian. I'm interested in you. Really interested in you. I just don't want you to get hurt."

That made Sebastian grin. "I'm the one who's supposed to be protecting you."

"That doesn't mean I can't worry about your safety too."

"Huh. Trust me. I can take care of myself. I'll be fine. You're the one we have to worry about, here."

"Still." Speaking of which, Zane pulled out his cell phone—his phone, not the burner phone, of course—to check the time. "Crap. If I'm going to make the ballet, I've got to get back to the hotel, get cleaned up, and head out."

"Sure. No problem." Sebastian sounded disappointed. Which was more gratifying than Zane could have anticipated. Maybe the guy really was as into him as he claimed to be. Although he was still perplexed over why Sebastian hadn't jumped his bones already. God knew he'd been throwing out all the signals he could possibly lob at the guy without coming right out and suggesting they stop, drop, and fuck.

Sebastian turned off the lights and music, and they climbed the secret stairs in silence, leaving the magic behind.

Disappointment coursed through him. He'd really hoped Sebastian would make a move on him down there. God knew it was the perfect setting for an illicit affair.

They reached the top of the stairs, and Sebastian turned around abruptly. Zane started and overbalanced backward, teetering on the top step. Sebastian reached out lightning fast to grab his arms and haul him forward into the tiny office. Zane slammed against a male chest made of pure brawn.

"Thanks," he gasped.

"You okay?"

No. "Yes." Zane looked up into Sebastian's blue on blue gaze and the world stopped revolving for an instant. An infinite universe of possibilities swam in those eyes. Passion. Possession. Permanence. All the things Zane craved and feared. All the things he desired but did not deserve. He wanted this man. And he could think of a hundred reasons they shouldn't be together—

"Stop overthinking it," Sebastian muttered as their mouths met. He swept his strong arms around Zane, drawing him up against that muscular chest, into a possessive, carnal kiss. This was no tentative first peck. This was tongues and teeth and lust, a frantic slide of wet lips and the hot, sharp pull of being inhaled by Sebastian. Zane could crawl inside that kiss and never come out. He gave himself over to it, shocked at how damned good it felt to be owned and worshipped, dominated and cherished, all at the same time.

He should have known the guy would kiss with as much intensity as he did everything else. This voracious embrace had nothing to do with finesse and everything to do with raw, desperate need. But shockingly, Zane was every bit as desperate as Sebastian, straining into the kiss, opening up his body, mind, and soul to the moment. He wanted Sebastian, and he freely gave himself over to both the kiss and the man.

Zane let his hands roam across Sebastian's back and slid his palms under Sebastian's soft polo shirt. He gasped at the heat and vibrating tension of the man beneath. Skin. He wanted skin. All the skin. Naked bodies. Sweat. The loud, slapping sounds of hot sex—

Sebastian's mouth tore away from his, and Zane actually whimpered in frustration.

"You'll be late," Sebastian muttered.

"Late to what?"

Sebastian laughed against his temple, a pained sound. "Late to the ballet."

"Oh." Belatedly, his brain started making logical connections. The burner phone. An anonymous order to go to the ballet and bring the plates. Which he was 100 percent ready to be rid of. Hell, right now, he didn't even care if he got the million bucks or not. He just wanted to be in the clear to get in bed with this man and crawl all over him. "Right. The ballet." A heavy-breathing pause. "But I'd rather be with you."

"Actually, that would probably be a terrible idea for any number of reasons."

"I've counted forty-two reasons why it's a bad idea," Zane said against the comfortable bulwark of Sebastian's chest. "How many have you come up with?"

"At least that many. So far."

"I bet you think we shouldn't be involved because I'll distract you from focusing on your job and protecting me." Zane sighed. He pulled his hands away from Sebastian's waist and felt bereft.

"Keeping you safe would be high on my list."

"I hate this."

"In my experience, doing the right thing often sucks," Sebastian replied wryly.

"I'll cut out before the encores and final bows," Zane murmured, "and be back at the hotel before eleven. Wait up for me?"

"Count on it."

The dark promise in Sebastian's voice sent shivers of delight down Zane's spine while frissons of guilt traveled up it. He hated lying to Sebastian, and the man struck him forcefully as the type to hate being lied to. No doubt about it, he was playing with fire to get involved with him. But when had he ever been able to resist dancing in the flames? Life had always been one giant dare to him.

The ride back to the hotel was freakishly awkward, with both of them clearly immersed in dirty thoughts and second-guesses. They didn't speak, which was just as well. At the slightest provocation, Zane would have fallen on Sebastian, ripped down their pants, and demanded to have hot, gnarly sex then and there, in the back of the car on a busy street.

The elevator ride up to the suite in the Waldorf was worse because the confines were close, forcing them to stand shoulder to shoulder, staring blindly at the electronic floor display. It took every ounce of willpower Zane had to keep his hands off Sebastian. And if Sebastian's labored breathing was any indication, he was waging the same struggle. As they let themselves into the suite, Sebastian said gruffly, "I'll have Etienne drive you to the theater. That should save you a few minutes."

"You don't have to."

"I made you late by showing you the speakeasy. Let me make it up to you."

Zane blinked. Sebastian wanted to do things for him now? "Umm. Okay. I'll be ready to go in two minutes."

"Two?"

"I'm a runway model. I can do a full down-to-bare-ass-naked change, including shoes, in sixty seconds if I have to."

Sebastian seemed arrested by the mention of him bare-ass naked. And just like that, the simmering tension between them broke over into a hard boil again. Zane had to physically shake himself to tear away from Sebastian's side.

He had to meet the counterfeiter. Hand over the plates. Be done with his short second career as a smuggler. He just wanted his life cleared out so he could serve himself up to Sebastian on a silver platter, and then pray Sebastian could forgive him for dumping the plates and extricating them both from involvement with potentially dangerous bad guys.

Zane was surprised to realize his hands were shaking as he hurried through putting on the counterfeiter's designer suit. He considered the briefcase and its metal plates. How was he going to sneak those out of here?

He shrugged back out of the suit jacket and draped it over his arm. If he bunched it up a little, he could hide the slim attaché case beneath it. And if he was lucky, he wouldn't run into Sebastian on his way out of the suite.

He peeked out of the bedroom. The coast was clear. Gliding fast and silent, he headed for the hallway door and slipped outside. The elevator took a lifetime to come, and he winced at the loud *ding* announcing its arrival. He jumped inside the thing and angled himself to hide the briefcase and suit coat from view. At long last the doors slid shut, and he let out a loud sigh of relief.

On the assumption that Etienne was loyal first and foremost to Sebastian, Zane kept the briefcase wrapped in his jacket in the car too.

The ride uptown to the ballet was not long, but the crowd in front of the big marble edifice was terrible.

"Do you want me to take you around to the VIP entrance?" Etienne asked.

"No, that's fine. I'll just jump out here. Thanks so much for the ride. And tell Sebastian I'll take a cab back to the hotel later. There's no need to keep you from whatever you have planned this evening."

Etienne grinned at him in the mirror and didn't elaborate.

"I hope she's hot, man," Zane said as he slid out of the car.

He turned to face the daunting prospect of finding an international criminal in this crush of suits and gowns. It was hard to believe one or more of the patrons dealt in counterfeiting and the other crimes Sebastian said went along with it.

He strode up to the Will Call window, gave his name, and picked up the ticket shoved through the slender opening below the glass. "Just out of curiosity, can you tell me who left this ticket for me?" he asked the attendant.

She typed into a computer and squinted at the screen. "Nope. You're lucky it became available, though. That block of seats is held entirely by season-ticket holders. They rarely miss premieres."

Wow. The counterfeiter had put this meeting together fast. Zane didn't know if that was good or bad. Maybe it meant a team of assassins wasn't waiting for him inside the theater, then. Yes. It was definitely good that this rendezvous was so short notice.

"Thanks." He grabbed the ticket and headed inside. Once in the theater, he slipped into a restroom, where he donned the suit jacket. Ensconced in a toilet stall, he took a quick peek at the engraved plates. Their fronts, the ones congratulating the recipient on being Salesperson of the Year, looked made of brass. But when he turned them over, they were shiny and silver-colored. The carved detail on them was stunning. Which, he supposed, was the point. He lifted one out of the case and was surprised to feel how heavy it was. They must be stainless steel or some equally dense metal.

His seat turned out to be in the orchestra, center section, only about a dozen rows from the stage. *Dang.* Give the counterfeiter credit for great taste in seats at the ballet. As the house lights were going down, an amazon of a woman, a few inches over six feet tall and broad-shouldered, wearing a turban of the same turquoise spandex knit as her dress and undersized-for-her-face diamond-rimmed glasses, slipped into the vacant seat on the aisle beside him. A spider brooch the size and shape of a real tarantula was pinned to the front of the turban, and the dozens of diamonds crusting it looked real.

"Oh good," she murmured in a contralto voice. "I'm glad my son's seat didn't go to waste. He has a cold and couldn't come tonight."

"I hope he feels better soon," Zane murmured politely. "And thank you for making the seat available."

There was no more time for small talk as the orchestra launched into the prelude and the stage lights came up.

The woman beside him stepped out several minutes before the intermission, murmuring about beating the crowd to the restrooms, and he sat alone to watch a breathtaking adagio. The romance between the prima ballerina and her leading man—a dark-haired, muscular Russian star who reminded Zane of Sebastian—was fraught with sexual tension that did nothing to ease Zane's own lust. Uncomfortable and frankly horny, he uncharacteristically stayed in his seat during the intermission and did not go out into the lobby to see and be seen.

Truth be told, he was scared to meet the counterfeiter. He was no secret agent to be running around making million-dollar handoffs.

The three-minute bell had chimed and the crowd was shuffling back in to their seats when his left pocket vibrated. The burner phone. He pulled it out and peered at the screen in the diminishing lights. An address he didn't know scrolled across the screen. Then: *One hour after the show ends. Bring the plaques and come alone.*

When he tried to text a response, he got a message back that the phone he was trying to contact was not in service. The person at the other end must have turned off his phone immediately after sending the text. *Drat.*

He typed the address into a maps program, and the screen lit up just as the music started again. The patron on his right harrumphed in annoyance at the light, and he closed his phone hastily, his thoughts racing. The address was only a few blocks away, a tiny side street. For that matter, it could be an alley from the looks of it. It was a perfect spot for a secret meeting. He would deliver the plates and Sebastian would be none the wiser. The money would be handed over to him for services rendered, and then he could get on with his life.

Sebastian would understand if he made the handoff and bailed out on being a hero, right? Sebastian's friend would probably be pissed, but that wasn't Zane's problem. The friend could figure out where the plates had come from some other way that didn't involve him or Sebastian being hurt or killed.

And truth be told, this whole mess wasn't Sebastian's problem either. Heck, for all Zane knew, Sebastian's friend was one of the counterfeiters and was using the excuse of Sebastian protecting him to actually protect the plates. Although in response to that notion, his instincts suggested that Sebastian was too uptight and honorable to hang out with master criminals, let alone be one himself. However, the guy had come from one of the poorest parts of London and risen to spectacular wealth in a surprisingly short period of time. Maybe Sebastian had criminal connections after all.

As hard as he tried to talk himself into it during the last half of the performance, Zane knew deep in his heart that Sebastian would be furious if Zane made the delivery alone. He hated the idea of getting Sebastian in trouble with a friend almost as much as he hated the idea of betraying Sebastian's trust. No question, it all boiled down to a choice between Sebastian and the cash. A life free of financial worry, or an uncertain future. His safety versus Sebastian's trust.

Was losing Sebastian worth a million bucks? Zane was stunned that he actually had to think about the choice. He barely knew Sebastian Gigoni.

And yet, he knew enough. Sebastian was unlike any man he'd ever engaged in an actual relationship with. He would be stable and steady, a commitment kind of guy. All in. Real and lasting relationship material. Sebastian was an adult, not a flaky model or starving artist. He would also be demanding at times, with ironclad ethics that would be a pain in the ass to live with now and then. But honestly, Zane found that challenge appealing. And the man kissed like a god.

Was he ready to step up to that kind of a relationship? Had he finally grown up himself? The temptation was incredible. But he couldn't turn his back on the million dollars. It represented an education, financial stability. A secure future, dammit.

The ballet ended, and the woman beside him dived out and rushed up the aisle just as the last note sounded. Zane wasn't as fast and got caught in the crush of people trying to leave. Of course, his trepidation might have made him hold back a little on trying to leave the auditorium.

He was so nervous, he made another stop in the restroom to pee a teaspoonful and check on the currency plates again before he reluctantly made his way to the now-mobbed lobby.

It took him a while to file out of the theater and into the night. Good thing the counterfeiter had given him an hour to get to the rendezvous site. Long enough to imagine a thousand things that could go wrong at this meeting. What the hell had he been thinking to agree to it and not tell Sebastian about it?

Clutching the briefcase tightly, he walked away from the broad plaza in front of the theater. The address, which he headed toward on foot, was in a largely business area. At night these streets were empty of pedestrians, and traffic was thin. He ducked under construction scaffolding that created a tunnel over the sidewalk and cast it in deep shadows. Under the cover of the darkness, he risked a glance over his shoulder. Was that a man skulking back there in a recessed doorway?

He waited a moment, and when the shadow didn't move, Zane silently declared himself paranoid. He moved on. Only a block or so ahead now was the side street he sought. His steps slowed again. Was that a man ahead of him?

It made sense that the counterfeiter would bring a security guard or two. Like Zane should have. It was sheer insanity to be out here like this without Sebastian. He sorely missed having a strong, confident, competent partner in this enterprise.

He frantically reviewed everything he could remember about self-defense strategies and moves for average civilians to protect themselves. But who was he kidding? He was going to freeze up and forget all of it if somebody jumped out at him and attacked.

He turned the corner onto the street. It was indeed more of an alley than a street. Tall, blackened brick walls rose in a narrow canyon. A delivery truck blocked the exit perhaps fifty feet into the alley off the main street. Its lights were off and its engine was silent. It was parked and not going anywhere. At a glance, the truck cab looked empty. Zane picked his way around it nervously.

Only a few yards beyond the truck, the street opened up into a tiny square ringed by the utility entrances to various businesses and apartment buildings.

He seemed to be alone. Was he in the right place? He pulled out the burner phone and double-checked the address in his own cell phone's mapping program. Yup, he was definitely in the right spot. Where, then, was his contact? He fidgeted nervously, wondering how long he was supposed to just stand here and wait.

He'd been there for what felt like hours but was probably only a few minutes—long enough to jump at every damned noise and get thoroughly terrified—when, without warning, a male voice rang out in the darkness.

"Don't move. Stay where you are."

CHAPTER EIGHT

As a voice shattered the silence of the night, Sebastian reacted sharply from the top of the building overlooking the alley. Out of breath from racing up a half-dozen flights of stairs at top speed, he'd only been here a few seconds before that voice spoke out of the darkness.

He didn't see the source of the sharp order, and the acoustics of the alley, tucked in between these tall buildings, made the noise bounce around so much he couldn't tell anything about the location of the owner of that gruff voice. He scanned across the neighboring rooftops fast. Nothing.

Hastily, he laid his soft-sided rifle bag down on the roof and pulled out the short-range sniper's rig. He flopped on his belly fast, draping his body over and around the fully customized Wilson Combat AR-10. Flipping down the integral bipod stand to support the rifle's barrel, he planted the weapon's butt against his shoulder and focused through the sight. He scanned the alley again, this time through his low-light sight, in search of the speaker. *C'mon, Zane. Get him to talk again.*

Nada.

On the assumption that the person here from Erebus would have to make physical contact with Zane to actually take the printing plates from him, Sebastian scooted over to the edge of the roof and lay flat, the tip of his rifle poking over the flat edge and angling down into the open space in the alley where Zane stood.

It felt weird as hell to be training a lethal weapon on Zane like this. He didn't think of the guy as a hostile, but in this situation, he had no idea who was a bad guy and who wasn't. For now, he had to assume the worst about Zane and hope for the best.

Worst case would be Zane recognizing and being all buddy-buddy with whoever was here to pick up the plates. Best case: the Erebus contact would try to kill Zane. Bizarre best case, but this whole situation was a bit bizarre. At least then Sebastian would know Zane wasn't part of the criminal syndicate.

Zane stood not far from the rear of a delivery truck randomly parked in the alley, which was a worrisome potential wrinkle in this op. If Zane was grabbed and thrown in the truck just before it sped away, it would be up to Etienne, waiting in an SUV down the main street, to follow the truck and not lose it.

"Did you bring the case and the plaques?" the voice demanded.

Sebastian zeroed in on a dark loading dock beyond the truck. He saw no movement, but the space was plenty wide and deep enough to conceal several men.

"Of course I brought them," Zane answered. "I'm trying to make this go as smoothly as possible for all of us."

Crap. This is the actual handoff. He'd hoped this was just a quick meeting to set up a final time and place for the exchange of the plates and perhaps a payoff to Zane for his service.

What was Zane thinking? They'd talked about this. Sebastian was supposed to go along and spot the counterfeiters, follow them away from the handoff. Find out where they lived and who they were. That was all. No drama. No violence. Minimal physical danger to Zane.

Even with an impeccable source within Erebus, Peregrine Cardiffe needed any physical evidence against Erebus that they could get, not to mention they needed the identities of all the Erebus employees they could get. When they cut the heads off the snakes, they needed to get all the heads, all at once. Of more immediate importance, on the off chance that Zane wasn't a member of Erebus and actually was an amateur, he needed professional protection.

Yet, there he was below, barging into a rendezvous completely alone. It would serve him right if he got shot.

Except the idea of Zane being injured or killed tied Sebastian's gut up in knots he didn't want to examine too closely.

The voice came out of the shadows once more. "Put the case down on the ground and step away from it."

Yup. The speaker was definitely hiding in that doorway. If only Zane was miked up and had an earpiece. Sebastian would give anything to be able to whisper to him to ease back, beside the truck, to prepare to use the vehicle's bulk for cover if this thing went to hell in a handbasket. *Get the guy talking*, he silently urged Zane. *Distract him. Put him at ease.*

"How am I going to collect my payment for delivering the goods?" Zane asked.

Payment? What payment? Apparently Zane had been a busy camper: either he'd made a prior arrangement before he came to New York, or he'd been talking to the counterfeiters on the sly and arranging some sort of payoff for making the delivery. Wasn't he the clever one?

An urge to swear—loudly—passed through him. At least bringing up the subject of payment was a great misdirect away from the security concerns of this moment.

"Bank transfer," the voice bit out.

Ha. Not bloody likely. Which meant this alley was a kill zone. If Zane were wired for sound, Sebastian would tell him to get the hell out of there, right now.

"You don't have my account number," Zane shot back.

C'mon, Zane. Make the leap of logic. If the guy can't pay you, he intends to kill you. Get. Out. But no matter how hard Sebastian thought the words, he couldn't seem to make Zane hear them.

"Getting your bank account number is child's play for my people."

My people. An organization, then. Big and powerful, if banking information was so easy to obtain. Confirmation that this was, indeed, an Erebus operation, perhaps? Although the choice of words was interesting. *My people* seemed to exclude Zane, as if Zane didn't work for that organization.

Hope leaped in his gut. *Please God, let Zane not be one of the smugglers.*

Zane declared boldly, "I'm not handing over the plaques until the funds transfer to my account is complete."

Shit. He did *not* just threaten the voice! *Take it back, take it back,* Sebastian silently chanted. His hand tightened around the stock of his high-powered rifle, and he had to forcibly relax the muscles in his palm and wrist, struggling to settle back into the calm readiness of a shooter.

Zane didn't take the words back.

And the tone of the guy in the doorway shifted markedly. "Put the briefcase down," he barked. "Step away from it and don't look back. I'm feeling generous tonight, and I'm going to let you walk out of here alive... *if* you leave right now."

Nonononononono!

Sebastian watched in horror as Zane set the case on the ground. It was his only lifeline! The voice was just making sure it wasn't handcuffed to Zane's wrist before he shot Zane. Frantically, Sebastian trained his weapon on the doorway. Sure enough, a dull glint of metal emerged, followed by a large man training a pistol in a two-handed grip in Zane's direction.

Sebastian double-tapped his trigger without hesitation, sending two high-caliber rounds into the shooter, who went down hard.

And then all hell broke loose.

Zane spun and ran. Two more men stepped out of the doorway, both armed, shooting down the alley at Zane's retreating form. Sebastian grimly took aim at the first guy and shot him once. The guy shouted out and staggered but didn't go down.

Dammit. Sebastian, already targeting the second man, was forced to swing his weapon back to the first guy and put two more fast rounds into him. But the second guy got off a volley of shots, accompanied by flashes of light and explosions of sounds, in Zane's direction.

Zigzag, Zane! Sebastian screamed silently. He dared not shout it aloud and give away his exact position. Operating on autopilot lest his panic overcome him, Sebastian zeroed in on the second shooter, who'd taken off running after Zane, which meant he was moving almost directly away from Sebastian.

He exhaled hard, and when his lungs were empty and his chest still, he pulled the trigger. The running man screamed, falling and rolling behind the truck, out of Sebastian's line of sight.

Crap. Sebastian grabbed his gun, jumped up, and ran along the roof edge, peering down every dozen steps or so, hunting for a sight line on the last man.

Zane's silhouette slipped around the corner of the alley and out of sight. Abruptly, one more man stepped out from that recessed doorway, snatched up the briefcase, and sprinted back. He was wearing a hat that completely shadowed his face. *Dammit!*

Sebastian took a fast shot at the guy but missed. He only succeeded in making the man duck as chips of brick flew in his face. A door slammed, heavy and metal-sounding, and the alley went silent.

Swearing, Sebastian threw down his rifle and raced for the stairwell into the office/shop building. He had to get a look at the man with the briefcase. Surely he wouldn't circle back and use the truck in the alley. Its license plates were clearly displayed, and Zane had seen them and could report them. No, the man would use some different getaway vehicle. There was a loading dock on the south side of the building. Had the man parked a set of wheels in there?

He ran down the five flights of stairs at top speed, skipping a half-dozen steps at a time, using the rails to catch himself as he bounded downward. He heard a squeal of tires as he burst out onto the ground floor. *No!* This link to Erebus couldn't get away!

Sebastian raced for the south end of the building, slamming against the locked door that had to lead to the loading area. He lost time circling back to find a pedestrian exit. As he threw open the emergency exit, an alarm sounded, splitting the night with piercing noise.

Ignoring it, he ran outside in search of the vehicle he'd heard leave the scene. The street was empty.

Quickly he called Etienne. "Any sign of a vehicle fleeing at high speed?"

"Not from here. But I do have eyes on Zane. He ran about a block from the alley and then hunkered down behind a pile of trash in a covered entry."

"Pick him up. Take him back to the hotel. I'll meet you there."

Sebastian ran down the street to the east, not really expecting to spot the fleeing vehicle. He reached a major thoroughfare, still reasonably busy, and gave up. No telling what car had been in that loading dock. What a mess. He'd lost the counterfeiter, and Zane had handed over the damned plates. Their main lead was gone, and Erebus would disappear into the shadows once more. It could be years before they got another chance to identify a member of the organization and pull at that thread. Unless, of course, Zane was one of them and led him to his superiors within Erebus.

Disgusted, Sebastian raced back to the building he'd used to surveil the meeting in order to pack up his rifle and sanitize his perch on top of the building. He glanced down into the alley. The truck was gone. More shocking, though, was the fact that no bodies were lying down there. He hadn't specifically been trying to kill anyone tonight, but he'd dropped three men. At a minimum, he'd injured them all badly enough that none of them would have been ambulatory. Someone had to have been waiting in that truck to clean up the bodies. As soon as he got clear of this place, he'd call Pere and have his guys run the plates on the truck. Ten to one they'd be stolen, though.

The urgent problem now was to clear out of here before cops responded to the building alarm he'd set off. He had maybe two or three minutes at most before someone arrived to check it out. Working fast, he wiped down the whole area to destroy any fingerprints and used a handheld battery-operated vacuum to pick up any stray hairs or skin cells he might have left behind. Using a high-powered flashlight, he searched quickly for threads or fibers. Clean.

A siren became audible. Hefting the rifle case over his shoulder, he ran down the stairs once more. Pere was going to be deeply disappointed in him. The Wild Cards, Inc. had gone to great lengths last year to place a guy undercover inside Erebus, high within the crime ring. The mole could only take so many chances—like revealing the existence of those currency plates—before he was discovered.

Worse, Sebastian knew from personal experience that undercover operatives had an expiration date. Even the best of operators got lost in their roles or so exhausted by keeping up the charade that they eventually slipped and made a fatal mistake.

This mess was his fault.

He'd known something was up when Zane suddenly had to go to the ballet. He should have listened to his gut, dammit. But he'd figured this rendezvous would only be an information dump. He'd had no idea Erebus would move so fast to get the plates back. And Zane had shown every indication of wanting to take him along for the actual handoff.

God, he'd totally misread Zane, who'd turned out to be a hell of an actor—and a hell of a liar. Zane had never intended to take him to this meeting at all. Betrayal and disappointment roiled in his stomach in a toxic stew.

That didn't automatically condemn the guy to being an Erebus agent, of course. But tonight sure made it look probable that Zane was at least in cahoots with Erebus, if not an employee of the consortium outright.

He should have seen that there was much more to Zane than met the eye. *Dumb, dumb, dumb.*

He'd been so besotted by the model, so dazzled by his beauty and sophistication, that he'd been totally hoodwinked. That made him worse than dumb. It made him a gullible fool.

He slipped out into the alley to avoid the police who were pulling up to the front door of the building. Moving stealthily now, he made his way to the north exit, turned onto the street, and made his way forward, walking as casually as he could, to a major thoroughfare, where he hailed a cab. He collapsed in the back of it, glaring at the city outside. Reluctantly he admitted to himself that his infatuation with Zane hadn't helped matters. He'd been blinded by the guy's looks and charm. *Okay, fine. And by my own out-of-control lust.*

He was batting oh-for-two tonight. He'd lost the plates and the lead they represented on Erebus, and he'd lost a shot at an honest, real relationship with one of the most attractive guys he'd ever met. *Dammit!* He smacked his palm hard on his gun case, and the stinging pain jolted him out of his momentary loss of control.

He had to talk to Zane. Question him. Maybe he'd gotten a decent look at the speaker's face before the gunfire erupted. There had to be something salvageable out of tonight's fiasco.

Sebastian's mind raced as it kicked over into damage-control mode. By the time he got back to the hotel, he had a plan. And it started with Zane Stryker spilling everything he knew about Erebus, no matter what it took.

He paid the cabbie, strode into the Towers, and rode the elevator upward in grim silence. He paused in front of the suite door to gather his resolve. He could do this. *No mercy.*

CHAPTER NINE

ZANE WAS going to barf. His hands shook almost too much to pour himself a shot of vodka. And his legs felt in imminent danger of collapse. He'd been genuinely scared a few times in his life, but nothing like this. When those gunshots had started—and he'd been standing out there all alone and exposed in that alley—and there'd been nowhere to hide, nowhere to run—

He slammed back the vodka and poured himself another one. The fiery pain in his throat distracted him momentarily from his terror. But as the alcohol hit, his already disjointed thoughts jumped around even more wildly. He'd been so grateful when that car pulled up beside him and Etienne yelled through the rolled-down driver's window for him to get in, he'd about fainted on the spot.

And now he had to face the music. Sebastian was going to be so mad he'd gone to the meeting alone and, furthermore, double-crossed him. He wouldn't be happy to hear about the black burner phone either.

Truth be told, Sebastian had been nothing but decent to him from the very beginning, and the man seemed to really care about his safety. He genuinely liked the guy. Respected him, even. And here he was backstabbing him. Talk about feeling like a schmuck.

After this fiasco, he was determined to come clean about the whole thing to Sebastian, though Zane had no idea how to make this mess right. But he would find a way to make it right between them if it was humanly possible.

The suite's door opened and he whirled, his hands coming up defensively. Which was a joke. He didn't know the first thing about fighting or even defending himself. He'd learned young to charm everyone and be a shameless clown. Keep 'em laughing, always be on stage with all eyes on him, and then nobody would beat the shit out of the gay kid. It was a frantic, exhausting existence, but it had worked in its own way.

Sebastian barged into the suite, looking mad enough to kill someone. Steam wasn't exactly coming out of his ears, but it might as well have been, given the blackness of the scowl on his face and the tightness of his square jaw. Zane's terror at facing Sebastian was abruptly joined by waves of guilt.

"Are you all right?" Sebastian asked tersely. "You didn't get shot?"

"No," Zane answered, startled.

"Are you sure? It's not uncommon for people not to realize they've been shot in the adrenaline rush of the moment. Have you checked yourself over for blood?"

Zane looked down at his shirt, alarmed.

"Turn around," Sebastian ordered, striding toward him.

Zane braced himself for he knew not what. Sebastian was visibly furious but ran his brisk, efficient hands over Zane's back, down his ribs and legs, quickly frisking him. It dawned on Zane that Sebastian was probably checking as much for a concealed weapon as he was for injuries. He definitely felt both phones but made no comment on them.

Disappointed, Zane turned to face Sebastian and walked across the room to put a coffee table between them. Not that the knee-high table would slow down Sebastian one bit if the man lost his temper. Still, it made him feel marginally safer.

He looked up warily, and Sebastian's arms were crossed, his jaw clenched, and his stare accusing. His silence was definitely more unnerving to Zane than a screaming fit would have been.

The silence stretched out between them until he couldn't stand it any longer. He burst out, "I found a cell phone in the pocket of the suit. I got a message to go to the ballet, and during the intermission of the performance, I got another message to meet someone in that alley."

More intense, brooding silence out of Sebastian. Dammit, he didn't know what more the guy needed to hear.

"I know I should have told you," Zane blurted. "I'm sorry. But I just wanted to get it over with, and the guy on the phone said to come alone."

Still nothing out of Sebastian.

"I know you wanted to go with me. But I didn't want to mess it up. And I wasn't sure I could trust you."

That got a reaction out of Sebastian. First a look of disbelief, and then, "*You* couldn't trust *me*? That's laughable. If I was one of the bad guys, I could've killed you and taken the plates for myself at any time."

Sebastian paced the length of the living room and back with taut, agitated movements, looking with every step like he was about to explode.

Zane winced and took a deep breath. He was the cause of Sebastian's rage, and Sebastian was not overreacting. "Look. I didn't know who you were when you whisked me out of the airport. Then I was freaked-out when I saw what was in my suitcase, and more freaked-out when you said some international crime ring was using me. And then you hinted that they might kill me instead of—"

"Instead of what?" Sebastian asked sharply.

He would really rather not mention the offer of a million dollars. He didn't want to seem like a greedy money-grubber to this ultra-wealthy man. Not that it mattered now what Sebastian thought of him, of course. He'd already blown it between them pretty thoroughly. If only there were a way to make this right.

He mumbled, "I had no way of knowing if you were one of them or not."

"Me? How do I know *you're* not one of them?" Sebastian demanded back.

"What?" Zane stared at him, shocked.

Sebastian closed the distance between them and got right up in Zane's business, nose to nose with him. "Time for some straight talk. And I have extensive training in detecting deception, so don't even try lying to me. Are you an agent of Erebus?"

"I've never heard that name, let alone am an agent for whoever that is." He added desperately, "Do I seriously strike you as some sort of secret agent type?"

"No. And that's what worries the hell out of me. I don't know how good an actor you are. How much did you make them pay you to deliver their plates?"

Damn, damn, damn. He really didn't want to bring up the money.

But he sensed that if he wasn't completely honest with Sebastian, right here, right now, then that was it between them. Sebastian would never trust him again.

"I didn't make them pay me anything. They texted me on that burned phone like I said before. They said they would pay me for the delivery or they would kill me."

"How much?"

"A million dollars."

"Son of a bitch."

Zane snorted. "Look. I'm getting old. I've got one more season in me, and then I'm done as a fashion model. I'm broke, and I really need that money to start a new life. Build a new career. It was nothing personal against you, I swear."

Sebastian stared at him a long time. He eventually muttered, "I wish I could believe you."

"What do I have to do to convince you?"

"That's the thing. Nothing you can say will help. I have no way of knowing if you're lying or telling the truth."

"What about this?" He pulled out the burner phone and shoved it at Sebastian. "Here's their damned phone. The texts are still there. Read them."

Sebastian took the phone and grimly scrolled through it. "They could've given you this burner and sent you those messages to make you look innocent."

Zane stepped back and took a turn around the living room in frustration of his own. Then he came to a stop in front of Sebastian, and they stared at each other in a standoff so fraught with tension, Zane felt on the verge of shattering. This was real life. He'd just been shot at. Bad people had tried to kill him. This was no hypothetical, semicool spy adventure.

Their stares clashed while their heavy breathing synced up. Sebastian's fists clenched and unclenched, and Zane's stomach muscles clenched and unclenched in response. Tendons corded in Sebastian's powerful neck, disappearing inside his collar. A pulse throbbed in Sebastian's temple, and Zane was startled to realize that his own heartbeat had sped up to match that metronomic pulsing of hot blood in Sebastian's veins.

"How did you know I would be in that alley?" he asked.

"I followed you, of course. The ballet? Really? A ticket becomes available out of the clear blue, when you're sitting on massively valuable and illegal printing plates that an anonymous bad guy wants back?"

Zane had to smile a little. "Hey, it wasn't my idea."

"Here's the problem: If you're telling the truth about not being part of Erebus, you're in more danger than ever. Just because they've got the plates now doesn't mean they won't want to silence you permanently."

"But I did what they wanted. I didn't tell anyone and I met them. Hell, I even came alone to the meeting as far as I knew."

Sebastian shrugged. "This isn't about what you did or didn't do. It's about powerful and paranoid criminals covering their tracks."

He heard Sebastian. He knew in his head that his logic was perfectly sound. But his heart refused to accept the idea of him being in mortal danger. He didn't choose this! He didn't do anything to deserve this.

"Why did they use someone outside their circle of trust to smuggle the plates in the first place?" he asked the universe.

He was surprised when Sebastian actually answered. "That's easy. The feds and various international law enforcement agencies are crawling all up in Erebus's business right now. There was no way one of their known guys could've made it into the United States without being detained, searched, and arrested. They had to use a mule."

"Why me?" he blurted. "God knows I've done some stupid shit in my life that should've gotten me dead. But I've been doing better the past few years. I finally got my life together, and then bam. Out of the blue. These criminals choose my suitcase to hide their damned contraband in."

Sebastian sighed. "In my experience, life is rarely fair. You caught a bad break. It happens."

"Seems like bad breaks are all I catch. When am I finally going to catch a good one for a change?"

Sebastian seemed to understand that the question was rhetorical and didn't answer it. Instead, he said soberly, "If I'm going to keep you alive, I need you to be honest with me."

"You're still going to protect me? Why? I thought your only interest was in seeing who came to pick up the plates from me. Now that these Erebus guys have shown themselves, don't you have what you need?"

"Not exactly. The guy with the briefcase got away from me. I expected him to leave via that truck in the alley, and I had Etienne stationed in the street, watching the truck. But the plates were taken to a second getaway vehicle, and I lost them."

"Oh."

Sebastian sighed heavily. "Yeah. Oh." After a pause, he added, "But even if I knew exactly where the plates had gone, I couldn't very well abandon you to whatever dire fate Erebus has planned for you."

That made him stare. "Why not?"

Sebastian stared back, looking unwilling, or maybe unable, to express why in words. Did the man have feelings for him, or was he hoping to pick up the trail of the bad guys again when they came to kill him? Was this personal, or was it purely business? Did he dare hope that Sebastian felt something more than casual lust toward him?

"Tell me everything," Sebastian declared. He sat down on the sofa and got comfortable, as if he planned to stay here until Zane told him all he wanted to know.

Everything? Like how he'd initially planned to collect the million dollars behind Sebastian's back and ditch him once he had the money? *No, thank you.*

Desperate to distract Sebastian, he took a step closer, bringing them chest to chest. "First, tell me something. Was it you who shot at those guys in the alley? It was, wasn't it? You saved my life, didn't you?"

Sebastian's gaze slid away, and Zane stepped to the side, into his line of sight, forcing Sebastian to look at him. Quietly, sincerely, he said, "Thank you. No one's ever done anything even remotely like that for me before."

Sebastian snorted. "I should hope not. But you're welcome. I'm sorry the handoff didn't go more smoothly. I should have done more to protect you. To be there for you."

For you. The words resonated through Zane's soul like rolling thunder. Sebastian had potentially *killed* for him tonight. That was so intense, Zane didn't know how to even begin to react to it. Words failing him, he shook his head in disbelief. While on a moral level it was appalling that it had come to a dangerous shootout, on some deep, personal level, it was kind of amazing.

"I'm sorry I put you in a situation where you had to shoot somebody."

"It's not that big a deal," Sebastian mumbled. "I'm a soldier. It's what I do."

"You're a retired soldier. It's what you did. I dragged you back into a world you left behind a long time ago."

It was Sebastian's turn to stare. "How did you know that?"

"If shooting people was still routine for you, you wouldn't have been so upset when you got back here."

Their gazes met once more, this time infused with understanding. Dawning knowledge of each other. Sharing the adrenaline rush of having survived a lethal confrontation.

"Are we okay?" Zane murmured.

"No. We're not." Sebastian surged to his feet as if he was too wound up to sit still any longer.

"What can I do to make it right?" He stepped forward, meeting Sebastian as he came around the end of the coffee table.

"You don't owe me anything, Zane."

"But what if I still want to express gratitude to you?" He reached out, hands contacting Sebastian's chest. Pectoral muscles jumped beneath his palms, bunching into tense wads. Sebastian's hands came up, whether to push Zane's away or hold him closer, Zane couldn't tell. But he didn't wait. He took the last step forward into the circle of Sebastian's arms and pressed his body against the wall of muscle that was Sebastian.

Was it a cheap ploy to use sex to distract Sebastian? Maybe. Except he really did want to make Sebastian feel better. And maybe to burn off a little of the driving need pounding insistently through his own veins. He was a physical guy. His life revolved around how he looked, how he moved, how his body was perceived. His body was his tool, his platform for experiencing life. It was the most important thing he could share with Sebastian. And he could only hope Sebastian understood the gesture.

Sebastian drew in a sharp breath that cut across the tense silence. "Zane—"

"Don't pull away from me. I'm not trying to seduce you unless you want me to. But you need to look at me. See me. I'm right here."

"Trust me. I see you. I can't look away from you."

His pulse leaped hopefully. "I'm not going anywhere, and I didn't lie to you about who I am. I'm not one of the bad guys. I'm not one of them."

"Do I dare believe you?"

"Yes. Take the leap of faith." He added desperately, "I'm with you."

Sebastian's arms swept around him, and his mouth swooped down, capturing Zane's in a hard, frantic kiss. He found himself kissing back just as urgently. He'd nearly died tonight, and he was in desperate need of reassurance that he'd made it. That he was still alive.

Sebastian's hips ground against his, and he ground right back. Lust and relief mingled explosively.

"You scared the hell out of me," Sebastian muttered against his lips.

Zane captured Sebastian's lower lip between his teeth and bit down lightly. "How do you think I felt when gunshots rang out and I had no idea where they were coming from, or who shot them, or who they were targeted at? I was sure I was going to die in that alley."

Sebastian turned with him, pushing him back against the wall beside the sofa, trapping Zane with his hands braced on either side of Zane's head, the cool wall at his back and Sebastian's burning heat at his front. "You would have died if I hadn't been there. As soon as you set that briefcase down, you were dead."

"But you saved me," Zane whispered. A pause, and then he risked adding, "Let me save you back."

Sebastian stared at him in something akin to shock, and Zane wrapped his fingers around those amazing arms on either side of him. He waited for Sebastian to pull away, but when he didn't move—and in fact looked rooted to the spot, frozen—Zane slid his hands down Sebastian's arms and reached for the buttons of his dress shirt.

Still giving Sebastian plenty of time and space to stop him, he moved slowly. Carefully. Never breaking eye contact, he popped open the buttons by feel, one by one, working his way down that magnificent chest.

He pushed the starched cotton back, revealing dark skin and curly black chest hair, then ran his fingers through the silken strands, groaning under his breath at how sexy Sebastian's chest was.

"Are we good here?" he murmured. When he'd been young, slender, and pretty, he'd been the target of several attempted assaults. He'd been lucky and smart—not to be too drunk or stoned to fight off his would-be assailants—and he'd been a big fan of conscientiously obtaining consent ever since.

Sebastian didn't answer right away, and Zane stilled, not moving his hands as they lay on his muscular chest. "I'm not proceeding without explicit consent. I don't want there to be any more misunderstandings between us, and certainly not about this. Do you want me to stop or keep going, Sebastian?"

A shudder passed through Sebastian, palpable under his palms. "Keep going." The words were no more than a breath of a sigh, but they were enough for him. Thank God.

He pressed his hand flat against Sebastian's chest and felt a heartbeat under his palm, pounding hard and fast. *Ahh.* Not as calm and unaffected as he looked, huh? Emboldened, Zane reached for Sebastian's belt buckle. It opened and he tugged, relishing the sexy slither of leather as it slid free of his hard waist.

Still staring into those dark, increasingly turbulent eyes, Zane opened Sebastian's fly. Unzipped it. Slid his fingers down inside the elastic of Sebastian's silk boxers. More crisply curling hair, thick and warm. And then he found and closed his fingers around Sebastian's rock-hard erection. He slid down the shaft and then found the heavy, hot sac behind, cupping Sebastian's balls and giving them a light squeeze. He pressed his middle fingertip to the spot just behind Sebastian's scrotum, rotating in a tiny circle.

Sebastian gasped and his hips rocked forward eagerly and then away in caution, or maybe embarrassment. Hard to tell behind the white-hot blaze of lust in Sebastian's eyes.

Zane slipped his other hand into the waist of Sebastian's trousers, reached around Sebastian's hips, and pushed the fabric down off those narrow, hard hips and ass of steel. Slowly, he sank down between Sebastian's corded arms.

He couldn't resist an urge to taste all those acres of bronzed flesh and rippling abs as he sank, inch by inch, to his knees. He took Sebastian's hard-on into his mouth, just the tip, swirling his tongue around the sensitive flesh, tickling the underside with quick flicks. He raked his teeth lightly down the less sensitive shaft and then slurped his way back up it, soothing where he'd just nibbled.

A hand plunged into his hair at the back of his head, not pressing him forward or trying to restrain him, thankfully. He recognized it for the silent plea it was, and smiling, he closed his eyes and took all of Sebastian into his mouth. He forced his neck muscles to relax and swallowed past the gag reflex as Sebastian's prodigious cock filled his mouth and pressed against his throat. He backed off just enough to breathe and used his right hand to grasp the base of Sebastian's erection tightly, substituting for his mouth.

Using his left hand to cup Sebastian's balls as well, Zane used his lips, tongue, teeth, and fists to drive Sebastian out of his mind. He wasn't gentle with Sebastian's junk. Not yet. Right now, it was all about making the man go wild with pleasure. He relished seeing Sebastian squirm and then writhe, totally out of control and at his mercy as he grasped Sebastian's entire package tightly and made it his. He played Sebastian's body, driving him to pant, and then groan, and then shout with pleasure.

It was an outrageous turn-on to look up at Sebastian, his forearm braced on the wall and his forehead braced on his arm. His eyes were closed now, his jaw clenched so hard he looked like he might crack a tooth. That long, tanned torso undulated and jerked as Zane sucked and soothed, nipped and pulled, driving Sebastian from the edge of pleasure to the edge of pain and back again, mercilessly driving him to lose all control of his body and soul, and to surrender both completely.

People might think the guy getting the blowjob was in control, but Zane knew better. He owned Sebastian in that moment, and he was so turned-on by it that his own erection threatened to explode.

Concentrating on the task at hand, he increased the speed and pressure of his mouth sliding up and down that slick, hard shaft. He tightened his hand on Sebastian's balls and demanded silently that Sebastian come for him. Sebastian fought it for a few seconds, but he wasn't able to hold out, and with a shout and one last shuddering surge, he plunged forward into Zane's mouth.

Zane reveled in how long Sebastian's orgasm lasted, how violently he erupted, and how utterly spent he was as Zane slipped out from under him and stood up. Sebastian stayed there—forearm against the wall, trousers around his ankles—panting, for long seconds. It was a beautiful sight, one Zane would never forget as long as he lived. Sebastian looked like a Greek statue, a warrior at rest after battle. Still standing but not unscathed, his defenses stripped bare, his naked soul exposed.

This was the real Sebastian. Stripped of power suits and money and authority. The flesh-and-blood man, spent and satiated, his mind blown. And Zane had done that to Sebastian. A surge of pride, of personal power, of having—for once in his life—gotten it right with the right man flowed through him.

Now he could only pray that Sebastian would forgive him and not turn his back on him. He had never felt more exposed or vulnerable in his life, even though he was the one still fully clothed.

CHAPTER TEN

NO. WORDS.

None.

What had just happened to him?

Sebastian was staggered by the violence of his reaction to Zane. He'd been completely helpless in the face of what just happened between them. He didn't *do* powerless. He never lost control, and he never, ever, got involved with a man he was half convinced was one of the bad guys.

Problem was, if Zane wanted to distract him, wanted to convince him they were on the same team, the guy would have done exactly what he just had.

Sebastian yanked up his pants and headed over to the bar. He poured himself a double shot of the vodka sitting on the counter, using Zane's glass. He threw it back in distaste, then poured himself another.

"You okay?" Zane asked from the doorway.

"No. I've got to call my friend and tell him I fucked up. That I let you out of my sight and lost the plates. Erebus is in the wind, and his undercover operative risked his life for nothing to tip us off about those currency printing plates."

"We didn't lose the plates," Zane said matter-of-factly.

Sebastian froze.

Turned in slow motion.

Stared at Zane. "I beg your pardon?"

"Oh, I still have the plates. I took them out of the briefcase before I went to the meeting."

Sebastian's mind went completely blank. "Come again?" he mumbled.

"I have the plates. They're right here." He reached into the Italian suit coat and pulled the pair of metal plates out of an inner pocket.

"Why didn't you say so sooner?" he burst out.

"You were so busy accusing me of being in cahoots with those Erebus assholes that I didn't get a chance. And," he added a little reluctantly, "I was mad enough at you for accusing me that I didn't feel like telling you just then. And then later, we got, umm, distracted." He flashed a quick, shy smile that was completely endearing, not to mention disarming. He added seriously, sincerely, "I'm sorry I didn't tell you about that."

"What on earth possessed you to keep the plates?"

"I was worried they might try to kill me in the alley if I just handed over what they wanted. I wanted to get the lay of the land, see if I was in any danger before I coughed up their stupid plates. If they hinted that they were going to shoot me, I was going to pretend to have stashed the plates somewhere else."

Sebastian rolled his eyes. "In that scenario, they would have kidnapped you and tortured the location of the plates out of you."

"Yeah, well, I don't think like a crime lord. That possibility didn't occur to me."

Zane isn't a criminal mastermind.

Sebastian strode forward and wrapped up Zane, plates and all, in a bone-crushing hug of relief. "Thank God, and thank you. Maybe you can still get out of this alive, and maybe we can still figure out who the bastards are who tried to kill you." His knees actually felt weak, he was so relieved.

"You're welcome," Zane gasped. "A little air, here."

He set Zane back down on his feet and kissed him soundly on the mouth.

Bad idea.

Their gazes connected, and all the heat and crackling attraction from before was right there again, snapping and popping between them. An urge to lean in, to carry Zane down to the floor, to return the favor and make love to the man until neither of them could stand, let alone walk, nearly overcame him.

He needed to keep his wits about him. Think about the mission, not get distracted by Zane's mesmerizing mouth and the things it did to him. Sebastian took a hasty step back, gratified at the disappointment shining in Zane's transparent and so-expressive eyes.

Focus on the job. "Why did you take the plates out of the briefcase?"

"No arrangements had been made for paying me, and that made me suspicious. When models work for newcomers in the fashion industry or upstart photographers, we learn fast to get paid up front, before we do the work. We're perceived as easy to stiff because we have no real means of fighting back. Particularly for Americans in Europe, who are unfamiliar with the legal systems and not likely to get much help from local police anyway. The whole setup for the meeting just came across as sketchy. I listened to my gut."

"God bless your suspicious gut," Sebastian declared fervently. "First thing in the morning, when the banks open, I want to put those plates in a safe deposit box and get them away from you. That way no one should come after you with guns blazing again."

"And tonight? How much danger am I in, given that I've still got these stupid plates?" Zane asked, frowning.

"Hard to tell. As far as I can tell, nobody followed you back here. I think they were too busy fleeing the shooting before the cops got there and getting that briefcase to whomever sent them to fetch it."

Zane let out a sigh of relief, and Sebastian added in warning, "But that doesn't mean they haven't been following you already, or maybe tracking your position based on the location of the burner phone they gave you. I'd like to take a look at that phone, by the way. I doubt we can learn anything from it, but it's worth checking it out and making sure there is no GPS function built into it."

"They could be on their way here to kill me? Right now?"

"Breathe, Zane. We're in a posh hotel with excellent security people. They can't just barge in, magically figure out what room you're in, and break in here. And even if they managed all of that, they'd still have me and Etienne to contend with."

"Etienne? Is he some kind of soldier too?"

"My dear man. He's ex–French Foreign Legion. Even I wouldn't want to tangle with him in a dark alley. He kicks my butt on a regular basis, and if you'll forgive me for being blunt, I'm no slouch at hand-to-hand combat."

"So he's your bodyguard?" Zane asked.

"Not officially, but we look out for each other. Have each other's backs. He was the first guy I hired when I had enough money to pay someone to help grow my business. We've been together for a long time."

"Friends with benefits?" Zane murmured. He sounded like he was trying to be blasé about the question, but sudden tension thrummed through him.

Sebastian laughed. "Dude. He's so straight he could double as an arrow."

Zane exhaled hard. "Glad to hear it."

"Were you jealous? Of me?" he blurted.

Zane answered breezily, "Do I strike you as the jelly type? Not even."

Hah. Zane was totally feeling territorial about him. Which was. So. Cool.

Truth be told, he was feeling pretty territorial about Zane too.

Aloud, he said, "I'll give Etienne a call. Ask him to come up to the suite. He and I will stay up tonight and guard you. That, and I'll call the hotel security guys and let them know you've got a crazy stalker, and we need eyes on the security cameras in the Towers all night."

"Wow. It must be nice to have that kind of clout."

"It's not nice needing to have that kind of clout," Sebastian retorted. "Go to sleep. If you hear gunshots, lock yourself in your bathroom and don't come out until I give you the all clear."

"What if you die?"

Sebastian snorted. "Then it won't matter. The bad guys will break down the door and kill you too."

Zane's eyes went wide and frightened.

"I didn't say that to scare you. Between Etienne and me, you couldn't have much more hard-core protection. He and I have both been to hell and back a few times. And believe me, the devil's scared shitless of him."

Zane laughed reluctantly. "Be careful."

"Count on it. I'm not losing you after I've just found you."

Zane looked nearly as startled as Sebastian felt. Where in the hell had those words come from? They'd just slipped out. This was still a mission, and he was still supposed to be protecting Zane's life. This was neither the time nor the place for a romantic entanglement.

But as the long hours of the night passed and he sat in the dark, gun in his lap, watching the front door, his mind kept wandering back to the encounter between him and Zane earlier. He'd had some decent sex in his life, but he'd never experienced anything remotely as intense as that. It was as if Zane had reached inside his gut and pulled his heart out. He'd felt... things... he'd never felt before. Gratitude. Empowerment. *Need.*

He didn't do need.

He'd learned a very long time ago that needing anyone was a weakness that others could and would exploit. He relied on himself and nobody else.

And yet he needed to do that again with Zane. In fact, he needed to do more than that. And he needed to do it almost worse than he needed to breathe.

It wasn't just about the sex, although the sex was great. It was about the warm feeling in his belly he got from being around Zane. He couldn't remember the last time he'd felt that way about anyone.

It was a long, *long* night.

MORNING BROUGHT Etienne back up to the suite after he went down to the kitchen to personally fetch their breakfast. He knocked on the suite door, and after Sebastian checked through the peephole to verify it was the Frenchman, he opened the door. Etienne pushed in a cart loaded with food, all vetted and free of drugs or poison. Knowing Etienne, the guy had tasted each dish himself, just like in medieval times. Sebastian dug in, hungry as hell after last night's excitement.

Zane came out of his room, rubbing his eyes, hair sticking up, and looking about twelve years old. Sebastian couldn't help grinning at him. "You look like Dennis the Menace."

"I am a menace." Zane tried to make a threatening face and Sebastian burst out laughing.

Etienne's eyebrows sailed up, and that was when it dawned on Sebastian that he hadn't felt this good, or laughed like that, in a long time.

"Eat, you two," Sebastian declared. "I'm calling my bank and arranging to go in before they open to make a deposit."

"I have a safe deposit box at my bank," Zane declared. "And I'd rather keep the plates there."

Sebastian leaned back, staring speculatively at him. Now why would he want to put the plates in his own bank? Why did he want to retain control of the plates? "Mind if I ask why?"

"They're my responsibility. They were put in my luggage. I'm happy to give you all the access codes to the box, but I'm not foisting my problems off on you."

Sebastian shrugged. "You didn't foist anything on me. The Wild Cards asked me to meet you at JFK and track those plates."

"Who are these Wild Card people, anyway?"

"London-based security firm. They do all kinds of personal protection and solve problems for clients with enough money to pay to make problems go away."

"How do you know them?"

"I worked for them right after I got out of the British Army. I saved every penny I made with them so I would have enough to move to America and buy my first real estate property. Good company. Great employer."

"But you don't work for them now?" Zane followed up.

"Haven't in a while. I'm just doing a favor for an old friend to handle this… whatever this is."

"It's definitely a problem," Zane responded. "I wish I had the cash to throw money at this one and make it go away."

"Hang in there, Zane. We'll get rid of these Erebus guys for you."

They traded smiles over the orange juice, and it was so damned romantic he could hardly stand it.

It was barely 9:00 a.m. when the three of them headed out. Etienne took point, and Sebastian hovered protectively next to Zane. They hustled him and the plates down into the parking garage and quickly into the town car.

It took about an hour at the bank to sign all the paperwork, show identification, get escorted into a small armored room, and wait for Zane's safe deposit box to be delivered pneumatically.

Long enough for Sebastian to wonder why a self-described broke high-fashion model had his own safe deposit box in a city where they were notoriously expensive to maintain. Suspicious, Sebastian peeked into the box when it arrived. He spied an old watch, a few men's rings—including a wedding band and a class ring of some kind—and several small flat cases. "What's in those?" he asked.

"My grandfather's medals from World War II. He willed them to me along with this deposit box, which is paid for in perpetuity, and the other stuff in it."

"What are the papers?" It was none of Sebastian's business, but he never had been great at controlling his curiosity.

"I don't really know. Old bonds."

"Treasury bonds or private bonds?" Sebastian asked with interest.

Zane shrugged. "I was twenty when Gramp died. He was the only member of my family speaking to me at the time. I was in Paris when he died, and it took me over a year to get back to New York to take possession of this box of stuff. I was busy modeling and never got around to investigating the bonds. The bank said they're not valuable."

"Mind if I take a look?"

"Nah."

He unfolded the old, delicate papers. Indeed, most of the papers were corporate bonds that didn't look worth much. But one piece of paper caught his eye. "This looks like a deed of some kind. Here in New York. Do you know the property?"

"No."

"Want me to look it up for you?" Sebastian offered.

"Sure."

Sebastian typed the address and deed number into his cell phone and tucked the deed back into the deposit box. Zane put the plates inside and sent the box back to the vault.

They emerged into bright morning sunshine, and Zane sighed with relief. "I'm not gonna lie. That feels good."

"Glad to have those plates off your chest?"

"Literally off my body? Yes."

"The Erebus guys are still going to make a run at you to get them back," Sebastian warned. "Don't let down your guard yet."

"I'm counting on you and Etienne. I would be less than useless if I had to defend myself from a violent attack."

"Never fear. I've got your back."

"Too bad you don't have my backside," Zane muttered under his breath.

Sebastian wasn't sure whether he was supposed to hear that, so he didn't respond. But he would like to take possession of the man's backside too. Aloud, he said, "Now we have to figure out how to let the bad guys know you don't have the plates anymore and that they'll have to deal with me from here on out."

"Maybe we can text them with the burner phone," Zane suggested.

"It looked set up so they can't be traced through it, which means you probably won't be able to contact them directly."

"You could rent a digital billboard in Times Square and put up a message that you've got the plates now," Zane teased.

"Great idea. I'll get right on that." They traded grins, and Sebastian felt like a million bucks. How long had it been since he'd had someone he could joke around with like this? Etienne was a loyal friend, but playfulness was *not* one of his driver's main qualities.

In a jovial mood, they returned to the hotel. Etienne left them, heading for a big truck across the parking garage while they headed for the elevator.

"Stand back a bit while I clear the suite, okay? It's just a precaution."

Zane nodded and struck a sexy pose against the wall beside the door. The man could turn his body into living art in the blink of an eye. No wonder he was one of the top fashion models in the business.

Sebastian opened the door to the suite—

—and stopped cold. The place was trashed. As in utterly destroyed. Cushions were ripped open, drawers on the floor, furniture knocked over, the paintings torn off the walls.

"Get back," he ordered Zane. "Run. Into the elevator. Fast."

"Why?"

"Go," he bit out, shoving Zane down the hall.

"My portfolio—"

"Leave it. I'll buy you a new one."

"You can't! Those photos took years to collect—"

"If whoever trashed the place is still in there, they'll kill us both."

"Oh."

They sprinted down the corridor, and he jammed the elevator button. The doors didn't open immediately, which meant it had already left. *Damn!* He grabbed Zane's arm and yanked him into the fire escape stairwell. When Zane opened his mouth to speak, Sebastian pressed an urgent finger to his lips for silence.

Sebastian went first, running downward at top speed, and to his credit, Zane kept up pretty damned well. They burst out of the bottom of the stairs into the parking garage, and Sebastian raced to the town car. He used the keyless entry number pad to open the doors and ordered, "Get in the back and stay low. Buckle your seat belt but lie down."

He found the spare key taped under the dashboard, backed out of the parking spot, and left the garage as fast as he could without squealing the tires and attracting undue attention. They turned out into the street, and he accelerated hard.

"Ow!" Zane complained. "Can I sit up now?"

"No! Stay down."

"What the hell is going on?"

"Someone was in our room. The suite was ransacked, and I wasn't about to stick around and see if the bastards were still in there."

"Oh." A pause. "Crap."

Sebastian concentrated on driving and watching the rearview mirror for a tail. He ran through multiple lights turning red and turned left in front of oncoming traffic, cutting it close enough to get honked at a half-dozen times, before he was convinced they weren't being followed. Now to get off the road and take Zane someplace safe.

He guided the car toward the Upper East Side.

He pulled into another underground parking garage, this time entering a code on a keypad beside a wrought iron security gate to gain entry. Once parked, he got out and opened the back door for Zane, who looked disheveled after getting thrown around the back seat of the car for the past hour. Sebastian held a hand out to him.

Zane took it, and Sebastian steadied him as he climbed out of the vehicle.

"You okay?" Sebastian asked quietly.

"Not really. I have to admit I'm a little rattled. Where are we?"

"Someplace safe."

"Are you sure about that?"

Sebastian smiled reassuringly at him. "Yeah. I am. C'mon. You're gonna like this place."

They climbed into an elevator that took both a key and Sebastian's palm print to operate. It whisked them up forty floors to the penthouse. They walked down a short hallway. Sebastian waved at the security camera, then used a retinal scanner and a lengthy number sequence to open the locks on a steel door.

He opened it and ushered Zane inside. After gesturing for him to stay put, Sebastian cleared the entire apartment, checking under beds, behind doors, and in all the closets and cabinets that could possibly hide a human being.

Finally he came back to Zane. "We're alone in here. You're safe."

Zane walked forward, down wide, shallow steps into the sunken living room. A floor-to-ceiling wall of windows overlooked the East River, and another wall of windows looked out at Manhattan's skyline.

The panoramic view never failed to impress Sebastian, and it seemed to have the same effect on Zane.

"It's like we're on top of the world."

"Just on top of a building."

"The penthouse?"

"Yup. And there are no sight lines from any surrounding buildings to see in here, which means no one can take a pot shot at you either."

Zane let out a deep breath. "Am I correct in assuming that you live here?"

"Why do you assume that?"

"This place is just like you. Spare. Classy. Sleek. Lots of hard angles and contrasting textures. Modern as hell."

Sebastian glanced around the condo. His interior designer had decorated the place, and he'd always been deeply comfortable here, but he'd never stopped to consider that it might be because this place was a reflection of him as a person.

The colors were muted, creams and grays with a touch of blue. Lots of glass and brushed nickel. Highly polished cream marble floors. Thick flokati rugs gave textural contrast and were deep and plush underfoot. "I'll take that as a compliment. And yes, this is where I live when I'm in New York."

Zane frowned. "But it's not your home?"

Home? What was that? He merely slept somewhere and kept his stuff somewhere. That didn't make anyplace a home, though, he supposed. He shrugged.

Zane wasn't satisfied, apparently, because he pressed, "Where do you spend most of your time?"

"Here, I guess. I've got a place in Switzerland where I ski, and I've got a funky little beach house in the Florida Keys when I need to unwind and stare at my toes for a while."

"So this is your home."

Sebastian answered slowly, "The last place I called home was a one-bedroom flat in the worst slum in London. I slept on the couch in the living room while my mother got stoned in the bedroom every night and I listened to her puke her guts up every morning. I guess I've never been much into the whole concept of home after that."

"Dark stuff, dude." Zane tilted his head. "Do you need to hug it out?"

Sebastian swore at him luridly in a thick, East London burr.

Zane laughed. "I'll take that as a no."

Sebastian watched Zane cautiously as he gave himself a tour of the open-concept space. A short hallway led to the bedrooms, but otherwise the place was mostly without walls. On one of the few walls, however, hung an eight-foot-tall painting, alabaster with splatters in all the muted colors of the condo. His decorator had called it the inspiration piece. It had cost a bloody fortune. But he did like the colors.

He glanced back cautiously at Zane. Did he like the place? Hate its lack of softness? Hate its intense masculinity and industrial vibe?

Lord, he felt vulnerable letting someone see into his private life like this. Even if he had had his dick firmly planted down said person's throat not too long ago and was plotting how to get his dick there again at the first possible moment.

This was a mistake. He'd never let anybody inside his inner sanctum like this. This was his private space. His refuge from the world, or, as his interior designer had called it, his *ivory tower of isolation.*

Even if he were inclined to let someone into this part of his life, it wouldn't be a high-strung high-fashion model who blithely ignored all of his instructions and cautions and seemed determined to deal with the counterfeiters on his own.

If Zane were just an airhead, Sebastian could put down the maverick behavior to naïveté, or even good old-fashioned stupidity. But behind that pretty face hid a quick mind and plenty of common sense. Why had Zane gone to that meeting alone? As much as Sebastian didn't want to admit it to himself, it didn't take a rocket scientist to see the answer.

Assuming Zane wasn't in league with Erebus—and Sebastian was inclined to believe the man based on the genuinely blank look he'd given Sebastian when he'd dropped the name last night—Zane must really want the money the counterfeiters had dangled as bait to gain his cooperation. And apparently Zane had no problem aiding and abetting international criminals for the right price. Which set Sebastian's teeth on edge. Erebus was not just a crime ring. It was a bunch of bad, *bad* people.

The trusting-voice angel on the other side of his skeptical mind argued back, *Who are you to judge somebody else for being willing to do anything for money? You remember what it's like to have nothing and be so desperate you'd sell your soul for a few quid.*

Yes, he knew exactly how much poverty sucked. He got how financial insecurity weighed on a person. Hell, he remembered what it was like to go hungry. To have nowhere to sleep. It made a person do things they wouldn't otherwise do. It was hard to believe a successful model like Zane was dead broke, but that was apparently the case. Why else would he have gone to that meeting in the alley and risked his life for the sake of a payday?

Sebastian would gladly offer the guy money—or a job if Zane was too proud to take a handout—but he got the distinct impression Zane wouldn't agree to either option. He was nothing if not stubbornly independent.

Which Sebastian could respect. He'd dragged himself up and out of the gutter by sheer force of will and damned hard work. Zane obviously had the hard work angle wired. He'd risen to the top of an insanely cutthroat field that routinely ate its young, from what Sebastian had heard of the fashion world.

Hell, he was no lily-pure idealist himself. Real estate could be a rough-and-tumble business, and he occasionally had to pass a little cash under a table to grease the wheels. But he made a point of always paying his workers decently and on time. He paid fair prices for the buildings he bought, he always worked to and above the building codes, and he made damned sure his building managers were pleasant, helpful, and kind to his tenants. Ethics mattered to him. A lot.

But what about Zane? Was his attempt to play ball with the counterfeiters mere financial desperation or something deeper? Something fundamentally amoral in his character? As hot as the guy might be, a lack of core ethics was a deal breaker for Sebastian.

Zane made no secret of having used drugs heavily for a few years, but he also made no secret of having cleaned up his act. Sebastian could respect that. And even though Zane had lied and concealed having the burner phone, he'd come clean readily enough last night when Sebastian asked him to tell everything he knew. Honestly, he got the impression Zane wasn't a natural liar.

Dammit. He'd been an idiot to let last night's hot encounter happen. It muddied the waters between them, and it definitely muddied his judgment. He could hardly see Zane for the lust blinding him.

Did he dare trust his judgment at all where Zane was concerned?

The hell of it was he didn't know the answer to that one.

Zane paused in front of the splatter painting. "Nice drop cloth."

Sebastian snorted. "That's the most expensive drop cloth in the recorded history of drop cloths."

"Actually, it makes me think of a snowstorm at my grandparents' house upstate, after Christmas, when deep winter has set in. It gives me the shivers, but I'm safe and warm in this room while the storm's outside."

"You get all that from a bunch of paint splatters?" Sebastian asked.

Zane grinned at him. "That's how art works. It evokes emotions and memories. Same with fashion, done well. It's art. It evokes feelings in those who wear it and those who see it."

"Huh. I never thought of clothing as art. To me, clothes are mainly a remedy for nakedness."

Zane groaned. "Have you never seen a Dior original? A Valentino suit perfectly tailored?"

"Umm, no. I don't think so."

"Oh Lord. I have my work cut out with you. You're missing the finest pleasures in life, my dude."

Sebastian opened his mouth to make a snappy retort, but a cell phone vibrated in the deep silence, and Zane jumped about a foot in the air. Under his Italian tan, his face went ghostly pale.

"What's wrong?" Sebastian asked quickly.

"That's the burner phone ringing," Zane whispered in panic, as if whoever was on the other end could hear him. "What do I do?"

Chapter Eleven

ZANE PULLED out the burner phone and stared at it in horror. Did he dare take the call? Surely the guy at the other end knew by now that the currency plates hadn't been in the briefcase he handed over.

Sebastian said, "Answer it. Demand payment before you'll deliver the plates. Make sure the counterfeiter knows the plates are in a safe place now, and not in your personal possession."

The phone continued to ring insistently.

Zane nodded at Sebastian and picked up the call, setting up the speaker function so Sebastian could hear too. "Hello?"

"Where are the damned plaques?" a voice snarled.

"Where's my damned money?" he responded in as threatening a tone as he could muster.

"Don't get cute with me, pretty boy. You'll be dead before you know what hit you."

"Then you'll never get your plaques back," Zane said lightly, even though he felt like he might barf any second. Sebastian nodded encouragingly and made a hand gesture for him to continue talking. He took a deep breath and continued, "Surely you don't think I've still got them on me, do you? What are those, anyway? Surely there's something wrong with them if you're willing to fork over so much cash for them and you've got armed guys shooting up alleys."

"That's none of your concern, and that shooter wasn't ours."

"Then who the hell was it?" he blurted. It seemed like a logical question if a guy didn't know it had been Sebastian on that roof. Maybe it would convince the bad guys he was still working alone and give Sebastian a little cover.

"We're working on that." A pause. "Where did you put the plaques?"

"How stupid do you think I am? I hid them. If you kill me, you'll never find them."

A long, pregnant pause was the only response on the other end
of the call. He could practically hear the person on the other end of the
line reassessing him, reevaluating how to deal with him, now that he'd
shown himself not to be a complete patsy.

At length the voice said, "Where do you want the money delivered?"

"Electronically transfer it to my bank account. You bragged that
you would have no trouble finding my account information, so find it.
Pay me. And then we'll talk."

Sebastian mouthed, *Hang up.*

Zane was more than happy to do so. He pushed the button that
disconnected the call and threw the phone down onto the cream sofa,
staring at it in distaste.

It started to ring again.

"Don't answer," Sebastian told him. "Let them stew. They've
blown their first, best opportunity to get the plates, and now they're
going to have to play by your rules."

"I have rules?" he asked.

"You do now."

"Will they really pay me?"

Sebastian shrugged as he pulled out his own cell phone. "I'm
counting on it."

Zane openly eavesdropped as Sebastian made what looked like an
overseas phone call. "Hey, Pere. It's me. I need you to watch for any big
deposits to a bank account. They'll be from an Erebus source. Payment
for the printing plates." A pause, then, "They fucked up the exchange and
now we're dictating the rules of the game." Sebastian lifted the phone
away from his mouth. "What's your checking account number, Zane?"

He rattled off the digits.

Sebastian repeated them into the phone, adding, "Right. Zane
Stryker. Erebus is going to have to find his account and then wire money
to it. Maybe your guys can connect the funds transfer to an account
Interpol didn't freeze in last month's sweep. I'm interested to see where
this money comes from, given how locked down most of their assets are,
and given how thorough your inside man was in finding their accounts
around the world."

Clever. Zane smiled in approval at Sebastian.

Sebastian gave a brief account to the caller of last night's failed
handoff, editing it a bit so Zane didn't come off as a hopeless amateur

and portraying him as brave and helpful. The call ended after Sebastian asked Pere to look into reports of any guys shot in alleys last night in Manhattan.

"Now what?" Zane asked Sebastian.

"Now we wait."

"I have the photo shoot this afternoon at 4:00 p.m.," Zane reminded him. "It'll run till around midnight. I already agreed to do it, and I can't back out."

Sebastian frowned. "This could work to our favor. You're undoubtedly going to be under surveillance from here on out. If Etienne and I act as your bodyguards and make you obviously and visibly difficult to kidnap, the counterfeiter may have no choice but to fork over the money for the plates."

"Difficult to *kidnap*?" Zane echoed in alarm.

"They'll have to keep you alive long enough to tell them where the plates are stashed. They can't just kill you, now."

"Uhh, good?"

"That's very good news. Snatching a person is a much trickier proposition than a straight-up murder." Sebastian added, "Now that we've got Martin watching your bank, we want to force a money trail to happen."

"Martin?"

"Martin Wylde. He and Peregrine Cardiffe founded and co-own Wild Cards, Inc. Martin is in charge of the intelligence gathering and analysis for the firm. He has assembled and trained an excellent computer surveillance team."

"Why haven't you mentioned him before?" Zane asked.

"Didn't know if I could trust you to keep quiet or not. He doesn't want anyone to know that he or the Wild Cards are tracking the currency plates."

"Remind me to thank your friend if I ever meet him," Zane said.

Sebastian grinned. "Will do. Which reminds me. I have another call to make. I'll be in the office if you need me."

Sebastian disappeared behind a sleek stainless steel door and left Zane to wander the penthouse. It wasn't huge, probably around three thousand square feet—three bedrooms, three-and-a-half baths—but it was three thousand square feet of pure luxury. And then he discovered the terrace, which was close to the size of the entire condo. It was a shaded oasis with full-size trees in giant steel planters and grasses, flowers, and even an herb garden in long, low planters around a swimming pool. The pool was black, long and narrow for swimming laps, with an infinity edge and glass fencing that meant someone in the pool could look out at the skyline of Manhattan at night without any obstruction of the view.

And then he saw the knee-high edge of what looked like a hot tub. He peeked under the removable cover and steam rose up. *Yes.* He could seriously use a good soak. He felt like one giant knotted muscle. On impulse, he stripped down and eased into the deep, hot, bubbling water. It had a faint saltwater odor. Perfect. No harsh chemicals to dry out his skin.

He lay back in the tub, resting his head on one of the neck pillows dangling along the water line, and closed his eyes. He let the foaming jets soothe away the stress and tension of the past few days until he was utterly boneless.

Without warning, the water level rose in the tub sloshed around him. He opened his eyes and was shocked to see Sebastian submerging, shirtless, into the white bubbles. *Please God, let him be entirely naked under the bubbling surface of the water.*

"Wait! I didn't get to see you climb in. Do it again!" Zane complained.

Sebastian grinned. "Your loss. Gotta be on the ball if you want to see the good stuff."

"Dammit."

Sebastian sat diagonally across the square tub from him, giving them both plenty of room to stretch out their legs and soak unimpeded. The afternoon was warming up fast, and Zane was close to overheating when Sebastian heaved out of the hot tub in a flash of muscular ass that made his heart pitter-patter. Several long running strides, and Sebastian dived into the swimming pool. He came up shaking water out of his hair and eyes and hung on the edge of the pool, grinning.

"Come on over here and jump in. I dare you," Sebastian declared.

Zane's eyes narrowed. He pushed out of the hot tub and strolled over to the pool, enjoying a moment of raw exhibitionism, confident in how great his body looked. And Sebastian was not shy to take in every detail of his physique. Those dark eyes lit up like torches, and Zane's own grin widened as he reached the edge of the pool.

"Should I dip a toe in first?" he teased.

Sebastian shrugged. "Real men dive in headfirst all at once."

Zane laughed. "Well, then…."

The shock of the icy-cold water on his well-cooked skin ripped the breath out of his lungs and, as he surfaced, wrung a noise reminiscent of a dying chicken from his throat.

"Good God almighty," he groused. "That made an innie of my naughty bits and an outie of my belly button!"

Sebastian laughed. "Going from hot to cold and cold to hot is good for you. It stimulates lymphatic flow."

"It stimulates fucking heart failure." Zane threw his head back, dipped his hair in the water, and slicked it back with his hands. "This is one to check off my bucket list. Skinny-dipping in Manhattan in broad daylight."

"No one can see you."

"Damn. I may have to leave it on the list, then. What's the fun if no one's looking on and being jealous as fuck?"

"Don't I count as a witness?" Sebastian asked. The sexy timbre of his deep voice made Zane's toes curl against the bumpy pebble bottom of the pool.

"I don't know. Are you jealous?"

"Seeing as how I own the swimming pool, not so much. But I am a little jealous at the idea of other people getting to see you like this. Does that count?"

"You most certainly do count, Mr. Gigoni." He swam over to hang on the side of the pool next to Sebastian. The cool water swirled around his body deliciously, and the hedonist in him reveled in the sensation.

"God, I never get tired of looking at you," Sebastian murmured. "You're too perfect to be real. Are you sure you're not a hologram?"

"Yes, I'm sure. And thank you." He couldn't resist adding in a tone that dared Sebastian to react, "Are you planning to do something about it, or are you just gonna look at all this hotness?"

He might as well have dangled a steak in front of a starving tiger. Sebastian turned, splashing water, and hooked his hand behind Zane's neck, dragging him forward into a kiss. Zane braced for something carnal and aggressive, but Sebastian surprised him by kissing him gently, seductively, almost reluctantly. Or maybe that was just Sebastian taking his time.

Sebastian sipped at his mouth, moving his lips and tongue lightly, almost teasingly, sampling him like a fine vintage and savoring him, if the groan emanating from the back of his throat was any indication. He did that to Sebastian? Joy unfolded in Zane's belly.

"You taste good," Sebastian mumbled.

Some people had a sweet tooth—he'd always had a taste for salty snacks, and today was no exception. "I taste like salt, and so do you," he retorted, enjoying the silken slide of lips on lips and exploration of tongue on tongue.

"Saltwater pool and spa. Hence the salty taste," Sebastian replied, licking at the corners of Zane's mouth.

"Shut up and kiss me," Zane whispered.

Sebastian's laugh was low and charged. He turned and pulled Zane's naked body against his. The solid heat of Sebastian and the liquid cold of the water mixed together in a sexy cocktail that turned him on ferociously. Belly to belly, chest to chest, buoyant and weightless, they kissed with their entire bodies, twining around one another both physically and emotionally.

Zane wanted this man so bad it shocked him. He loved Sebastian's strength and intelligence and badassery. He loved how private the guy was, how he wasn't stuck-up. Goodness knew he had a right to be. He might be ridiculously successful, but he was 100 percent a self-made man, and not many people could say that.

Sure, the guy had some trust issues. Maybe that came with the territory of being rich. How was a person to know if people liked them for themselves or their money? He'd seen it before in the super-rich. Although Sebastian's trust issues seemed deeper than that. Like he didn't trust people to stick around.

Zane knew the feeling. His family had abandoned him when he'd needed them most. He'd been a confused young kid, trying to figure out who he was, scared of the fact that he fantasized about making out with boys and not girls, and they'd been ashamed of him. They'd hidden him from their friends and family and they'd hidden from him. He'd been an embarrassment, swept under a rug to the best of their ability.

They made a hell of a pair, him and Sebastian. The long-in-the-tooth model and the ex-soldier real estate tycoon. But they were both survivors. They'd made something of themselves in spite of the lack of support from their families. They'd succeeded against all the odds in each of their chosen careers. What were the odds that they were emotional wrecks in the exact same way?

He knew one way to find out.

Zane was busily considering the logistics of sex in the pool when Sebastian stunned him by turning him loose and pushing away, porpoising over to the end of the long, narrow pool.

Well, hell. Had he done something wrong? He'd thought their kisses and naked bodies in the pool were hellaciously hot. If Sebastian was half as turned-on as he was, the guy had a seriously overflowing rudder under his boat right about now. He watched Sebastian swim back and forth, knifing through the water with powerful, smooth strokes. He glimpsed flexing shoulder muscles, a long, ridged back, clenched buttocks, and the bottoms of Sebastian's feet flashing as he kicked.

Was Sebastian playing hard to get? Or was he more hung up about being gay than he was letting on? Zane had always been a live-and-let-live, anything-goes sort of kid, long before he'd known he preferred boys to girls. Once he'd made peace with who he was, it hadn't been much of a stretch to kiss the boys in the corner of the gym instead of the girls. But he could see Sebastian as the kind of kid who identified with being strong and macho. Realizing he was gay must have been a hell of a shock to him.

The idea of slow-walking Sebastian into his full sexual potential exploded across Zane's mind with all the flash and excitement of a comet. *Oh, man.* That could be an amazing trip. And it would be the perfect thank-you to Sebastian for saving his life. He would save Sebastian's in return—just in another way.

Seducing the reclusive rich dude—it sounded like the script from a movie. And yet the billionaire was only a few feet away from him and unquestionably in need of rescue from himself. *Yup*, this was going to be fun.

Unfamiliar excitement unfolded in his gut. He rather liked the idea of doing something generous for someone else for a change. Most of the time, people were too busy sucking up to him to give him an opportunity to do anything for them. It was one of the downsides of being beautiful. He was often perceived as a trophy and not an actual human being.

Sebastian swam laps with smooth, powerful strokes that were mesmerizing to watch. Zane was a runner when he bothered to exercise outside of what was needed to maintain the body sculpting. It helped keep his muscle long and lean. While there was a market for buff male models with bulging biceps and pecs, the high-fashion industry demanded lean body types that clothes hung on elegantly. Even the clunkiest of fashions could look decent on a thin enough model.

Across the pool deck, he spied a glass-front cabinet holding folded towels, and he hopped out of the pool, fetched one, and wrapped it around his hips. He strolled over to one of the curving steel-mesh chaise lounges and stretched out on it to watch Sebastian swim. He lost count of the number of laps but guessed Sebastian went at least a mile before hopping out of the pool himself.

Sebastian was his polar opposite, dark to his light, brawn to his beauty, all raw masculinity to his androgynous elegance. Maybe that was why Zane found him so completely captivating. Sebastian was everything he'd wished he'd been as a kid. When the other kids had been bullying him and picking on him for being scrawny and thin, interested in things the other boys weren't, he'd desperately wished to be big and strong enough to make them all shut up.

Sebastian flopped, naked, beside him on a chaise, eyes closed and face raised to the sun. Damn. He'd swum off his hard-on.

"I'll bet you never got beat up as a kid, did you?" Zane asked wistfully.

"All the time."

Zane stared. "Really?"

Sebastian cracked open one eye. "You thought being a gay kid in the street gangs of London many years ago went well for me?"

"It's just that you're so big and strong."

"I am now. And besides, when a half-dozen other kids jump you all at once, no matter how big and strong you are, there's not much you can do but take the beating and hope they don't kill you."

"Jesus, Sebastian."

"Times have changed. Now I could probably give a half-dozen punks a run for their money."

"Is that why you joined the Army? To learn how to defend yourself?"

"I was young and stupid. I thought fighting was the way to be a man. I know better now. It's being able *not* to fight that makes a person a man."

Zane was staggered. How many people could come from as rough a background as Sebastian and come to the same realization? "You're a remarkable person," he murmured.

"Ha. I'm a low-class thug—all dressed up and the rough edges polished off these days—but I don't fake out anybody. The rich, classy people in this town won't have a thing to do with me."

"And you're sure they're not intimidated as hell by you?"

"Intimidated? By me?" Sebastian snorted.

"You do realize that you exude a serious badass vibe, right? You walk around on your toes with fists already half-formed, almost like you're daring someone to mess with you. The upper-crust snobs are probably scared silly of you."

"I do not walk around like that!"

Zane laughed. "Let's recall that I'm a runway model. I make my living portraying various images by how I walk. I study human movement professionally. And I'm here to tell you, you walk like a pissed-off commando looking for an excuse to pound someone into dust. With your bare fists. And you're going to enjoy it…."

"I am a commando. Or at least I was."

"Exactly. And it's who you portray yourself as. It's why they steer clear of you. They don't know what to do with someone like you. That kind of self-possession and capability is completely outside their experience."

"Huh." Sebastian looked thoughtful. "Should I change up how I walk, then? I wouldn't have any idea how to do that."

Zane waved a breezy hand. "Oh, learning how to walk is easy. I could teach you a world-class runway walk in a few hours. The question is, why would you?"

"I don't understand."

"Do you really want to change yourself to suit them?"

Sebastian frowned at him.

Zane frowned back. "Why not be yourself? I happen to find you so irresistibly sexy I can hardly keep my hands off you most of the time."

Sebastian looked startled at that. It took a moment for pleasure to replace the surprise, in fact.

Zane warmed to his topic. "What you think about yourself is what you project to other people. If you think you're beautiful, others will see you that way. If you think you're worthless, that's what people will see when they look at you. If you're at peace with who you are, other people will be too."

"That's all psychobabble crap," Sebastian declared. "I am what I am, and they'll never accept me or like me. Period."

"You have possibly the most negative outlook on life of anyone I've ever met," Zane declared.

"Where I come from, that's a compliment," Sebastian responded dryly.

"I didn't mean it as one."

"Yeah. I got that memo."

"As much as I would love to sit here analyzing why you pretend to be such a curmudgeon, I have a job to get to," Zane announced. Seducing Sebastian would have to wait for later. But then… then he was going to blow this man's ever-loving mind.

CHAPTER TWELVE

SEBASTIAN LOOKED around the chaos of the photo shoot in dismay. The abandoned warehouse it was being staged in, complete with broken windows and an entire missing wall, had upward of a hundred entry points, not to mention more possible hiding spots for a sniper than he could count. It was a bodyguard's nightmare. The space was cavernous, with blindingly bright light stands illuminating a huge piece of gray canvas hanging from a wall. Dozens of chains hung from the ceiling, and models in various stages of undress hung, tangled in the chains, all sprawled in awkward poses, many of them upside down.

Rock music blared, a relentless, pounding beat that gave him a headache. Makeup artists painted models with streaks of gray and silver body paint. Photographers shouted at the models to *Work it, baby!* And raising his voice over all the din, an impossibly young-looking Asian man orchestrated the chaos. Sebastian gathered he was Kato, the actual designer of the clothes being photographed tonight. A dozen people did nothing but scurry around carrying tablet computers, and Sebastian had no idea what any of them did.

They all looked like children to him, though. *Jeez*, he felt old all of a sudden. Yet another reason to stay the hell away from Zane. The guy lived in this young, hip, fast world—was an integral part of it—and he emphatically was not. Hell, people had called him an old man before he even left London in his teens. He'd had to grow up early. Fun was not part of his vocabulary. Never had been. He didn't do *young*, let alone playful.

Zane was currently climbing a ladder and then being wrapped in chains. Slowly, carefully, Zane tipped off the ladder, dangling upside down by a chain around his waist and another around one of his legs. It looked freaking precarious, and the gym mats on the floor looked completely inadequate to the task of breaking a fall if one should happen.

"Give me a smile so I can check the contrast, Zane," the main photographer called. He made an adjustment to his camera. "Okay, I'm ready. Go for it. Give me torture. Ugly. Weird angles. Postapocalyptic madness. Great. Fabulous. Love the vibe. More sex. Give me dirty. Bondage. Nasty. Oh yeah…."

Sebastian tuned out the patter. It was all he could do not to rush forward, grab up Zane, and set him safely on his feet. If he slipped out of those chains, he was going to land on the top of his head and break his crazy, stupid, beautiful neck.

It was close to 2:00 a.m. when the photo shoot wrapped up. Final lines of cocaine and beers were passed around as the designer congratulated everybody on a spectacular shoot. Sebastian did have to admit that some of the test shots he'd glimpsed on computer monitors the photographers used had looked pretty amazing.

Sebastian sidled up to Zane, clustered with the other models, chatting.

Zane exclaimed to him, "God, that was an amazing shoot!"

"It looked as uncomfortable as hell."

"Oh, it was. Terrible head rush. But have you seen the prelims? They're insane."

"Prelims as in preliminary pictures?" Sebastian queried.

Zane started to answer, but just then a female model draped herself over Sebastian and all but climbed him. He cringed a little and looked up in time to catch Zane's amused expression. *Traitor*.

He murmured to the girl as he reached for her arms around his neck, "You flatter me. But I'm old enough to be your—well, let's go with uncle."

She giggled, and he used her distraction to attempt to extricate himself from her possibly high or drunk advances.

Zane clearly thought the whole situation was hilarious and smirked at him unsympathetically.

Returning the female hand from his asscheek to its owner, Sebastian said to Zane, "Ready to go?"

"Been ready. You were the one tangled up with the new girl."

"How do you know she's new?"

"Experienced models never partake of controlled substances on a shoot. Just because shit's available doesn't mean it's professional to do any of it. That girl's pretty, but she'll never go anywhere in this biz."

"That's cold."

"That's the truth."

"Fair." Then Sebastian asked, "Did you have fun tonight? I couldn't tell if you were bored hanging up there or homicidal."

"We were told to give them no emotions."

"Did it hurt hanging in those chains?"

"Like a bitch," Zane replied. "Intense shoot, right? My God, I'm famished. But I can't wait to see the ads. They're going to cause a sensation."

"Yeah. Sure. We need to leave before the crowd thins out."

"Why?" Zane asked. "Shoot's over. Now's when everyone can professionally let down their hair a little. Have a beer."

"Can't. Working," Sebastian muttered.

"Aww, c'mon. Loosen up. Live a little." Zane did a little bump and grind in front of him. It was sexy as hell. And yes, his breathing sped up more than he liked to admit.

Sebastian bit out under his breath, "I'm carrying a concealed weapon. It's illegal for me to consume alcoholic beverages."

Zane rolled his eyes and then grinned broadly, leaning into him flirtatiously. "Do you have any idea how hot that is?"

"Are you stoned?" Sebastian demanded.

That snapped Zane out of his hyper mood. "No. Absolutely not. I don't do drugs anymore. I've been clean for years."

"So you're just hyped up from the work?" he asked, trying to understand.

"That, and this is who I am when I'm working."

"Fair. I get that. I was just worried that being under the kind of stress you've been experiencing and having access to the smorgasbord o' drugs over there had been too much for you."

Zane glanced over at the big table with literal bowls of party drugs sitting on it. "Actually, I'm not the least bit tempted. The job went great without chemical help, and I gotta say, my personal life's looking up these days."

The comment threatened to derail Sebastian's determination to get Zane out of here at the earliest possible moment and use the crowd for cover. "Good, because we need to go. I need you to come with me," Sebastian ground out. "Now."

"Fine." Zane sulked as Sebastian hustled him across the big, exposed warehouse and stuffed him into the back seat of a nondescript sedan. "Party pooper," Zane added for good measure as the car pulled away from the industrial lot.

"That's me, the old party pooper," Sebastian allowed dryly. "So damned boring keeping you alive. What *was* I thinking?"

Zane dropped the hyper model persona, which was a bit startling to see. One minute he was a flaky kid, and the next he was an intelligent and articulate adult. "I'm sorry. I was being an ass back there. I can't tell you how much I appreciate you looking out for me like this. You could've dropped my ass when I went behind your back to that meeting, and you didn't. You're a good man, Sebastian."

"Umm, thanks." Well, hell. Now he was a little bit embarrassed at how prickly he'd been back there. Had he been more jealous than he'd realized?

His consideration of that rather unpleasant possibility was interrupted when Zane asked, "What happened to the snazzy town car? I was starting to enjoy being chauffeured around in a bougie limo."

"This car won't be as conspicuous. Harder to follow."

"Are we being followed?" Zane blurted in alarm.

"Not if I have anything to say about it," Etienne said grimly from the driver's seat.

Sebastian leaned back, his knees banging into the seat back in front of him. "This car may look like crap, but it has a police car engine, armored body, run-flat tires, and light-diffusing windows. They make it look like you're seeing inside the car, but you're actually not. A camera outside the vehicle can't snap a picture of us sitting inside it."

The last remnants of Zane's ebullient mood evaporated, and Sebastian felt like shit for puncturing the guy's balloon. He threw Zane a bone. "You looked great in the photo shoot."

A laugh. "If you hang me upside down, nothing can sag. It's why I took the job."

"It looked uncomfortable. Was it?" Sebastian asked curiously.

"Oh God, yes. Blood rushing to my head, chains digging into my sides. Trying to pose in defiance of gravity while keeping the damned clothes where they're supposed to be—that was one of the rougher photo shoots I've ever done."

"I'm relieved that it's over. I was worried you would slip and break your neck."

"Me too," Zane replied.

A pause, then Sebastian confessed, "I'm glad you didn't."

"Didn't what?"

"Break your neck."

Zane laughed. "I'm glad I didn't either."

The temperature in the back seat climbed a few degrees, and Sebastian had to turn away from the come-hither look Zane was shooting him sidelong. Temptation to reach out and inhale all that crackling energy Zane was throwing off nearly overcame him.

"We've got company, boss," Etienne injected.

"Behind us?"

"Yuppers."

Sebastian jolted and turned around to peer out the rear window. He turned sideways, bracing one knee on the floor and his elbow against the seat back, which was awkward and tight, but necessary. "Which vehicle?"

"Dark SUV about four cars back."

"You know what to do." To Zane, he said, "You might want to brace yourself. This could get rough."

Zane grinned. "That's what they all say."

Sebastian rolled his eyes and was saved from having to respond by their car abruptly flinging them sideways as it screeched around a corner at high speed at the very last second. He all but ended up lying in Zane's lap.

"Sorry," he muttered. "I can't wear a seat belt and have the freedom of movement I need to watch for tails."

"No apology necessary. I like having your face in my lap."

Etienne snorted, a sound suspiciously like laughter. Chagrined, Sebastian merely pushed upright and tried to brace himself better.

The next turn threw Zane into his lap; however, he suspected Zane had let himself be flung there intentionally. Zane took his sweet time pushing upright, using Sebastian's thigh to hoist himself back to vertical. "Mmm. Nice," Zane murmured as he retreated to neutral territory on his side of the car.

Sure enough, the SUV turned and wove through traffic behind them, giving itself away.

Etienne hit the gas, and their car leaped forward, swerving in and out among the other cars. They turned back and forth, wending their way across the city. "They're making no secret of being back there, boss."

"You think there's another tail?" Sebastian asked quickly.

"I do. I just haven't spotted it."

"Are they working a rolling box around us?"

"Possibly."

"What's a rolling box?" Zane interjected.

"A loose net of several cars, in this case probably five or six of them, that drive parallel to us a block or two offset from this street, possibly a car or two trying to stay in front of us. That way, no matter which direction we turn, one of the cars can quickly and easily get eyes on us. The other cars adjust, and we're centered up in the box again, until we make another turn. But they never lose us."

"Ugh," Zane grunted as Etienne swerved around a truck, slamming Zane against the passenger door.

Sebastian asked Etienne, "Are you heading for the nearest ditch point?"

"Yes, sir."

"Ditch point?" Zane interjected again. "What's that?"

"We've created a few predetermined spots around the city for ditching tails, paparazzi, and homicidal exes."

"You have homicidal exes?" Zane asked in surprise.

"Not me. But Etienne does."

The driver grinned in the rearview mirror. "What can I say? I'm French, and I love the ladies."

"So he's a lothario, in other words?" Zane retorted.

Sebastian nodded. "Exactly. Serial cheater."

"Dude. Not cool," Zane told Etienne.

"I can't help myself. Women, they are an addiction in my blood."

Zane shook his head. "I like sex and lots of it, but even I know to ride only one horse in the stable at a time."

Sebastian murmured, "I've tried for years to tell him that, and it falls on deaf ears. And don't disturb him. The kind of driving he's doing right now takes intense concentration."

Zane nodded and went quiet. Meanwhile, Sebastian lost sight of the SUV behind a pair of delivery trucks and craned to see around them.

Urgently, he made mental lists of the car makes and models behind them, looking for cars he'd seen before to pop up again.

They drove a few minutes in terse silence. He didn't speak and let Etienne, an experienced combat driver, do his job without distractions. The SUV showed up again, but it had fallen back, perhaps a block away from them now. Etienne stopped turning and relied solely on speed to put distance between them and their tail. By not turning, he froze the other vehicles in the box on their own streets where they couldn't help the SUV behind them to keep them in sight.

Etienne's tactics were buying them the lead they needed for the ditching tactic to work.

"How much longer to the garage?" Sebastian asked.

"Three minutes," Etienne supplied.

"Zane, we're going to pull into a parking garage soon. You and I are going to jump out of the moving car, and Etienne will lead our pursuers away from us while we get out of there on foot."

"Sounds dangerous. Shouldn't the three of us stick together? I thought there was strength in numbers."

"There usually is. But in this case, we're going to divide and conquer our tails. Trust me. I won't let anything bad happen to you. Just stick with me and do what I say. Okay?"

It was a critical moment. If they were going to successfully evade the counterfeiter's thugs, he had to have Zane's cooperation. They would have to move fast, and Zane would have to follow his instructions exactly.

Would Zane's independent streak rear its ugly head, or would he actually do what Sebastian asked of him quickly and precisely? He got that the guy hated being told what to do. But in this case their safety, possibly their lives, rode on it. *Trust me, Zane. Just this once.*

He bit out, "When we get to safety, you can ignore me all you want. But right now, I need you to trust me completely and do as I say. Please."

Zane stared at him, eyes wide with worry. Eventually he nodded. "I do trust you."

Thank God. Maybe they would get away from the counterfeiter's people after all.

"Next block, I'll make the turn," Etienne announced. "Brace for impact."

"Impact?" Zane squawked.

Sebastian knew what was coming. He and Etienne had practiced this emergency procedure in the past until they'd perfected it. The car turned right into an alley and turned right again, immediately and violently, into a parking garage with a sharp down ramp. The car's tires left the ground as the vehicle launched itself airborne down the ramp. It slammed down to the concrete and then skidded around the first U-turn into the parking facility. Etienne hit the brakes hard, slamming Sebastian and Zane against the back of the front seat. The car accelerated across this parking level, braked without leaving any more skid marks, and turned again, descending into the bowels of the garage.

"Egress on my mark," Etienne announced.

Sebastian unlocked his door, and Zane copied him. "When Etienne gives the signal, open your door and fall out of the car. Curl into a ball and roll. Get back to your feet as soon as you can and follow me. We'll be running for a stairwell."

To Etienne, he said, "Take it slow. Zane's never done this before."

"Got it," the Frenchman replied tightly.

God willing, Zane hadn't had enough time to overthink what came next or think up any logical reasons not to jump out of a moving car in the middle of a high-speed chase, because Etienne called, "On my mark. Three. Two. One. Go!"

Sebastian burst from the car, praying Zane had done as he'd been told. He leaped to his feet, looking around desperately in the dimly lit space, and spotted Zane climbing to his feet maybe twenty feet away as well. "This way!"

Zane sprinted to him, and they darted to the stairwell only a few yards to their left. They dived inside, and once there, Sebastian jammed a thin key into the door lock and twisted it, breaking the key in the lock.

"Jesus! You just broke steel!"

Sebastian grinned. "Sorry to disappoint you, but that's a breakaway key. Designed to jam locks."

"Vandal," Zane retorted. "Up or down?"

"Down."

They raced two levels down, and Sebastian scanned the space. The garage was silent. Etienne had reversed direction on the last floor and would now be heading back up to street level and out another exit, where he would try to lead their tails away from here.

Moving cautiously now, Sebastian eased into the garage. Crouching and using parked cars for cover, he led Zane over to an elevator and punched the Up button. Sebastian pulled his service pistol from its holster and held it ready as the doors slid open.

Empty. Exhaling hard, he slipped inside with Zane. Using a fireman's key to override the normal commands, he closed the door and sent it directly to the tenth floor of the building without stopping. While the car rose, he jumped up and bumped a ceiling tile out of place. He jumped again, yanking it down.

"I knew you were a commando, but I didn't know you were a secret agent too," Zane commented.

"I'm a man of many talents."

"Say that to me in bed. I dare you."

Sebastian's gaze snapped to Zane's. An urge to press him back against the wall, kiss him senseless, and then have his wicked way with Zane roared through him. From between clenched teeth, he muttered, "Don't distract me."

Zane subsided but looked well satisfied with himself.

When they got to the tenth floor, Sebastian jammed the tile between the elevator doors so they wouldn't fully close, disabling the car.

"Hurry," he urged Zane in a low voice.

"Where the hell are we?"

"One of my buildings that's under renovation." He added, "I hope you're not afraid of heights."

"Why?"

"Follow me." He led Zane through the construction debris of the unfinished floor to a sky bridge that was also unfinished. "The subfloor is laid, but there's been a delay getting the glass panels for the wall delivered. Hang on to the guide railing, move quickly, and don't look down. Stay on my heels. Got it?"

"Umm, okay."

Sebastian paused to scan the scantily lit street outside and saw no movement. At this time of night, the city was as asleep as it ever got. Walking fast, he crossed the sky bridge in the dark. Taking his own advice, he avoided looking down between the gaps in the plywood boards laid flimsily over the sky bridge's steel frame. There was one tense moment when a gust of wind hit them, buffeting him badly. He could only pray Zane wasn't knocked off his feet behind him. He pressed on grimly. They couldn't stop out here, exposed and vulnerable, ten stories above the ground.

They reached the vestibule at the far end of the sky bridge, and Sebastian punched in a number code on a lock pad. The door opened to reveal a long hallway. He hurried to the stairwell and climbed three stories with Zane on his heels. He used another number pad to open a locked, unmarked door and let Zane out into an unfinished floor in the second building. The space was wide-open, with steel poles at intervals, dangling electrical conduits, and exposed ventilation ducts.

On the far side of the room, what looked like a giant box, perhaps thirty feet square, filled a corner.

"What is this place?" Zane asked.

"Thirteenth floor. It doesn't exist."

"Excuse me?"

Sebastian explained, "This building doesn't officially have a thirteenth floor. The elevator goes from twelve to fourteen, and the windows are arranged so the building appears to have one less floor than it actually does."

"Do you own this building too?"

"No. But I renovated it and sold condos in it a few years back. I still own this floor. It makes for a decent safe house because I have the only elevator keys that will open the doors onto this floor. In fact, this entire floor doesn't exist on any but a few obscure architectural plans conveniently buried deep in the bowels of City Hall."

Zane strolled around in the dim light seeping in through the tinted windows. "How are we supposed to eat or use the facilities?"

Sebastian grinned. "Come with me."

He led Zane over to the box, more specifically to the steel door on the far side of it. He opened a complicated sequence of locks and identifications that were as close to undecryptable as were available today.

He tugged on the heavy steel door and it swung open ponderously. "Step into my parlor, said the spider to the fly," he misquoted.

Zane passed him, and as he did so, motion-activated lights illuminated the interior of the safe room. Or safe apartment, as the case might be.

Sebastian gave him the nickel tour of the one-room space, which took about ten seconds. "Bathroom is over in that corner behind the partition. Kitchenette is behind you, along with a pantry of nonperishable foods. I had Etienne stock the place with some fresh foods earlier today, in case we had to hide out here. That stuff will be in the refrigerator."

Zane stood in the middle of the space and turned in a slow circle, taking in the sofa, flat-screen TV, desk, dual-screen computer, and bed. "You've thought of everything for riding out the apocalypse in comfort, it seems. Why on earth do you even have a place like this? Are you one of those doomsday prepper guys?"

"I'm not worried about doomsday, but call me a pessimist." He shrugged. "I do like to be prepared for contingencies, however."

"Well, hell," Zane declared. "All we need is a gaming console to hook to the television, and we'll be set for life."

Sebastian grunted. "Sorry. No games in here."

"I'm deeply grateful that you take these kinds of precautions, regardless of the deep-held paranoia they suggest."

"I'm not paranoid!"

Zane stepped close to him and pressed his fingers against Sebastian's lips. "No worries. I like you the way you are. And we can make up our own games to pass the time. It's perfect."

Games? What games?

CHAPTER THIRTEEN

AFTER THE steel door closed and faint pressure on his eardrums announced that they were sealed into the panic room, Sebastian placed a quick phone call on a landline to report to Etienne that they were safe. Apparently the maneuver to dive into the parking garage had successfully thrown off their tails as well. Etienne was currently on his way back to his place and, no doubt, whatever woman du jour was at his apartment waiting for him.

Zane waited until Sebastian had hung up the old-fashioned wall-mounted phone to ask, "So, we're safe in here? Nobody knows where we are?"

"Correct," Sebastian answered.

"And the plan is for us to spend the rest of the night here, undisturbed?"

"Yes," Sebastian answered a little less certainly. "Why do you ask?"

Ahh, he did so enjoy stringing Sebastian along. It was good for the man to get nervous now and then. He was entirely too self-assured for his own good. It made for an ego that tended to run away with itself.

"I'm hungry," Zane announced. "Let's see what Etienne brought us."

He moved over to the tiny kitchen in the corner and spied a picnic basket sitting on the counter. Gotta love the Frenchman's style. He opened the picnic basket and peeked inside.

God bless Etienne. Like any self-respecting Frenchman, he'd included a bottle of wine with the salami, cheese, assorted fruits, croissants, and pastries. Zane fished around in a drawer and found a corkscrew—of course. Every properly stocked panic room came with one of those.

The cabinets yielded a pair of wineglasses. During his search for those, Zane found a couple of pillar candles and a box of matches as well. While they were probably meant for a power outage, they would lend the picnic a romantic ambience, and he grabbed them too.

He carried everything over to the coffee table in front of the couch, efficiently popped the cork on the wine bottle, and poured a rich red burgundy vintage into the glasses. Damn, Etienne had fine taste in wine.

"Since we're safely tucked in for the night, can I convince you to take off your gun and have a glass of wine with me, Sebastian?"

"You can, and I will, thank you."

Zane unapologetically watched Sebastian shrug out of his suit jacket and pull a sinister-looking pistol out of the leather holster strapped across his chest. Truth be told, he nearly hyperventilated at the sexy sight of those broad shoulders, starched shirt, and well-worn leather. It was all so damned masculine.

Who would have guessed that a macho military type could be so wildly attractive to him... and actually be attracted back? He just wanted to wrap himself around all that yummy brawn and feel safe and protected for once in his life.

He had barely finished lighting the candles when Sebastian said, "Computer, dim the lights to ten percent."

Zane rolled his eyes. "Of course you have a completely automated safe house."

Sebastian grinned. "I like my tech toys."

Zane waggled his eyebrows. "Toys, huh? Duly noted."

Sebastian snorted. "Perv."

"What? Are you saying you don't like toys?"

"I wouldn't know."

Zane stared. "Just how repressed are you, dude?"

Sebastian scowled. "I'm not repressed!"

"Sounds like it to me. Have you ever had a threesome? Gotten tied up or tied someone up? Dressed in a costume of any kind? Role-played?"

"No. But that doesn't make me repressed. That makes me private."

"I dunno. You sound severely uptight to me. I think we need to loosen you up a little."

To that end, Zane picked up his glass and gave it a swirl. He sniffed... *oh, my.* He sipped, smiled, and sniffed again. "Holy wine country, that's a smooth vintage. Are you a fan of fine wine, Mr. Gigoni?"

"I am. You?"

"When I can afford it. Unfortunately, my tastes usually run ahead of my wallet."

Sebastian shrugged. "I thought it all tasted like vinegar until I discovered the good stuff. Only way I can drink wine is to drink expensively. Even then, I only sip at it. Side effect of having an alcoholic parent; I'm not a fan of getting drunk."

"Or of losing control?"

"Correct.

"Fine. Then we'll just sip at this magnificent wine together," Zane replied.

Sebastian's eyes lit with gratitude and maybe even a little newfound respect. "Are you seducing me?"

"By keeping you sober?" Zane asked humorously.

"I guess so." He waited for Sebastian to protest, or to get up and leave their impromptu picnic, but instead, the man very deliberately and slowly picked up his wineglass and took a long sip from it.

Zane grinned. He bloody well knew an invitation when he saw one. "Well, then, Mr. Directness, what do I have to do to get you to play along with me?"

"I'm already playing along with you."

Zane rolled his eyes. "I'm talking about you getting in bed. Naked. Doing dirty things to each other. Expanding your experience and making you a little less uptight."

Sebastian didn't move a single muscle, but his pupils dilated hard and fast. *Ha.* He wasn't as immune to Zane's suggestions as he was trying to pretend.

"What kinds of dirty things?" Sebastian finally mumbled.

Zane shrugged. "Depends on what you like. Are you a vanilla pudding kind of guy, or do you like to live on the wild side?"

"I'd say it's pretty wild to be gay, wouldn't you?"

"Maybe where you come from. It's not such a big deal here."

"Lucky," Sebastian retorted.

"The good news is it's the twenty-first century, and we're in a nice, forward-thinking city where very few people care who anybody else sleeps with."

They toasted to that, and he emptied the last of the bottle into Sebastian's glass.

Inside the reinforced walls of the safe room, the silence around them was profound, sinking deep inside him. Zane rarely slowed down enough to experience such stillness, and he stared into the steady flame of the candle, the moment mesmerizing him. It was actually kind of magical. He murmured wonderingly, "I feel alone."

"I'm here with you," Sebastian replied, sounding surprised.

"I get that. I mean, I've lived in big cities most of my life, and I'm always aware of being surrounded by crowds of people. For once, I feel completely isolated. As if we've stepped out of the city into a private world all our own."

Sebastian nodded slowly. "It does feel that way a little."

Zane reached out and laid his hand on Sebastian's shoulder. "Do you mind if I put my hand here? I feel a need to be connected to someone else."

"Go ahead." Sebastian's shoulder muscle bunched into a mass of hard knots.

"Are you always so tense?" Zane asked.

Sebastian shrugged, but the movement did nothing to relieve the terrible tension beneath Zane's fingers. "Turn away from me," Zane ordered.

Sebastian complied, and Zane gave him a shoulder massage, taking his time, gradually working his way toward Sebastian's neck, kneading gently at first and then deepening the massage, digging his thumbs into the thick muscles, working out the kinks one by one.

At last, Sebastian groaned and his head fell forward, a reluctant release of the held tension.

"Better," Zane murmured.

He massaged his way up Sebastian's neck to his hairline and then down the center of his spine to his shoulder blades through the fine cotton of his shirt. The man really did have a gorgeous physique. A photographer would have a ball capturing all the bumps and curves of his musculature. He could see the images now. Black-and-white photos, extreme lighting angles, all the shapes of Sebastian's muscles cast in light and shadow.

"If you ever get tired of modeling, you should take up being a masseur."

Zane chuckled. "I'll keep that in mind. If you'll take off your shirt, I'll work on the rest of your back. It's a mess, my dude. You're all knots and kinks."

Sebastian shrugged out of his empty gun holster and shirt, his back still to Zane, who gulped at the sight of all those acres of ridged muscle—much better than the mental imagery he had a moment ago. The power he would have as a lover… *yowza*. His breathing accelerated until he felt a little light-headed. Or maybe that was just the wine hitting him.

"Have you got some kind of oil in here?" he asked. "Something to keep me from making your skin mad?"

"No idea. I didn't stock the joint. A disaster expert did."

"Back in a minute." Zane poked around and found a jar of coconut oil in the kitchen cabinet. Perfect. "It's about to smell like a beach in here."

"I like beaches," Sebastian murmured.

"You wanna lie down so I can do this right?"

Without answering aloud, Sebastian moved across the room to the big, Sebastian-sized bed and stretched out on his stomach. His frame sprawled across much of the king-sized mattress, reminding Zane of just how large a man Sebastian was. He scooped out a small blob of the congealed coconut oil and rubbed it between his palms. It melted in seconds, and hesitantly, he laid his oiled palms on Sebastian's back.

The scent of coconut rose around them. He could almost feel a salt breeze on his face, and it was no stretch to imagine palm fronds fluttering in a breeze and the rolling rumble of the ocean. Starting at Sebastian's neck where he'd left off, Zane massaged his way slowly down Sebastian's torso, kneading away the stress and tension. And at the same time, his own tension drained away. The concentration of the moment was simple and complete, and he relished being in it. He worked his way down each of Sebastian's arms, all the way to the fingertips. Then he took another slow journey up Sebastian's spine to his scalp.

His almost zen state was only interrupted when Sebastian groaned in pleasure and said, "I don't know if it's just you or the wine and you, but I haven't felt this good in a long time."

Zane murmured, "I've only gotten to about half your body. Think how great you'd feel if I massaged your legs."

"Go for it." Sebastian started to sit up, but Zane pushed him back down.

"Relax. I'll get your pants for you."

He plunged his hands under Sebastian's stomach to unbuckle his belt and unzip his fly. As tempting as it was to cop a feel while his hands were so close to Sebastian's privates, he refrained. Instead, he slowly stripped the wool fabric off Sebastian's hips, hooking the silk boxer shorts at the same time. He pushed the clothing down over ripe buttocks and slipped the pants down Sebastian's powerful thighs. He stopped when the pants and boxers tangled around Sebastian's ankles.

"Need me to kick them free?" Sebastian asked.

"Nope. I want your pants right there." Zane shoved Sebastian's knees apart and knelt on the tangled fabric, effectively turning the pants into ankle bindings and pinning Sebastian in place.

Sebastian tugged once against the restraints, realized what Zane had done, and went tense from head to foot.

"Relax, already," Zane murmured, leaning forward and starting over at the top of Sebastian's head and massaging down his back, past his hips, and all the way down to his toes this time. The turn-on of having Sebastian Gigoni sprawled out naked beneath him, totally relaxed, was almost more than he could stand. "I won't do anything you don't like or want."

He wanted to put his mouth on all that skin, to slurp off the musky sweet coconut oil, to take Sebastian into his mouth and drive him out of his mind again. But he bided his time, working his way up Sebastian's calves, lingering on the backs of his knees—which turned out to be ticklish—and up the backs of his thighs.

He re-oiled his hands and went to work on Sebastian's glutes. He worked gradually toward the tight crevice between his cheek muscles, drawing a finger down into the crack again and again until Sebastian finally relaxed and gave him full access to his nether regions. Zane worked the oil into the whole area, daring to dip his middle finger a tiny bit into his tight anal sphincter.

A gasp.

Zane smiled and dribbled a bit of the coconut oil onto his finger, still lodged just inside the tight opening. The oil ran down his finger, dripping onto the clenched muscles. Using his other hand, Zane massaged it in all around his finger. And then he dipped a little deeper.

This time Sebastian hissed a sharp breath in through his teeth.

"Tell me if I hurt you," Zane murmured.

"Uh-huh," Sebastian panted.

"Uh-huh, I'm hurting you or uh-huh, I'll tell you?"

"I'll tell you." Sebastian's vocal cords sounded stretched on a torturous rack of pure pleasure.

Thoroughly enjoying himself, Zane eased his finger a little deeper, turning it back and forth as he inserted and removed it, in and out, left and right, until Sebastian was groaning in the back of his throat and starting to squirm. Pressing forward with his finger, rotating and hooking the tip to catch Sebastian's prostate from the inside, Zane massaged up and down, stimulating Sebastian slowly and mercilessly.

Sebastian was swearing under his breath now.

Using his unoccupied hand, Zane reached beneath his other wrist and captured Sebastian's balls, rolling them gently in his palm. They were hard as rocks and practically vibrated with tension. Given that the guy'd had an epic orgasm yesterday, Zane had to admit he was impressed. Poor man was loaded for bear and ready to blow again. He reached lower still and grasped the hot, throbbing column of Sebastian's cock.

Sebastian's hips surged up off the bed, and Zane leaned forward, using his body to press him back down. He dragged his well-oiled fist downward to the base of Sebastian's erection and back up to the tip, tugging lightly on his whole cock.

"What do you like, Sebastian?" he asked. "Do you like it slow and sensual or hard and fast?" He demonstrated both as he said the words.

"Yes," Sebastian groaned.

Zane smiled against Sebastian's back and bit the skin beneath his mouth lightly before pushing back up to his knees.

"What do you like?" Sebastian mumbled from between gritted teeth.

Leisurely pumping his fist up and down the rigid hot flesh filling his hand, he answered, "Honestly, I prefer to bottom. I love being driven into hard and deep. I'll like it when you spread me wide, grab my hips, and pull me up to you as you take me like you own me. I'll love it when you tell me not to come until you tell me to. When you reach around me to stroke me to climax at the same time you explode inside me. I like it dirty, and raw, and hot as hell."

With every word he uttered, Sebastian became more agitated, his hips grinding more urgently into the mattress.

Zane leaned forward to whisper in Sebastian's ear, "Would you like that? Do you want to bend me over and do me like you've never done anyone before? I can take anything you can dish out. I don't want you to hold back. I dare you to lose control. If I turn you loose, will you do that?"

"Yes. Oh God. Yes," Sebastian groaned into the pillow.

Using one hand to fumble in his back pocket, Zane found his wallet and pulled out a condom before he dropped the wallet on the floor. Sebastian lifted his hips as Zane tore the packet open with his teeth. He reached under Sebastian's hips, sheathed him in ridged latex, and rubbed Sebastian's now safely protected cock with more coconut oil. Then, at long last, Zane moved off the pants that had been holding Sebastian down.

Instantly Sebastian surged upright, rolling off the bed and to his feet, his erection standing up proud and huge. A burst of trepidation coursed through Zane. Maybe he shouldn't have dared Sebastian to lose control.

"Clothes. Off," Sebastian said, low and dangerously.

CHAPTER FOURTEEN

SEBASTIAN WAS so blinded by lust he could hardly breathe, let alone form coherent thoughts. Never, not once, had he ever cut loose in the way Zane had given him permission to. Hell, dared him to do. Sex had always been a hasty thing for him. A secretive, furtive physical release to be taken as quickly as possible and then left behind so he could get back to his regularly scheduled life.

But tonight, they were completely alone. Locked in. Nothing but time stretched in front of them. And the man had just told him to try out every fantasy he'd ever had. This could take a while. All night even.

Frantic to get Zane naked, he helped Zane disrobe when he didn't do it fast enough. His T-shirt went flying and Zane's jeans skinned off his hips.

"Commando?" Sebastian blurted. "I pegged you for thongs."

"Nah. No cock pockets for me. I like to live dangerously," Zane purred.

When Zane was fully naked, Sebastian just had to stop for a moment and look. "You're living art," he murmured reverently.

Zane smiled a little. "Thank you. I'm glad you find me attractive."

That sounded like a canned response. Guy must get told all the time how pretty he was. His automatic answer bothered Sebastian.

"It's more than just how you look, Z. It's how you carry yourself. How you move. How… aware you are of yourself and the world around you. It's not just how you look." He searched for the right words to express himself. "It's… who you are. You're so much more than just a pretty face. You're smart and mouthy and disrespectful. Just cocky enough to be hot, but not so much as to be arrogant. I'll bet people underestimate you a lot, don't they?"

Zane looked startled. And then something akin to gratitude shone in his light green eyes. "Yeah. I guess they do."

"Erebus sure as hell did." Sebastian snorted. "I'd lay odds they thought you were some half-witted pretty boy who would do exactly as you were told and be completely cowed by the first threat they muttered at you."

Zane grinned. "Oopsies. The pretty boy didn't go along with the program, did he?"

"Thank God," Sebastian murmured fervently.

"Wonder if the pretty boy will go along with your program tonight. Shall we find out? Are you man enough to tame me?"

He really didn't need the dare. But it was a fucking turn-on. As if he wasn't already so hard he could barely stand under the pressure of the blood pounding through his fully loaded surface-to-ass missile.

Sebastian grabbed Zane by the shoulders and dragged him forward for a deep, carnal kiss that was all restless mouths, clashing tongues, and seeing who could suck who harder. Zane was clearly as turned-on and ready for this as he was. Abject gratitude made his knees weak until impatience to be inside this man, to possess him and mark him forever, to make Zane *his*, overcame him. Still grasping Zane's shoulders, he guided him forward, away from the bed, over to the back of the leather sofa.

"You okay with this?" Sebastian muttered.

"I'm the one who dared you. Show me what you've got, big guy," Zane challenged.

Laughing, Sebastian pushed him down, face-first, over the sofa back. "Where's that coconut oil?"

"Shit. Over by the bed."

"Don't move," he ordered Zane.

Sebastian raced to the bed, grabbed the oil, and turned back. The sight of Zane's lithe body bent over the sofa, sculpted thighs spread wide, his body offered up to Sebastian in willing sacrifice, made something in his heart crack open.

He stopped, taking a moment to memorize the sight of this amazing man offering himself to him. "I'm glad as hell I didn't sleep with you when we first met," he said in awe.

"What?" Zane asked. "Why?"

"Because you'd have been a trophy then. A notch on my bedpost. 'Hey, look at me. I fucked the hot model dude.'" Zane frowned, and Sebastian added hastily, "But now I know you. I'm attracted as hell to you. I want *you*. The person. Not just the poster boy. This means so much more to me."

"Don't go making me all emotional and sappy, now, Seb. I plan to blow your mind tonight. Give you a night you'll never forget."

A rush of emotion poured through him, and he stepped forward slowly. He leaned down over Zane and dropped a single, slow, reverent kiss between Zane's shoulder blades. "It's already a night I'll never forget. In case I forget to say it later: thank you."

Zane wiggled his ass impatiently against Sebastian's crotch, and they laughed together.

He took his time lubing up Zane's ass and returned the favor of massaging oil into Zane's privates until the guy was doing his own squirmy dance on the sofa.

"Would you beg me to take you if I asked you to?" Sebastian asked. His voice was more breathless than he'd expected. Dang, Zane made him hot.

"You don't have to ask me to beg, Sebastian. Please, for the love of God, fuck me."

"Is the dare still on?" he asked, fingering Zane much the same way he'd been fingered earlier.

"You don't play fair," Zane panted.

"I don't want to hurt you. At least, not too much."

Zane groaned and his legs collapsed, planting all his weight on the sofa back at exactly the right height for Sebastian. He couldn't resist any longer. He placed himself at the small, rosy entrance, as perfect and beautiful as the rest of him, and pushed a little.

Zane groaned again.

"Are you sure you can take me?" Sebastian asked in concern. "I'm not exactly tiny."

"Take it slow and give me a little time to adjust."

And that was what he did. Bit by bit, he pushed past the first resistance. Zane was panting hard, and he paused, waiting for the muscles gripping him to relax. When they did, he eased deeper. The heat, the tightness of Zane's body, the sight of those pale buttocks clenching and unclenching—it was almost more than he could stand. Gritting his teeth, Sebastian eased all the way into Zane, seating himself to the hilt. Just knowing that he was buried inside Zane was nearly enough to make him come. He stood perfectly still, fighting for control, fighting off the massive explosion his body was begging to let loose.

Zane began to squirm a little around him, and Sebastian grinned. He would take that as permission to proceed. He withdrew partway and then pushed forward all the way in a slow, smooth stroke.

"You okay?" he checked in.

"God, yes." Zane shuddered and let out a long groan. "Again. Please. Again."

Sebastian obliged, putting a little more force into the thrust. Most of his lovers cried uncle at about this point, declaring him too big to get rowdy and insisting that he stick to little baby rocks of his hips.

"More," Zane demanded.

"You sure?"

"Fuck me hard or swear to God, I'll walk out of here," Zane complained.

Sebastian threw back his head and laughed. Finally, after all these years, he'd found a compatible lover. He thrust his hips forward hard, and Zane muttered, "Oh yeah. Better."

He hooked his fingers around Zane's hip bones, pushing him down into the sofa and at the same time pulling him back, deeper onto his cock. Zane's hips rocked rhythmically, and Sebastian took up the rhythm. As Zane picked up the pace, so did he. Flesh slapped on flesh loudly. Zane grunted a little as the thrusts deepened even more, and Sebastian realized, with no little surprise, that he was swearing in a steady stream.

Gritting his teeth, he tried to hold back, but damned if Zane didn't throw his legs even wider open and cry, "I dare you!"

That was it. He let go and pounded mindlessly into Zane's body, which clenched him spasmodically with each thrust, lifting to meet him, offering him everything. And he took it all.

Their bodies grew slick with sweat, and all elegance fled in the face of their mutual groans and their bodies slamming into each other. He'd waited his entire life to do this, like this, to this man. He just hadn't known it till now.

"Yes, Sebastian. Yes!" Zane cried.

Sebastian strained forward, seeking the core of Zane's pleasure. His entire body clenched and he gathered himself for one last, apocalyptic moment. "For you, Zane," he cried out.

Zane froze beneath him as well, quivering with his own imminent climax. Sebastian leaned forward, reached around in front of Zane to clutch his erection, and then went for the gusto, surging forward into Zane in a wild flurry, his fist moving in time with his hips, faster, faster, faster.

Zane shouted his pleasure just as his own explosion blinded Sebastian, emptying his entire soul in an exquisite, endless release of pleasure so intense it made his legs collapse and his spirit weep for joy.

At some point, he realized he was draped on top of Zane, no doubt crushing him.

"Can you breathe?" Sebastian gasped.

"Don't move."

Well, the guy could talk. He wasn't suffocating. They rested for a while, catching their breath. And it was… nice. Intimate. He started to pull out at one point, but Zane mumbled a protest, and he stayed put.

Then Zane's muscles flexed around him. Even in the satiety of the moment, that felt amazing. "Do that again," he muttered.

Zane's muscles flexed again, this time a little more strongly. Shockingly, Sebastian's cock stirred with interest. He propped himself up on his elbows on either side of Zane, still lodged deep inside him. His cock began to fill and harden again, his lust bright and sharp, highly sensitized by his recent climax.

He moved his hips experimentally. *Oh yeah.* He wanted Zane again, right now.

"Are you kidding me?" Zane muttered.

"Are you okay? Will I hurt you?"

"Never. If you were going to hurt me, you already would have."

"Still—" He started to pull out, aware that he'd already used Zane pretty hard.

"I double dare you," Zane declared.

He laughed richly. "Well, in that case…."

CHAPTER FIFTEEN

ZANE WOKE up slowly, into total darkness, disoriented by the utter
lack of any light, any visual reference to where the hell he was. He
moved slightly. Cotton sheet beneath his cheek. More cotton sheet over
his feet. He reached out with one hand and encountered warmth. Flesh.
Human skin.

Sebastian.

Awareness of where he was, who he was with, burst across his
mind. Along with reminders of last night. He was sore, his arms and legs
and ass achy, but whether that was from the epic sex they'd spent hours
sharing or from the strenuous photo shoot beforehand, he couldn't tell.

He rolled over onto his back, smiling up into the darkness. He
felt made love to from head to foot. And he pretty well had been last
night. Once Sebastian's reservations had been shattered, the guy was a
relentless and thrilling lover. Zane was flattered as hell that Sebastian
had felt comfortable enough to go to that intimate place with him, to bare
his fantasies and then act them out with him.

A pang of insecurity shot through him.

Surely, that wasn't morning-after regret. He wouldn't give up last
night for anything.

Poking at the nervous jitters in his gut, he identified their source.
Fear. Please God, let last night be more than a casual one-night stand
to Sebastian. So often in Zane's life, he'd been a conquest. A thing of
beauty to be pursued, possessed, and once conquered, discarded. That
was him. The throwaway lover.

He sat up quietly, trying to orient himself. If he was correct, the
bathroom was over that way.

"Need a light?" Sebastian mumbled sleepily beside him.

"I didn't mean to wake you. Go back to sleep," he whispered.

"Computer. What time is it?"

A male, British-accented voice answered, "It's 10:56 a.m."

Holy shit. Almost eleven in the morning? With no windows to let in any light, he'd had no idea!

"Computer: light, ten percent," Sebastian murmured.

Tiny halogen lights illuminated all over the ceiling of the safe house.

"Thanks," Zane murmured quietly, trying not to wake up Sebastian further. The guy'd had quite a workout himself last night and deserved to sleep as long as he wanted to.

He climbed out of the bed, used the restroom, and then wandered over to the kitchenette. Spying a coffeepot, he found pods of coffee and filters and popped some into the coffee maker. Blearily, he stood there and watched it brew.

He jumped when something warm touched his shoulder. Sebastian had come up behind him and leaned down to kiss his neck. "Good morning, Zane."

"Good morning, Sebastian," he replied, startled. While most of his lovers didn't throw him some cash and kick him out, they rarely showed actual affection the morning after either. But then, most of the guys he slept with came out of the fashion industry and were fully as self-involved as most models were.

"It is a good morning, isn't it?" Sebastian murmured against his shoulder, his lips moving lightly across his sensitized skin.

"Wow. You're sounding relaxed." He glanced over his shoulder, smiling at his lover.

"Aren't you?" A frown started between Sebastian's dark eyes.

"I am. Thank you for last night."

Sebastian laughed. "No, no. It's me who owes you the thanks. That may be normal for you, but I've never had a night like that in my life."

"Trust me. That wasn't normal for me either."

"Are you okay—" Sebastian started.

Zane turned around and slid his fingers down Sebastian's nose to his mouth to stop any more words. "I'm fine. Better than fine," he confessed. He started to lean forward, intending to loop his arms around Sebastian's neck for a good-morning kiss and whatever it might lead to, but a bell rang somewhere behind Sebastian, who tensed cautiously.

"What's that?" Zane asked, alarmed.

"Phone. Only a few people have the number. I've got to get it."

"Of course."

Sebastian moved away, and Zane fiddled with heating a frying pan and pulling eggs and bacon from the refrigerator. *God bless Etienne.*

Across the room, Sebastian said, "Go ahead. Oh, hey, Pere." He listened in silence for long seconds. Then, "That's great. Glad you've got a trail to work on. The plates? Yes, we've still got them. Why?"

The wait was agonizing this time as Sebastian was silent, listening. Zane mentally jolted as Sebastian said, "Yes, he'll work with us. He'll do whatever I tell him to."

What? Whatever Sebastian told him to do? Was Sebastian right? Had he really fallen so hard for the man already?

Dang.

Warning lights flashed and sirens wailed in his head. He knew better than to fall hard and fast for a guy, particularly after they'd just had great sex. He'd been so needy in his younger years he'd mistaken any attention from anyone as real caring. But he knew better now, dammit.

He'd worked too hard over the years to love himself, to recover from the mistakes and wounds of his youth. He was *not* going to fold up and give in to the old insecurities. Did he like Sebastian? Yes. Did he want to get to know the man better? Hell yes. But he was far from caring about the guy so blindly, trusting him so completely, that he would do whatever Sebastian told him to without questions of any kind, thank you very much.

A slow burn of anger started in his toes, rising inch by inch to consume his entire body. Jerkily, he pulled the bacon out of the pan and broke the eggs into it, wishing them slow, painful deaths. By the time Sebastian got off the phone, he was shaking with rage.

He'd thought they had something. An emotional connection, in spite of his initial goal of merely distracting Sebastian. He was crazy about the guy, but Sebastian was taking him for granted. And that was the one thing he knew better than to accept from anyone, especially his lovers. His eyes narrowed in fury. Spatula in hand, he wielded it like a sword as he turned to face Sebastian.

"What was that about?" he asked ominously.

"Wild Cards were able to track a deposit to your bank account from a numbered anonymous account in Cyprus. It's likely Erebus, since they have a major hub in Greece. The Wild Cards computer guys and the British government are unpacking the data now. If we're lucky, it'll lead to the consortium's last remaining bank accounts."

"The deposit's been made, then? The full million dollars?"

"Apparently."

"Wow." He was a millionaire, huh? Of course, if he didn't cough up the plates, he would be a dead millionaire soon enough. "I wonder how much taxes Uncle Sam is going to charge me on the money."

"Your main problem is going to be explaining to the government where it came from." Sebastian shrugged. "I mean, I suppose you can claim it as work income earned overseas. Unless you're audited, Uncle Sam shouldn't request receipts or contracts to prove where you earned the money. As long as you pay income tax on it, they probably won't care where you got it."

Damn. He hadn't thought of that when he'd told the counterfeiter to put the money in his regular, American, regulated bank account. As if he would have had any idea how to set up some illegal, anonymous offshore account.

"I have a great accountant," Sebastian continued blithely. "If you'd like me to set you up with him, he can help you figure out what to do with the money to protect it as much as possible from tax implications."

"How does that saying go? It takes money to make money, and it takes more money to hide your money?"

Sebastian snorted. "That's no lie."

He commented, "Well, I have to give this consortium of yours credit for keeping its word."

Sebastian made a sound of derision. "In the first place, not my consortium. And in the second place, yeah. Only after they tried and failed to kill you and then couldn't successfully kidnap you."

Details, details. If the money was in the bank, then he should probably move heaven and earth to find a way to deliver the plates and walk away from this mess alive. Of course, that also meant Sebastian's mission would be over and the man could walk away from him as well, and not look back.

His head and heart felt as if they'd gone to war against each other. He was pissed as hell that Sebastian didn't respect him as an adult in his own right and thought he could exert any kind of control over him.

His heart argued that he'd been the one to dare Sebastian to take possession of him. He couldn't throw the man under the bus for doing exactly what he'd asked him to do, could he?

Did Sebastian respect him or not? Should he believe Sebastian when he said he only wanted to help Zane extricate himself safely from this mess? Now that the money transfer had given the Wild Cards the financial lead they'd wanted, he could walk away from this whole situation, right? His part was done... he hoped.

Which meant Sebastian's obligation to protect him was finished too. Right?

What came next? Would Sebastian actually give him the respect he deserved and take their relationship to the next level? Or would the man walk away from him and never look back? Had last night been it? Did that phone call spell the end for them?

The old fear was back, along with insecurity slimy and roiling in his gut. Would he lose Sebastian now that this mess was more or less resolved?

One thing he did know. Sebastian respected strength. Intelligence. Self-control. Weakness did not impress Sebastian Gigoni.

The show must go on, baby. As if he was stepping out onto the runway, he plated the eggs and bacon, smiled brightly, threw his shoulders back, and carried the food over to the coffee table. He felt like a performing monkey, but he would be damned if he would show Sebastian his fears and hurts.

"So. What's on your agenda for today, Seb?"

"I need to check in with Etienne. See if he was able to get any identification on who was following us last night. Then I need to track down a top-notch engraver who can mark the plates in some subtle way that won't be obvious on casual inspection but which makes them useless."

"Won't the counterfeiters spot something like that?" he asked in alarm.

"Not if the plates are altered subtly. I don't know much about it, but Pere suggested that we could probably get them defaced and rendered unusable without a casual visual inspection being able to spot the flaw."

Zane was tempted to skip altering the plates and just hand them over, but that would make him an accessory to counterfeiting, and he highly suspected that was a serious felony, if not something worse, like treason.

"How about you?" Sebastian asked. "Anything you need to do today?"

"I was thinking about taking a nap."

Sebastian smiled knowingly, and Zane's insides melted a little. They both knew why he hadn't gotten much sleep last night. "All right, then," Sebastian said. "Sit tight here, and I'll be back in a few hours."

Thought he had him caged and cowed, did he? Hah. He was no domesticated house cat to sit around all day waiting for the master to come home and pet him at his convenience. No, sir. He was a goddamned tiger.

Zane gave Sebastian ten minutes to clear out of the building, and then he hurried to the door. Thankfully, it was designed to keep people out and not keep people in. He slipped outside and went down the stairwell to an actual, recognized floor in the building, where he caught an elevator and took it all the way down to the ground level. He walked out of the lobby, hailed a cab, and headed for the bank.

While he was in the car, he called his agent. "Janice, sweetheart, I need a favor."

"Anything, darling. I heard from Kato's people, and they're raving about your work last night. You're back, baby. I won't have any trouble booking you gigs after this. They said you were the only model who wasn't a complete bitch about the shoot."

He laughed. "Not for lack of desire to bitch, I assure you. I'm bruised all over. I won't be able to take any swimwear work for a couple of weeks."

"Duly noted. What favor do you need, sweetie?" she asked.

"Do you know someone in the jewelry business who could take a cast of a metal piece and make a duplicate superfast? And they'd need to keep their mouth shut about it."

"You planning on pulling a jewelry heist?"

He laughed, a little uncomfortable with how close to the truth that was. "Do I strike you as the cloak-and-dagger type, darling?"

That sent Janice into peals of laughter. "Actually, I know an artist who might be able to do what you need. She's a sculptor by training but makes costume jewelry for Broadway productions. Does that sound like what you're looking for?"

"My God, yes. She sounds perfect!"

"Lemme dig up her number. I haven't called her since I broke up with her a few years back. But I see her work all the time in theaters. She's freaking brilliant. High-strung artist type, though. Does way too many drugs. You be careful around her, okay?"

"Never fear. I'm clean as a whistle and planning to stay that way."

"I'm proud of you, kid. Have you got something to write with? You know you can't remember numbers for shit, sweet boy."

Maybe not when he was stoned out of his head, but sober, his memory was just fine, thank you very much. He memorized the number she rattled off and hung up quickly. On television, spies never wrote down phone numbers. No trail of evidence and all.

A quick phone call later, and he was scheduled to meet with the artist, a woman named Maya, in an hour. She sounded like she was coming down off some kind of hard-core hallucinogen and only partially checked in with reality. But she focused fast enough when he mentioned that he could pay well for her services. Must be broke and almost out of drugs.

He was jumpy the entire time he was in the bank gaining access to the plates. As he waited to be shown down to the vault, every new person who came into the bank made him nervous. He assessed everyone, wondering if each one was a shadow agent of the Erebus Consortium. Of course, he had no idea what an international criminal looked like.

Thank God he'd had the presence of mind to insist on putting the plates in his grandfather's safe deposit box so he could access them today. The safe deposit box arrived in the private viewing room, and he stuffed the metal pieces into his coat pocket, then left the bank quickly. Time was the enemy now. He had to get these things copied and back into the bank before Sebastian realized they'd been removed at all.

He could only pray Sebastian had no plans to take the plates to a jeweler for a couple of days. His impression had been that Sebastian's other business today would take a while, which meant he might not even get around to looking for an engraver until tomorrow.

Zane hailed a cab and gave the driver Maya's address, not far off Broadway. He jogged up five flights of stairs to a walk-up over a nightclub that was deserted and quiet right then. He didn't like involving anyone else in this mess, but he didn't know who else to turn to. And surely Erebus wouldn't go looking for an obscure jewelry artist tucked away in an obscure loft in an obscure corner of Greenwich Village.

Maya scowled darkly when he mentioned that Janice had given him her phone number. She burst out, "That rotten piece of shit. I oughta throw you out of here with a message for her to jump off the tallest building she can find."

"Why don't you tell me how you really feel?" he replied dryly.

Maya burst out laughing. "I like you. So why are you here? Please tell me Janice didn't send you to try to get me back."

Aloud, he said, "She did not send me here to beg you to take her back. I'm actually here because she said you're the finest sculptor and jewelry designer she knows."

"Bitch," Maya muttered with considerably less heat. "You need me to make you a piece of jewelry? What's it for?"

"Actually, I need you to make me an exact replica of something. As exact as you can possibly manage." He pulled out the pair of plates and set them down on the worktable in the middle of the cluttered industrial loft. "And I need them as fast as you can possibly do them."

Maya picked up the plates and stared at them in shock. "Do you know what these are?"

"Yes," he answered grimly. "That's why I came to you to destroy them. After you make the replicas, I need you to alter both the copies and the originals in some subtle way that will make them unusable. Do you have any idea how to do that?"

"That's easy. I'll just chisel an existing line a little deeper. Too much ink will fill it during the printing process and it'll make a fat, dark stripe on the bill. The plate will look fine until someone uses it."

"How fast can you make me replicas?" he asked.

"That depends. If you want me to make a cast and then fill it with stainless steel identical to this and temper it and cool it, that could take several weeks."

He swore. "I don't have several weeks. I have to deliver what looks like real plates to someone, possibly as soon as tomorrow, and then make sure they can never be used."

"Tomorrow? I'm not a magician!"

"Huh. Janice said you are."

Maya grinned. "Do you really want to mess with that person who's getting these's head?"

"What do you mean?"

"I can cast replicas of these suckers out of a nickel-titanium alloy called nitinol. It's the stuff magicians make bending spoons out of. At roughly human body temperature, nitinol bends and is easily breakable. You could warm the replica plates up next to your body, like in your shirt pocket, and then you could snap them in half with your bare hands.

Stuff's not too expensive either, and because of its special properties is very easy to cast."

"Perfect. Do that," he declared. "Can you make the impression thingy now that you'll cast the replica plates from while I wait?"

"I suppose so. As long as you don't hover over me. Makes me crazy to have people watch me work."

Huh. He couldn't imagine working without people watching him.

They negotiated a quick price, which he was pleased came to less than the two thousand dollars of the paycheck he'd just cashed. He didn't know much about banking rules, but he did know that large deposits like the one Erebus had allegedly dropped into his checking account last night took a couple of weeks to clear and become available. The federal government examined all large deposits to make sure they weren't drug money. He had no earthly idea how Erebus had explained away his deposit, and he hadn't had time to ask at the bank this morning.

Maya took the plates over to a table under a window and pulled out a wooden box about three times the dimensions of one of the plates. She took down jugs of clear goop and stirred them together in a bucket, then poured some of the goop in the boxes. She sprinkled the plates with a fine powder of some kind, blew off most of it, and then carefully laid them side-by-side in the goop. More goop went on top.

And then she strolled over to the refrigerator across the room, an ancient beast that had to have survived World War II, and opened the door. "Beer?" she asked.

"No, thanks."

"Weed?"

"Definitely no, thanks."

"Good for you. Getting wasted will be the death of me."

He flopped down on a decrepit sofa and held his breath as best he could while Maya lit up a joint. Thankfully, she sat over by the resin casts and didn't smoke for long. He was extremely proud of himself for surviving the temptation to move closer to her and inhale the blue cloud around her head.

"Is there anything we can do to speed this up?" he asked as she pulled out a flat tin container, opened it, and started rolling another joint.

"Nah. Resin's gotta harden. Won't take long. Relax. Take a load off. Tell me how you got no-shit currency printing plates?"

"It's a long story. I can tell you I am not a criminal, and I'm not going to let them fall into the hands of criminals. In a few weeks, when this is all over, I'll tell you the whole tale. You're gonna love it, especially the part where you're the heroine of the story. Please promise me you won't tell anyone about this."

"Who am I gonna tell? I mean, who'd believe me anyway?" she drawled.

"I mean it, Maya. Bad people want these things, and they would kill you if they found out you were involved."

"Dark, man."

Dammit. Was she too stoned on the weed to comprehend the seriousness of the situation? He should've made the danger clear before she'd lit up.

They sat in silence, Maya sucking down two more joints and Zane watching the big clock on the wall tick away maddeningly slowly.

"Okay," she announced abruptly. "We're done cooking."

Thank God. He felt ready to explode.

He followed her to the table this time, watching as she unscrewed the sides of the box to reveal a cream-colored gelatinous cube. Carefully, using a length of thread, she cut into it. The cube split open to reveal the currency plates inside, like a toy surprise. She lifted the plates out gently, and perfect impressions of each of their faces were left in the gel. She turned over the top piece of gel, revealing the opposite sides of each plate, complete with the engraved inscriptions for the employees of the year. After inspecting both impressions in the bright light streaming in the window, she declared them bubble-free and perfect.

"Great. You'll call me when you have the replicas?" he said, reaching for the plates.

"Not so fast. Lemme ruin those originals for you."

He watched in trepidation as she pulled out a set of metal tools that looked like dentist's picks and donned a headpiece that pulled magnifying glasses down over her eyes. "Are you sure you're steady enough to do this now? You've had a fair bit of weed, Maya."

She snorted. "That was just my wake-up weed. I don't get fucked-up until I switch to the hard stuff. Back off, okay?"

Riigghht. Note to self: stay the hell away from this woman in the future.

"Seriously, Zane, stand back and don't jostle me or the table. This shit's delicate work if you don't want it noticed right away."

He stood with his back against the door, holding his breath. It was a huge risk to deface the plates, but he would feel guilty for the rest of his life if he didn't.

The artist hunched over the engraving plates and placed the tip of a tool against the surface of one. She tapped the end of it lightly with a small wooden mallet, moved the tool, and tapped it again. She repeated the process a half-dozen times.

"Done!" Maya announced. "Damn, I'm good."

"You only worked on one plate."

"I only have to deface one plate. They can't print money if both plates aren't perfect. I messed up the back side of the bill, by the way. I figure most people will examine the front face first and be more familiar with what that looks like, anyway."

"Good thinking," he murmured.

He picked up the plate that was the back side of a twenty-dollar bill and peered where she pointed at a long border stripe that she promised was too deep to pick up the right amount of ink now and would make a giant blob on the bill if used. He would have to take her at her word. The plate looked exactly the same to him as it had before.

"I'll call you when the fakes are ready, pretty boy. Now get out. I gotta go shopping."

Somehow he suspected she wouldn't just be shopping for art supplies with the money he'd given her. "I need these fast. *Capisce*? Everything depends on this, Maya."

"I told you. One day. I'll cast them, polish them, and coat the back sides with brass. What joker put those sales award things on the back of the plates?"

Zane shrugged. "Not my circus, not my monkeys."

Maya laughed and shoved him toward the door.

"Remember, not a word to anyone," he warned.

"Mum's the word. Good news for you is I probably won't remember having done them in a week. That dough of yours is gonna buy me a whole lot of forgetfulness."

"Don't get trashed until you finish the plates, okay?" he pleaded. "It's life or death that I have the replicas right away."

"All right, all right. Don't get your panties in a wad. I've got you covered."

He scooped up the now allegedly unusable original plates and hurried back outside. A quick ride back to the bank, another quick visit to his safety deposit box, and the plates were tucked away safe and sound once more. He breathed a huge sigh of relief.

Now. How to explain his departure from the safe house? He turned over a few possible excuses and decided to go with the simplest, most obvious reason. He needed clothes to replace the ones that had been stolen along with his luggage. He still had several hundred dollars left over from the shoot. It wouldn't go far in New York, but it would buy him a few decent shirts and pairs of slacks.

He was about finished shopping when his cell phone rang a few hours later.

"Hello?"

"Where the hell are you?" Sebastian demanded. "I told you to stay put."

"Yeah, well, you forgot that I didn't have any clothes. As in none. I cashed my check from last night and bought myself some clean underwear. So sue me," he snapped back.

"You should have asked me or Etienne to get clothes for you. You risked your life by leaving the safe house." An irritated sigh. "Do you know the address of the penthouse?"

"Yes. I notice these things, you know."

"Meet me there. I have big news for you."

Zane glared at his phone. He hated when people were secretive like that. Curiosity was his greatest single downfall, and Sebastian had used it against him to perfection. Now he *had* to go back and find out what the big news was. Curse Sebastian!

Chapter Sixteen

Sebastian glared at his phone. What were the odds Zane had gone to get the damned plates? Surely, he wasn't that suicidal. He was going to lock Zane in a closet and not let him come out if he didn't quit running around on his own, though.

He couldn't wait to share his good news with Zane. Which was weird. He was used to being alone and having nobody to talk with about any aspect of his life. He kind of loved the excitement zinging around in his gut as he anticipated Zane's reaction to his good news.

Etienne had gotten the license plate number from the vehicle following them last night. The police had found the SUV abandoned this morning, and he'd convinced a friend in the police department to order it dusted for prints. They'd found fresh ones on the steering wheel. In a few hours, his friend in the department should have a name for him.

If they could track down Erebus's operatives in New York and get them to spill their guts, law enforcement agencies might just stand a chance of cornering and taking out the remnants of the slippery organization once and for all.

And then Zane would be safe, and they'd both be clear of this mess. How cool was that?

God, he couldn't wait to get on with his life… which would hopefully include Zane in it for a good, long time.

Wild Cards had been monitoring the police reports in New York for the past forty-eight hours, and no report of shots fired in any alley two nights ago had been filed. The counterfeiter had cleaned up all evidence of the failed handoff. Sebastian supposed he should be grateful for that, since any evidence could have led back to him and to some extremely awkward questions from the police.

While Etienne drove him home from the police station, Sebastian placed several more calls, this time to jewelers. When asked who the best engraver in the tristate area was, all of them unhesitatingly came up with the same name: Matteus Vanderpohl.

Sebastian got a phone number for the guy and called it. A man answered.

"I was told this was the phone number for an engraver, Matteus Vanderpohl," he said politely. "Have I got the wrong number?"

"No, you've got the right one. He just doesn't like to talk on the phone. What can I do for you?" the man asked.

"I have an engraving job I need done. A small and delicate one. I'm told Mr. Vanderpohl is the best engraver in the city, and I'm hoping he'll help me out."

"Of course, I'll be happy to schedule an appointment for you, Mr.—"

"Gigoni," he supplied. "Sebastian Gigoni." Although, as soon as his real name came out of his mouth, he regretted having used it. Not that he still owned any of the fake IDs the Wild Cards had made for him over a decade ago.

"Will tomorrow at 11:00 a.m. be acceptable, Mr. Gigoni?"

"Absolutely. What's your address?" Sebastian asked. He copied down the street address, which frankly sounded residential rather than commercial. "I'll see you then."

He made one last call, and this one made him smile. Sometimes it was awesome to be rich. The most amazing things could be arranged without any notice at all. He hung up just as the armored SUV Etienne was driving him in today pulled into the parking garage below his penthouse.

He was impatient as he rode the elevator up. God, he was besotted with Zane. He couldn't wait to see the guy.

Zane was there already, soaking in the hot tub on the terrace.

Sebastian strolled over to the hot tub, loving coming home to Zane lounging in it. He seemed more subdued than Sebastian would have expected after last night, though.

Personally, he was on top of the world today. He had never connected with any of his lovers like he'd connected with Zane. Physically—well, physically, they were dynamite together. And they fit together emotionally. He tended to be more serious and grounded, while Zane was dramatic and fun-loving. They balanced each other out.

And the sex had been fantastic. Zane seemed to know what he wanted to do almost before he did. Sebastian smiled. He never had been able to resist a dare. Zane might have pushed him to cut loose physically, but what had really cut loose were his feelings. He'd had no idea he had held them back so hard all these years. Today he felt like he could fly.

"So. What's your news?" Zane blurted.

Sebastian smiled and added *insatiable curiosity* to the list of Zane's lovable qualities. "They got prints from the vehicles that were at the handoff. The police think they'll be able to arrest the Erebus men there."

"And?" Zane asked, sounding confused.

"Once they're in custody, the feds can lean on them. Get them to roll over on their bosses. Expose the remaining Erebus members. If the whole bunch of them end up in jail, you'll be safe and this mess will be over."

"Wow! That's great! Join in the tub to celebrate?"

Lord, Zane was tempting. Sebastian sighed. "I've got a little work to do first. Rain check?"

"You've got it. Go make a few million dollars before dinner."

Sebastian dug through emails in his office while Zane dozed, naked, in a chaise beside the pool. Every few minutes Sebastian looked up, taking in the sight of Zane lounging outside. And to think that handsome man had been all his for the taking. He was counting the hours until he could realistically ask to do it again. He didn't want to fall on Zane like a starving wolf, but hunger for his lover gnawed at his gut until he could barely stand it.

He was saved by the doorbell. *Please let that be the gift I ordered for Zane.*

It was. Four young women wheeled in racks of clothing. "Put them over there, by the fireplace." He stuck his head out the sliding glass door wall and called, "Zane, I've got a surprise for you."

One of Zane's eyes opened lazily.

"You'll have to come inside to see it. And there are some women here."

A towel wrapped around his hips, Zane strolled across the deck, looking every inch like a big cat on the prowl. Sebastian never got tired of watching that slinky catwalk.

When Zane stepped inside, Sebastian gestured at the racks of clothes. "Pick out everything you'd like."

Zane spied the women and the designer clothing. "Hey, Jill. Katya. Good to see you both. I'm sorry, I don't know you two."

The other two design assistants introduced themselves quickly, and Zane flirted with them until they giggled. Then he turned to Sebastian. "Where did all this stuff come from?"

"I asked several designers to send over clothing for you. They all knew your measurements already, as it turns out."

"I used to get around in this town," Zane commented wryly.

"Choose. Anything you want," Sebastian said eagerly.

A frown passed across Zane's expressive features. Why wasn't he thrilled? Zane knew high fashion like nobody else Sebastian had ever met. Jeez, if someone had offered him a designer wardrobe when he'd been broke, he'd have been out of his mind with delight.

"Can I speak to you in private for a minute?" Zane murmured.

Confused, Sebastian gestured at his office. They stepped inside, and Zane pushed the door shut.

"Why did you do this?" Zane asked.

"Because you need new clothes after all of yours were stolen. And," he added, "I thought you would like it."

"I don't like feeling bought and paid for," Zane snapped. "And I told you I already got some more clothes."

"Bought and paid for? I never meant—"

"Regardless of what you meant, that's how this makes me feel. I've done a lot of stupid things in my life that I'm not proud of, but I am not a whore. I don't have sex with rich guys for money or gifts."

"I never thought you did!" Sebastian exclaimed, aghast that this was where Zane's thoughts had gone.

"I don't want your clothes."

"Zane, please," he said reasonably. "You need them. You lost everything you owned when your bag was stolen. I want to do this for you. Consider it a thank-you for helping with the investigation."

"I get what you're saying. But I can't accept them."

He rolled his eyes at that. "Other people can't have the pleasure of doing something nice for you if you won't let them. Don't deprive me of this happiness."

"That's a low blow," Zane declared.

"I never said I fight fair."

They glared at each other for several stubborn seconds.

"C'mon, Zane. Take the damned clothes as payment for helping out. I'll even bill Wild Cards, Inc. for all of it if that makes you feel better."

A long pause. Then, "That *would* make me feel better."

"Done. And now that we're doing this on Pere Cardiff's dime, please—for me—choose everything out there."

Zane grinned. "Is the guy loaded?"

"Makes me look middle-class."

"Got it. Well, in that case, let's go have a shopping spree."

No way was he letting Pere foot the bill for this. But what Zane didn't know wouldn't hurt him. He would quietly reimburse Pere for whatever tab Zane ran up. And in the meantime, he would have to figure out a way to get Zane to accept future presents from him. He wanted to shower the guy in beautiful, elegant things.

Watching Zane shop was an experience. He assessed each piece with laser attention to detail, mercilessly discarding the inferior pieces for their poor lines or poor construction. Once he'd winnowed down the selection to only the finest pieces, he then began creating outfits and looks. The design assistants offered suggestions and advice, and he laughed and joked easily with them while they put together collections for various occasions and levels of formality and informality.

And then it was time for Zane to try everything on. He retreated to Sebastian's bedroom with the first rack of clothes and emerged in a few minutes in a chic black-on-black suit that made him look like a fallen angel. He was so beautiful Sebastian could practically weep at the sight of him.

"Like it?" Zane asked him.

"Love it. Keep it," Sebastian answered promptly.

"Done."

Over the next hour, Zane emerged in several dozen ensembles. Sebastian was impressed at how decisive Zane was about the keepers and losers. As the girls hung up and racked the rejected clothes, Sebastian asked, "Have you ever considered designing your own clothes? You have a hell of an eye for fashion."

"It's one thing to see good lines. It's another to create them."

"Have you ever tried?"

Zane shook his head. "I confess I've thought about going to a design school, seeing if maybe I have what it takes. But until recently"—he gave a significant glance in the direction of the busy design assistants—"funds to pursue a formal fashion education were not forthcoming."

"I think you'd be a natural at it. You've got the eye for it and an artistic sensibility," Sebastian declared. "You should go for it."

A thoughtful gleam entered Zane's mint-green eyes. Sebastian would have offered to finance a line of clothing for him then and there if he didn't think Zane would throw it back in his face. But as it was, he bit his tongue. He could make a few calls, though. Maybe to that Japanese guy who'd hung Zane upside down. Zane seemed to gravitate to clothes with a similar aesthetic to that particular designer.

Another hour was spent picking out socks, shoes, ties, scarves, sunglasses, and even cuff links to go with the new wardrobe. Hilarity ensued as Zane picked out underwear from the selection that had been provided, modeling it over his clothes and, in a few cases, over his head. Who knew men's bikini briefs were so perfectly proportioned to be earmuffs?

At long last, the girls and their racks vacated the penthouse, leaving him and Zane alone.

"Thank you for going along with that," Sebastian said quietly.

"Thank you for arranging it."

"My pleasure." And he meant that.

Zane moved over to the fourteen-foot-tall glass wall to gaze pensively at the skyline turning rosy with sunset. Although Sebastian would love to know what Zane was thinking about, instead he said, "Would you mind indulging me on one thing if I swear it doesn't involve taking monetary gifts from me?"

Zane turned around to face him. "What's that?"

"Have dinner with me on the terrace."

For an instant Zane's expression was stubborn. But then he said graciously, "It would be my pleasure. How formal is the attire for this meal?"

Sebastian laughed. "After the education I got today on the nuances of formality in clothing, I leave that entirely to your discretion. If you'll excuse me, I'm going to the kitchen now."

"You're going to cook?" Zane exclaimed.

He turned back, frowning. "Well, yes. How else does dinner get prepared?"

"I call for takeout and food fairies make it magically appear at my door."

Sebastian grinned widely. "Dammit, you busted me. I'm actually a food fairy."

"Ha. I knew it! Want some help?"

"Do you know anything at all about cooking?" Sebastian asked.

"You saw my entire culinary repertoire when I made fried bacon and scrambled eggs for you. Does that answer your question?"

"Check. No tricky cooking assignments for you. How are you with washing dishes?"

"You can *do* that?" Zane exclaimed.

They retreated into the kitchen, laughing.

He let Zane chop a head of romaine lettuce for a salad but took the knife from him when Zane nearly amputated his own finger trying to slice a tomato. Sebastian pointed with the tip of the knife at a barstool. "You. Sit there. And don't get in my way. I'm armed and dangerous, got it?"

"Ooh. The badass commando has a knife."

Sebastian couldn't resist showing off. He finished slicing the offending tomato and then flicked his wrist, throwing the knife across the kitchen to stick in the butcher-block backsplash behind the sink.

"Shit!" Zane exclaimed as the knife flashed past his face.

"Never fear. It didn't come within three feet of you." Sebastian strolled over to the sink and rocked the knife handle, freeing it from the oak wood, and dropped it in the sink.

"You expect a lot of trust out of the people around you, don't you?" Zane asked.

He turned. That didn't sound like light banter. He answered in a similarly serious vein. "Yeah. I guess I do. I live as honorably as I can, and I expect my friends to believe in that. To believe in me."

Zane nodded slowly at him. "I think I believe in you."

"Thanks for the ringing vote of confidence. I'm so glad we got that straight *after* we had sex."

Zane hopped off the stool and came over to him, wrapping Sebastian in an embrace before he could decide whether or not to dodge it. "I follow my heart, Sebastian. You felt right to me, so I went with the moment. I'm following my heart again now. It's telling me you don't mean to be a rich control freak and that you really are trying to be a decent guy."

He mumbled into Zane's styled hair, "You know, if you tried examining logic, you would also come to the same conclusion."

"How so?"

"Because if I wasn't interested in you personally, I'd have offered you two million bucks to just give the plates to me. I'd still get to use the plates to trap the Erebus guys for myself and I wouldn't have had to deal with some pesky dude."

Zane lifted his head to smile up at him, an eyebrow quirked quizzically. "Thank you, I think?"

Sebastian stepped away from Zane, carefully setting him at arm's length. "If we're going to get any supper tonight, I have to get back to cooking. Otherwise I'm going to take you to bed right now and we'll starve before morning."

"Speak for yourself. I'm used to living on twigs and berries, remember?" Zane retorted.

Sebastian lifted a lid and stirred the pot of bolognese sauce. "Not in this house, you're not."

It didn't take much longer to cook and drain fresh angel hair pasta, toss it with the sauce, shred a hard, salty cheese finely over it, and dish up salads and only slightly burned garlic bread. Zane picked out a bottle of wine from the cooler and pulled the cork. They carried the whole feast out to the terrace, lit only by the shimmering glow of underwater lights in the swimming pool. At their feet lay the lights of New York City stretching away into the night. It was magical.

Sebastian had brought the occasional date to the penthouse, but he'd never been nervous over what the date thought. Tonight he was desperate for everything to be perfect. He served Zane a big plate of pasta that had Zane laughing in protest, filled his glass with a vintage burgundy he'd paid thousands of dollars for, and mumbled, "I'm sorry for the burned bread."

"Sebastian. Stop. Look at me."

Frowning, he sank into his seat and looked across the small table at Zane in alarm.

"That's the third time you've apologized for the bread being burned. I'll scrape off the black bits—which are only around the edge of the crust, by the way—and it'll be fine. Trust me. If I'd been in charge of toasting the garlic bread, fire extinguishers would have been involved."

A burst of laughter slipped out of him, and he finally relaxed a little. He just wanted everything to be perfect tonight.

"Everything's wonderful, Seb. Let's just relax and enjoy the evening together. Okay?"

He exhaled hard. "Okay."

CHAPTER SEVENTEEN

ZANE DIDN'T taste any of the supper, which was no doubt delicious, lightly charred garlic bread notwithstanding. Nor did he taste the superior wine. And frankly, he would have been hard-pressed to repeat much of what they talked about over the meal.

But he did register the way Sebastian's eyes glowed bluer than ever in the flickering pool lights. And the way he got a small dimple in his left cheek when he smiled at Zane. He noticed how Sebastian's powerful, callused hands ran ever so lightly over the delicate crystal stem of his wineglass. And how Sebastian seemed to hang on every word he said, as if what Zane had to say mattered deeply to him.

He hated lying to Sebastian about where he'd been earlier. But it wasn't like he had any choice. No way was he letting this Erebus bunch get their mitts on usable plates. They both were getting jerked around, he supposed. Him by Erebus, and Sebastian by the people who'd recruited him to deal with this situation.

The last remnants of his earlier anger at hearing Sebastian declare that he could get Zane to do anything dissipated. Neither of them was blame-free in this mess.

They lingered over the meal until the food was cold and the last of the wine savored. Zane never wanted their first official date to end. Full night fell around them, and the evening cooled quickly as high up as they were.

Sebastian stood up and spoke into his watch. "Computer, play relaxing playlist number two."

Soft music started, and Zane looked around for the source but didn't spot it. Must be hidden speakers. He shook his head. Sebastian and his tech toys.

"You have an unrelaxing playlist?" he murmured.

"I have a jack-me-up workout list and a piss-me-off list."

"Piss me off? Whatever for?"

"Sometimes I have to go into a meeting and kick asses, and I need to be in the proper frame of mind for that. After I spent my entire twenties working my tail off to become zen, it's an effort for me to get good and pissed off these days."

Sebastian stood and held out his hand formally, palm up, silently asking for Zane's hand. He complied, reveling in the strength and gentleness of Sebastian's touch.

"You're shivering," Sebastian murmured.

"I'm a little cold."

"I know a cure for that. Dance with me?" Sebastian murmured.

"I would love to."

Sebastian stepped forward, placing one hand on Zane's waist and another on his shoulder, like they were at a junior high cotillion.

"What are you doing?" Zane asked.

"Dancing with you. I want to get it just right with you."

Zane smiled and moved forward, wrapping both his arms around Sebastian's neck and plastering his body against Sebastian's from chest to knees. "*This* is just right."

"You're sure?"

He tilted his chin to one side and kissed Sebastian, relishing the stubble that grazed his cheek and the warm fullness of Sebastian's mouth. Everything about this man, this moment, was perfect. They swayed to the music, shuffling in a slow circle more than actually dancing, not that Zane cared as long as Sebastian kept kissing him like this, so slow and lazy, like they had all the time in the world together. Like this was the start of something very long-term.

Strange how quickly things had changed for him. Two weeks ago he would have laughed his ass off at the notion of finding true love and settling down forever. But now… things like commitment and long-term relationships suddenly seemed not only possible but within his grasp.

He checked himself sharply. Just because he was thinking that way didn't mean Sebastian was.

"What?" Sebastian murmured.

He lifted his head off Sebastian's shoulder and peered at him in the dim black glow of the pool. "What what?"

"You tensed all of a sudden like you'd thought of something alarming."

"Ahh." He stared fixedly over Sebastian's shoulder at the black sky. "I was just, umm, thinking about us."

"What were you thinking about us?"

"I was wondering if there is an 'us.'" He hesitated, then mumbled, "And for how long."

A long pause. Long enough that Zane pulled back to be able to stare fully into Sebastian's face. Dammit, he'd gone all inscrutable, and Zane couldn't read a thing in his expression. "Help me out, here, Sebastian. What are *you* thinking?"

"I'm thinking that I'm no good at this 'talking about my feelings' stuff."

Zane huffed. "It's not hard. You just blurt out what's in your gut and on the tip of your tongue to say. Go ahead. Give it a try."

Sebastian grinned ruefully. "We'll have to dance some more. I can't do this with you staring at me like that."

Zane promptly stepped forward and wrapped his arms around Sebastian's lean, hard waist, resting his head on Sebastian's broad shoulder. "Okay. I'm not looking at you. So let rip."

"Well, at the exact moment you asked me what I was thinking, I was wondering how to get you into bed again without sounding like some old horndog who's only interested in hot sex."

Zane chuckled. "That's easy. You ask."

"Yeah, but how?"

"You say something like, 'I find you incredibly attractive and you make me insanely horny. I think about you constantly, and I've imagined a hundred things I'd like to do with you and to you. I really like you. All of you. Not just your looks but your mind, your humor, your intelligence. I like the way you hold a wineglass, and how much I love to talk with you, and how you make me feel when I'm with you. Would you do me the great honor of retiring to the bedroom with me and exploring our mutual attraction for each other until we're both too fucking exhausted to stand up?'"

"Wow. That's quite a speech. I don't think I could remember all that."

Zane laughed and smacked Sebastian's upper arm. "Don't be a jerk."

Sebastian stopped moving to the music and took Zane's shoulders in his hands. He leaned back to look him in the eyes and said gruffly, "I'm no good at flowery words, but all of the stuff you just said? That. All of that."

Zane's insides melted into a puddle right then and there. "You see?" he managed lightly. "That wasn't so hard."

"Yeah, but did it work?"

He laughed a little. "Hell yes, it worked. What are you waiting for, Mr. Gigoni? Take me to bed."

They practically ran through the penthouse to a big, airy bedroom as sleek and open as the rest of the dwelling. Hastily they helped each other undress, laughing and kissing and teasing each other as ties and pants and socks went flying every which way.

Zane threw back the coverlet, and Sebastian practically jumped onto the mattress. He looked like an eager puppy, and Zane had to laugh. He stepped up to the bed and threw his leg across Sebastian's hips, straddling him and staring down at him. The humor faded from their gazes as they stared at each other. They had secrets between them. They still had big problems to iron out. Sebastian had good reason not to trust him completely, and he probably deserved the doubts. For that matter, he wasn't 100 percent sure why Sebastian was doing all of this either.

But this was real, this thing between them.

Very slowly, inch by inch, Zane bent down until his mouth paused a hair's width from Sebastian's. "Thank you for tonight," he whispered.

"The night's just getting started."

"I know. That's why I'm saying thank you now. Before I'm too wiped out and blown away to remember to say it."

Sebastian slipped his hand into Zane's hair and pulled him down the last millimeter. As their lips met, he murmured against Zane's mouth, "You're welcome. But I'm the one who should be thanking you."

Their lovemaking was a slow give-and-take, easy and sensual, tonight. They explored each other's bodies, learning shapes and textures, cataloging ticklish spots and the spots that drove their partner crazy. Sometimes Zane crawled all over Sebastian's muscular frame, and sometimes Sebastian surged up and returned the favor. At other times they wrestled playfully, Sebastian restraining his strength carefully, both evening the odds and protecting Zane from harm.

Zane was generally a bold and confident lover, but in the presence of Sebastian, he found himself unaccountably shy when they finally lay face-to-face with Sebastian looming over him, big and dark.

"Look at me, Zane."

He opened his eyes and stared up at Sebastian, fascinated by the ticking muscle in his temple. "Are you okay?" he asked.

"I want to be inside you so bad I could explode."

The shyness faded in the face of Sebastian's confession. "Well, don't explode. I want you inside me before that happens."

Sebastian positioned himself correctly and then slowly, inevitably, filled Zane to bursting. They stilled and traded the most naked, vulnerable gazes so far, while they registered and absorbed the joining of their bodies. His legs wrapped around his lover's hips in welcome and acceptance.

For the first time in his life, Zane truly understood the difference between sex and making love. The exhilaration breaking free of his chest, the sense of oneness with Sebastian, the almost religious nature of the moment overwhelmed him. He was utterly shattered. Moisture escaped the corner of his eye.

Shifting his weight to his left elbow, Sebastian pushed the hair off Zane's forehead and studied him in concern. "Are you okay?"

"I'm more than okay. I'm amazed. And humbled."

"Humbled? What for? You're the stunning high-fashion model. I'm just a hairy Italian dude."

Zane reached up to frame Sebastian's face. "Don't ever say something like that to me again. We're us. Just us. None of the rest of it matters. Okay?"

Something fierce and free passed through Sebastian's gaze, erasing all the doubts in his eyes. "Okay." A pause. "I'm completely addicted to you."

Not exactly a declaration of true love, but he would take it. He was addicted to Sebastian too. And maybe even more than that.

Zane groaned with pleasure as Sebastian began moving within him. Slowly at first, then with increasing force and urgency. The pleasure in his own gut built and built, climbing through him until it was clawing to get out, demanding release. He thrust up at Sebastian more and more frantically, chasing the pleasure he felt hovering just out of reach.

On and on into the night, they drove each other, pushing each other further and further toward the brink of something indescribable. And all the while, Sebastian stared down at him and he stared back, their gazes locked and their souls stripped completely bare. The intimacy of it was staggering.

And just when Zane didn't think he could take one more second of the pleasure overload, Sebastian paused, partially withdrawn from Zane's body. Zane froze as well, arched up against the hot, sweaty glory of Sebastian's body. Their gazes met one last time, and then Sebastian slammed into him with a shout, and Zane exploded as well. His entire body and soul emptied into the crashing moment of exquisite pleasure, so sharp and intense it was nearly painful.

Sebastian collapsed on top of him, and Zane wrapped his arms weakly around Sebastian's torso, hanging on for dear life as he slowly fell back toward earth.

Eventually he became aware of breathing. Of Sebastian's heaving chest. Of Sebastian's delicious weight pressing him down into the mattress. "Wow," he breathed.

"Yeah. That. Wow," Sebastian panted back.

Not tonight, but soon, he would tell Sebastian about making the fake plates. About hoping to keep the money now sitting in his bank account so he could finance a new future for himself. And just maybe, he would tell Sebastian that he'd fallen in love with him. He would come clean and there would be no more secrets between them. And when that was taken care of, he would be whole again. Whole and complete and truly loved for the first time in his life.

ZANE WOKE up feeling better than he could ever remember. He'd had some spectacular highs in his life—some drug-induced and some not— but none of them were even a pale shadow of the joy he felt now. There'd been no talk last night of the future or of long-term relationships. But there didn't need to be. He'd rocked Sebastian's world every bit as much as Sebastian had rocked his. In a state of bliss, he stared up at the ceiling, lazily enjoying the play of shadows on the ceiling as the air conditioner gently fluttered the gauze sheers over the floor-to-ceiling window.

"Good morning, sleepyhead," Sebastian said from the doorway. He was fully dressed in wool trousers and a crisply starched white shirt. There he was—the wealthy executive. *Hot, hot, hot*, a little voice in the back of Zane's head chanted.

Zane sat up smiling, the gray sheets pooling around his hips. "If I'm tired this morning, it's because somebody kept me up half the night, blowing my mind."

"Blowing your mind, huh?" Sebastian leaned against the doorjamb, grinning back.

Zane got out of bed and strolled over to him naked, enjoying the feel of Sebastian's fine cotton dress shirt against his skin. "Good morning to you too," he murmured and then kissed Sebastian.

Instantly Sebastian straightened, his arms going around Zane possessively. The kiss deepened, and Zane felt Sebastian's interest stir behind his zipper. But then Sebastian turned him loose and stepped back regretfully.

"Unfortunately, we've got an appointment in an hour."

"We do?"

"The engraver. We have to take the plates to him to see if he can tell us anything about who made them."

Zane's hope for a morning quickie evaporated. He'd hoped to put Sebastian in a good mood before he made his big confession. The magic spell of last night was broken, and the stress and worry of getting rid of those stupid currency plates rushed back in.

He opened his mouth to tell Sebastian that they needed to talk, to admit that he'd defaced the original plates, but Sebastian whirled away and strode toward the kitchen, calling over his shoulder, "Are you hungry?"

"After last night?" Zane called back. "No twigs and berries for me this morning. I could eat a horse."

"Go take a shower, and I'll cook breakfast for you."

"Deal. See you in a few."

Tonight. He would arrange for a romantic evening, maybe a little wine—correction, a lot of wine—get Sebastian drunk and mellow, and then he'd tell all. A plan in place, Zane caught himself racing through showering, shaving, and dressing because he was in a hurry to get back to Sebastian. Lord, he was a goner.

He stopped in the great room just outside the kitchen to absorb that thought. He *was* a goner. He was head over heels for Sebastian. *Son of a gun.* He sure as heck hadn't seen this coming when he'd been standing at that luggage carousel at JFK, panicking over where his suitcase had gone.

He stepped into the kitchen and into Sebastian's arms, pancakes and sausage forgotten. "You, sir, are a miracle. I'm so glad you came into my life."

Sebastian laughed. "Trust me. The miracle is all for me. I couldn't in my wildest dreams have imagined that a man like you would ever see anything redeeming in a guy like me."

"Consider yourself redeemed," Zane declared.

Sebastian snorted. "You don't even know the full list of my sins yet."

"So tell me all of them while I eat that delicious stack of pancakes I spy on the table."

Sebastian steered the conversation toward more trivial matters over the meal, which was just as well. It wasn't like Zane was in any huge hurry to confess all of his own sins. Nope. Wine first. Then true confession.

Tonight, though. He wanted the slate clean between them so their relationship had a solid foundation to build on.

After the meal, Sebastian made a quick call to Etienne to ask for the armored SUV to pick them up in a half hour. They would go to the bank first to get the plates and then to the engraver's house.

The safe deposit box was delivered to them in a private room at the bank, and Zane picked up both plates reluctantly.

"We'll only need one of them," Sebastian commented.

"Why only one?"

"Because that's all it will take for a topnotch engraver to tell us if the plates are accurate enough to print passable money, and if he can tell who made them. This way, if Erebus's people jump us while we're out in public, they'll only get half of what they need to counterfeit money."

Chilling, but logical.

And handy as hell. He happened to have one undamaged plate left to show to this engraver of Sebastian's.

Zane held out the undamaged front plate to Sebastian and, in secret relief, tucked the defaced back plate back into his safe deposit box. It crossed his mind to tell Sebastian what he'd done, but now was not the time. Sebastian didn't need to be distracted and angry at being left out of Zane's plans while they were out in public, exposed to Erebus and in danger.

They pulled up in front of an aging but still lovely brownstone north of Central Park. Etienne dropped them off and then drove away. In an abundance of caution, Sebastian carried the lone currency plate in his coat pocket as they trotted up the steps and rang the doorbell.

A man with short gray hair opened the door for them and introduced himself as Claude Vanderpohl. "My son is in his workshop this morning. If you want to leave your engraving order—"

Sebastian cut him off. "Actually, we want to speak with Mr. Vanderpohl directly. I'd like to ask his opinion on something. I'm told he's an expert on fine engraving."

"He is that," their host replied dryly. "If you want to try to speak with my son, you'll have to go see him." A shrug. "Maybe he'll want to talk with you. Maybe he won't." Claude led them toward the back of the long, narrow home. "Matty's workshop is back here."

They stepped into a dark room that felt tiny and cluttered but in fact was a rather spacious room that took up the whole back of the ground floor. Tools and gears and boxes of who knew what crammed the floor-to-ceiling shelves. They rounded a freestanding wall of shelving, and Zane spied a man sitting on a tall stool, hunched over and staring through a large magnifying glass on a brass stand at something small on the worktable before him.

"You have guests, Matty. Clients."

"Uh-huh." The engraver sounded singularly uninterested in the news.

Zane moved out from behind Sebastian to see Matty more clearly. He was older than Zane had expected, balding, and soft in body like someone who was mostly sedentary. Maybe in his early fifties. He still hadn't looked up.

"He's more likely to talk if I'm not here. He's angry at me for taking away a box of cookies he found in the kitchen." Claude retreated after that odd comment, leaving them alone with the engraver.

"Hello, Mr. Vanderpohl. My name is Sebastian Gigoni, and I'd like to ask you a question about a piece of engraving I recently—"

"I'm not Mr. Vanderpohl," the man at the table interrupted abruptly. "That's my father. I'm Matty." He looked up at them then, and Zane mentally drew a sharp breath as he looked back at the eyes of a child.

"All right, Matty," Sebastian said with admirable composure. "I thought you might like to see this." He laid the engraving plate, sales award side up, on the table in the circle of light shining down on it brightly.

Matty snorted. "That's terrible engraving. The depth of the letters isn't even, and the engraving wheel needed sharpening. I can tell because the edges are too rough. You shouldn't have used a crappy engraving machine. You'd have got a better plaque."

Sebastian nodded. "Thank you. But I have a surprise for you. Flip it over."

Frowning, Matty flipped over the plate. And gasped in delight. "Oh. Oh, that's so cool!" Excited, the engraver reached for a small monocular magnifying glass that he pulled over his right eye. He hunched over the plate in utter concentration.

"Is it real?" Sebastian asked.

No answer from Matty.

"What I actually need to know is will it work?" Sebastian tried again. "Will it print money that will pass for real?"

Still no reply from the engraver. He seemed lost in contemplating the plate. Inch by painstaking inch, he examined the plate like a connoisseur totally engrossed in a masterpiece.

Zane and Sebastian stood silently beside the table for a good five minutes, and still Matty said nothing. Bored, Zane began to register that the third cup of coffee at breakfast had possibly been a bad idea. Another several minutes passed in silence, and his bladder was really starting to complain.

"I'm going to go find a restroom," he murmured to Sebastian.

He headed back down the hallway but found only a kitchen, dining room, and living room. *Damn.* There was no sign of Matty's father either. Cautiously, Zane headed upstairs to the second floor. "Mr. Vanderpohl?" he called.

No answer. Deep silence enveloped the house. He poked his head through an open doorway and saw a bedroom. The bed wasn't made, and a woman's dressing table was messy with makeup, perfume bottles, and bits of jewelry. More importantly, however, to the right of the table, he spied a bathroom through an open door. He scooted fast through the space, feeling like an intruder. The bathroom was old-fashioned, with tiny hexagonal floor tiles and a mismatched Formica counter from the seventies.

He used the toilet quickly, flushed, and washed his hands hastily. He was rinsing them when he spotted the brooch. A glittering spider crusted in diamonds. Surely it was one of a kind. Which meant he'd seen that exact piece before. At the ballet.

He picked it up and turned it over. The stamp of an old and venerable design firm graced the back. No question about it: this had to be the same spider as the one on the turban of the lady he'd sat beside at the ballet. What were the odds of that?

Thoughtfully, he left the bathroom and headed back out into the hallway, relieved when he reached the stairs. He was about halfway down them when Claude Vanderpohl walked in the front door. "What were you doing up there?" the man barked.

Guilt speared into Zane. "I'm sorry. I had to use the restroom."

Claude frowned, clearly displeased, and Zane hurried back toward the workroom and Sebastian, eager to avoid their unpleasant host. There was something familiar about the man. The shape of his shoulders. And that facial bone structure. He never forgot a jawline....

It hit him just as he was turning into the dark, stuffy workroom. It was probably the spider brooch that led him to make the connection. The woman who'd sat beside him at the ballet and Claude Vanderpohl. They had to be siblings, for they had identical facial bones.

But then a flash of the cosmetics on the dressing table upstairs came to him. There'd been a lot of makeup on that table. And lots of contouring products in particular. And white glue. The kind drag queens used to paste down their brows... and a straight razor that would give an exceptionally close shave....

He moved over to the table quickly. "Matty, what's your mother's name?"

The engraver looked up from the plate, guilt and confusion plain on his features. "Umm"—his gaze slid away—"I can't tell you."

"Why not?"

"It's a secret."

"Is that because your father actually dresses up as your mother?" Zane asked gently.

Matty sat up, his hands moving without purpose across the tools laid out on his table. "Nonono. Can't tell. No cookies for me. Bad man. Go away!"

Matty's voice rose on the last words.

"It's okay, Matty," Sebastian said soothingly. "My friend was being bad and shouldn't have asked that. Do you want me to take his cookies away from him when I take him home?"

"Yes," Matty said emphatically. "No cookies for him."

Sebastian chuckled and nodded to the engraver. "All right, then."

Sebastian's attention was fixed on Matty, but Zane suddenly got a bad feeling along the back of his neck. Like he was being watched. He turned fast, just in time to see Claude close the hallway door. A snick announced that the door had been locked.

What. The. Hell?

And then it all fell into place, every piece suddenly forming a complete picture. There was no mother. Claude had been the "woman" beside him at the ballet. It had been Matty's ticket that miraculously became available, just in time for Erebus's contact to give it to him. Which meant the Vanderpohls at a minimum knew somebody affiliated with Erebus, or at least with the consortium's counterfeiter. Or maybe *were* the counterfeiters....

And the locked door abruptly made perfect sense.

He turned back to Sebastian and murmured, "I need to speak with you in private."

After the cookie outburst, Matty had returned to examining the currency plate in utter fascination, and Sebastian leaned down beside him to murmur, "Will it make a perfect picture?"

"Don't know," Matty mumbled. "Let's see." He rummaged in a wide, flat drawer to his left and pulled out a small rubber roller, a pot of what looked like black finger paint, and a piece of paper. He set about meticulously cleaning the roller and preparing the paper and ink.

Sebastian seemed interested in the process, but Zane physically grabbed his sleeve and gave it a tug. "Now," he mouthed. "I need to talk with you."

Frowning, Sebastian stepped around the stack of shelves in the middle of the room with him. "What the hell's so important that I can't watch a trial print?"

"Claude Vanderpohl was the woman beside me at the ballet. I sat in Matty's seat. Which means they know the counterfeiters, or are the counterfeiters. And Claude just locked us in here."

"What?" Sebastian exclaimed under his breath. He moved over to the door and tried the knob once, quietly. He returned to Zane's side, swearing under his breath.

It fell to Zane to state the obvious. "I think Claude and Matty work for or are part of Erebus."

CHAPTER EIGHTEEN

SEBASTIAN LOOKED up as Matty exclaimed on the other side of the shelf. To Zane he muttered, "Pretend everything is fine," and then he ducked around the shelf and joined Matty at the worktable.

"Whatchya got, buddy?"

"Look! It's perfect!" Matty exclaimed.

Sebastian stared down at the sheet of paper, and indeed, a perfect, albeit black, image of Andrew Jackson on a twenty-dollar bill stared back up at him. Nausea erupted in his belly. "Do you think a bank would take a note printed with that plate?" he asked.

"Well, duh," Matty retorted. "Nuh-uhh."

"Why not?" he asked.

Matty answered scornfully, "Money has two sides."

Sebastian grinned. "You got me there, buddy."

Matty grinned back archly.

Out of the side of his mouth, Sebastian muttered to Zane, "Keep him talking."

On cue, Zane smiled at the engraver and asked conversationally, "If I had the plate for the other side and it was as good as this one, and I made a twenty-dollar bill with them, would a bank believe it was real?"

Matty nodded. "You would need the right paper and ink and metallic threads and the ability to print holographic images."

From what Wild Cards' inside man had said, Erebus had already lined up all of that other stuff. To Matty, he said, "But if I had all of that stuff, could I do it?"

"You could print all the money you wanted."

"How long did it take someone to make this plate, do you suppose?" Zane asked.

Sebastian tuned out Matty mumbling to himself about how long various parts of the job would take him.

They had to keep Matty talking and not sending out any alarm calls until Sebastian figured out a way to get himself and Zane out of this locked, windowless room and away from the Erebus operative outside.

Vanderpohl was no doubt calling in reinforcements as they stood here. Maybe there was a window behind one of the built-in shelves. He commenced scanning the walls for any signs of exterior light. It would be unusual for one of these old brownstones not to have a rear window facing the yard or alley behind the house.

Matty counted on his fingers for a while and finally announced, "It took a really long time to make."

"Was this made by hand?" Zane asked.

"Only way to do stuff that fine," Matty declared.

"Could you make something like this?" Zane followed up.

Damn. No sign of a window. There must be a way to unlock the door from in here. Goodness knew Matty had every small hand tool under the sun. He must have a set of lock picks in here somewhere. Or maybe even a key.

Matty shrugged. "I made something like that once. The people who make money asked me to make a picture of someone they were thinking about putting on money."

"That's awesome!" Zane exclaimed. "Who was it? Do you have a picture of the engraving you made?"

Sebastian scanned up and down the shelves for something resembling a lock pick while Matty preened for Zane. It was hopeless. The room was so cluttered and random in organization, he would never find lock picks on his own. Did he dare try calling Etienne?

He asked casually, "Matty, do you have a key for the door?"

"No." His expression went closed, and he sat very still on his stool. "I guess I have to stay in here and work, then."

"Why?" Zane asked.

"When he locks me in, that's what I do. I make stuff."

"Like what?" Sebastian interjected.

"Watches and machines and stuff."

"Is there another way out of this room?" he asked.

"Nuh-uh. Just the door." Matty sighed. "I'm already hungry."

Zane patted his shoulder. "We'll get you out fast. And then you can share my cookies with me."

"Liar!" Matty shouted. "Your cookies got taken away like mine!"

Sebastian dived in to calm Matty. "I changed my mind. Both of you can have cookies when we get out of here."

Except Sebastian heard a voice outside the door. Make that several voices. And they were headed this way. Damn. No time to make a phone call. "Get back behind the shelf with Matty, Zane." He scanned the shelves urgently for a weapon, any weapon.

"You hide too!" Zane retorted. "If they shoot their way in, there's no reason for you to die."

Matty looked back and forth between them in confusion. "I don't want to die," he declared, his lower lip starting to tremble.

Zane wrapped his arm around the man. "Nobody's dying. We just want you to be safe. I'll protect you, okay? And then we can share our cookies. What kind is your favorite, Matty?"

"I like peanut butter. And chocolate chip."

"How about peanut butter-chocolate chip all in one?" Zane asked.

Sebastian found what he was looking for on the shelves. He pulled out a length of pipe that was heavy and sturdy, about the length of his forearm. The doorknob moved slightly, and he braced himself behind the door, gesturing urgently to Zane to keep Matty talking.

The conversation about flavors of cookies flowed around him, not touching him. All his focus was on that door and the men about to step through it. The knob turned.

All at once the door flew open, heaving toward him. He dived to the side, barely missing being smashed behind it. A big man spun into the room and launched himself upward into Sebastian's gut, lifting him all the way off his feet.

Sebastian chopped downward with his free fist on the back of his assailant's neck, too close to bring the pipe to bear. The attacker grunted and turned him loose, and he swung the pipe in a short, sharp chop. The man went down to one knee. Sebastian jerked his own knee up hard into the man's face, and the guy went down the rest of the way, flat on his face.

Sebastian spun but drew up short as Claude said, "Ah, ah, ah, Mr. Gigoni. We wouldn't want to get your friend killed, would we?"

A second man had burst into the room behind the attacker he'd dropped, and this one had a handgun trained on Zane.

Dammit. If Zane were a trained Special Forces operative, he would have known to throw himself behind Matty and use him as a human shield or hostage. But as it was, Zane stared in wide-eyed horror at the big bald dude with a gun pointed at him.

Sighing, Sebastian dropped the pipe and linked his fingers at the back of his neck without having to be told and moved over to stand beside Zane. One of the thugs took his cell phone.

"Hands up, Mr. Stryker," Claude snapped.

Zane mimicked Sebastian, and their elbows bumped. They traded glances, and Sebastian put all the reassurance he could into his own expression. It was false reassurance, but a panicked Zane wouldn't do anybody any good. A thug lifted the cell phone out of Zane's pocket as well. So much for a phone call to Etienne and a quick rescue.

Matty started to whimper behind them.

"Go to your room, Matteus."

"Can I take the plate they brought me?"

"No. Give me that."

"But they brought it for me. It's mine."

"You can have the entire bag of cookies in the bread box, but give me the plate," Claude bit out.

"Yippee!" Matty crowed.

"Where's the second plate, gentlemen?" Claude asked pleasantly. Not that he would stay pleasant for long, of course. Sebastian knew full well how this game went. Either he or Zane would be tortured until the other one broke and spilled the location of the plates. His gut turned to water at the thought of watching Zane suffer, his beautiful face and innocent civilian spirit broken and permanently marred by whatever these goons would do to him.

"Don't answer, Zane!" Sebastian cried. If Claude thought Zane knew the answer, maybe they would torture him instead, to make Zane talk. He would much rather take the pain himself and spare Zane.

Zane looked back and forth between him and Claude. Sebastian pleaded with his eyes. *Don't say a word.*

"Let's take this conversation somewhere more private, shall we?" Claude said. "Bring them along, gentlemen." The guards glared at them, the one Sebastian had dropped mopping at his bloody nose with a handkerchief.

Sebastian allowed himself to be prodded along behind Zane, and the two of them were taken downstairs into a low-ceilinged, unfinished basement that hadn't been updated since this house had been built. A hot-water heater clanked in a corner, and an air conditioner rattled in another. No one would hear them scream down here. Fear for Zane began to climb the inside of his stomach. He and Zane were in big trouble. Huge. He had to think up something and *fast*, or they were both dead. One of them would be tortured until the other one broke, then the second plate would be fetched from Zane's bank, and then they would both die.

"Mr. Vanderpohl, I need to speak with your superiors. If you could pass a message along to them, I would appreciate it."

Claude stared at him. "What could you possibly have to say to them?"

Ha. He'd all but admitted to working for Erebus.

"I would like to apply for membership in the Erebus Consortium. Tell them that."

Zane gasped, and Sebastian flinched. Surely Zane knew he was lying. That he was buying them time and a way out of this hellhole.

"How do you know that name?" Claude demanded.

"Does it matter? You dropped a priceless pair of currency plates into my boyfriend's luggage, and you didn't expect me to investigate and figure out who was behind that? I have resources, my friend. Pass the message."

A snort. "What reason would they have to even speak with you?"

"I have about a billion reasons in the bank," he retorted, "and assets and contacts worth more than that."

That silenced Claude. After a minute he asked, "Who are you again?"

"I told you. I'm Sebastian Gigoni. Google me."

He was faintly surprised when Claude did in fact pull out a cell phone and type into it. The man looked from the phone to him and back down at the phone. Must be comparing a picture of him to his face.

Without agreeing to pass the message along, Claude turned to Zane. "So. Tell me where the other plate is now, Mr. Stryker. I'm sure I don't have to explain that you will tell me sooner or later. All that remains to be determined is how much pain you will suffer between now and then."

Zane looked at Sebastian, clearly asking without words for guidance. Begging for Sebastian not to have turned on him, for Sebastian not to have thrown him to the wolves the minute the going got rough.

Implacably, never breaking eye contact, he stared back, willing Zane to trust him. *Play along with me. Please, please, believe in me.*

But doubt swam in Zane's light green gaze.

In turn, Sebastian eyed the pair of thugs, both of whom were upright, armed, and angry-looking. They had the cold, dead look in their eyes of men who could inflict pain without remorse. Especially the one Sebastian had taken by surprise and dropped. He looked eager for Zane to refuse to talk.

Sebastian sighed. Stripping all emotion out of his voice, he said, "We gain nothing by you holding out on these low-level flunkies. Tell them where the plate is."

Zane shocked him by saying, "Even if I tell you where it is, I'm the only person who can access it for you."

Claude stared at Zane, reassessing him and realizing he wasn't just a pretty face. "You will take both of these men with you. You have one hour to get the plate and come back here." He didn't bother spelling out what would happen if Zane failed to return with the plate. Billionaire or not, Sebastian would be a dead man.

"Do as he says. No tricks. No heroics," Sebastian said, low and urgent. "For real. Got it?"

"I do. Trust me, Sebastian. I won't let anyone hurt you."

And that was what scared the hell out of him. The last thing they needed was any sophomoric rescue plan full of ill-guided heroics, attempted by an amateur.

"Do exactly as they say—"

Zane didn't stick around for any more instructions from him. Instead he turned and left the room with the thugs. The last thing Sebastian heard as their footsteps retreated was Zane asking if the men had a car. He sounded shockingly calm, given the dire situation.

Like he had a plan.

Oh Lord. That could *not* be good.

CHAPTER NINETEEN

ZANE HOPPED out of the back seat of the car, armed thug in tow.

"No funny business, Stryker. I've got a gun."

He trotted up the flights of stairs to Maya's loft, trailed by his minder. Before knocking, he muttered, "She's the skittish type. Let me do the talking and don't scare her, or God knows what she'll do."

The thug nodded.

"What are you doing here?" she mumbled when she opened the door.

"I need to pick up the plate. Let me in." He pushed past her and took her arm, using his body to shield the grip from the thug standing in the doorway. He half-pushed her across the room. Talking low and fast, he said, "I need you to call Janice."

"Fuck that—"

He cut her off. "Shut up and listen. This is life and death. I need her to find a guy named Pere Cardiffe in England. He owns a company called Wild Cards, Inc. Tell him Erebus has Sebastian and me and they need to rescue us ASAP. Have you got all that?"

"What's this about?"

"I have no time to explain. Just do it. Pere Cardiffe. Wild Cards. Erebus. Can you remember all that? Sebastian and I will die if you don't."

"I'm not that fucked-up. I've got it."

"Let's go," the thug rumbled. "Clock's ticking."

"Coming," Zane called. To Maya, he murmured, "Get me the back side plate. Only the back side. Got that? Just one plate. And hurry. I'll take care of the guy at the door. Go!"

His urgency must have pierced her hangover, for she nodded and turned toward a chest of drawers under her big living room window as he headed for the door. "Be patient. She's pretty drunk."

Over his shoulder, Zane called, "Hurry, Maya."

"Sheesh. Cool your jets. Here it is. Be careful. Body heat makes it frag—"

"I know. Hush. Love you. Thanks." He kissed her cheek as he took the plate, unwrapped and sitting in a piece of newspaper, from her. Quickly, he slipped it into his coat pocket.

"Got it," he announced cheerfully. "Let's go."

His heart was about to pound out of his chest and his knees were in imminent danger of collapse, but he put on his cold, expressionless runway face and strolled down the stairs beside the armed thug, exuding what he hoped was confidence and cool detachment.

Please God let Maya make that call. And get the names right. And convey just how urgent it was that Janice pass the message to the people at Wild Cards, Inc. He could've asked Maya to make the call directly, but he was afraid Sebastian's friends would think it was a crank call from some drunk. At least Janice would be sober.

Now the trick would be to keep Matty away from this plate and to keep Claude from holding it too long, softening up the alloy, and breaking the plate.

They arrived back at the brownstone, and the thug ushered him inside. Claude was waiting in the living room now with Sebastian and three more armed men. *Crap.* Reinforcements had arrived.

But the good news was Sebastian wasn't in the basement being tortured. And apparently the two of them got to wait in the living room now, at least until a response to Sebastian's request arrived. That was a welcome change of status, at least.

"Do you have it?" Claude demanded.

"Of course," Zane answered. "Do you still have the briefcase the plates came in? We wouldn't want to scratch them and make them unusable, would we?"

Claude looked alarmed at that prospect and left the room, returning with the briefcase that had started this whole fiasco. He opened it on a coffee table and laid in the front side plate. Zane unwrapped the second plate and placed it in the second foam cutout, praying it would hold up to inspection side-by-side with a real plate. If not, he and Sebastian were dead.

The two plates winked up at him, shiny and crisply carved. Claude closed the briefcase, and Zane breathed a huge mental sigh of relief. He glanced up and caught Sebastian's quizzical look at him. The guy knew him too well. He'd figured out that Zane had done *something*, but he didn't know *what*.

Without asking permission, Zane walked over to the sofa and sank down on it beside Sebastian. "Are you okay, babe?" he asked.

Sebastian nodded. "I'm fine. You?"

"I'm fine now."

A perplexed frown quirked between Sebastian's brows, and Zane smiled back encouragingly, trying to convey that he had things under control. Now he could only pray that Janice didn't think he'd had a psychotic break and that she'd done as he'd asked. Lord, he hoped that call was enough to get a rescue ball rolling. It had been all he could think of in the heat of the moment.

There had been no way he could call the police. No sane law enforcement official would believe that counterfeiting plates had just shown up randomly in his luggage and that he was an innocent victim in this whole mess. And if Erebus was even half as powerful as Sebastian said it was, he and Sebastian might get free of Claude today, but they'd still be dead men. Erebus agents would find them eventually and take them out. This thing had to be finished and Erebus destroyed if he and Sebastian were ever to be safe.

Sebastian had asked to meet with the senior Erebus officials to interview for admission to the consortium. If they actually gathered, maybe the Wild Cards could send in some kind of cavalry and take out the lot of them. It was out of his hands now.

Oddly enough, he wasn't all that concerned for his own safety. Well, he was scared stiff, but his fear for Sebastian's safety was so much greater than his own jeopardy that it overwhelmed his personal terror at the notion of dying. What was up with that? Was this love?

Hell, even the money didn't matter anymore. When faced with a choice between a million dollars and Sebastian's safety, he couldn't give a crap for the cash. When they got out of here, he was going to tell Sebastian everything. No more secrets ever again. He made a silent vow to himself to that effect.

"You okay?" Sebastian muttered.

"Yeah. Just thinking."

"About what?"

Claude interrupted. "Quiet, you two!"

Was he in love with Sebastian? Truth be told, he'd never been in love in his life. He'd been in lust and had crushes, but this feeling was something entirely different. It wasn't rainbows and hearts and warm fuzzies, although he did feel those things when he thought about Sebastian. This was something else entirely. It was a *knowing*. Recognition of Sebastian as the one meant for him. It was solid, more fact than feeling, as if a fundamental truth of the universe had revealed itself to him. He loved Sebastian. And in knowing that, he also knew he would do anything—*anything*—to protect Sebastian and keep him safe from harm.

It wasn't a choice, wasn't a revelation. It was just the way the universe was wired. Sebastian was his, and he was Sebastian's. And with that reality came unquestioning, matter-of-fact willingness to die for the man he loved. *Huh.* Who'd have thought love would be this simple when he finally found it?

He surreptitiously squeezed Sebastian's hand. Sebastian's eyes lit with warmth. Oh, his gaze was still concerned and filled with a promise to get Zane out of there safely, but Zane recognized that glow in Sebastian's eyes. It mirrored the glow of love in his own heart. He mouthed, "I love you."

Sebastian mouthed back, "I love you."

Brilliant joy exploded in Zane's chest. As declarations of love went, it was the quietest one in history, but it was plenty for him. They sat silently on the sofa together, fingers linked between their knees, reveling in the moment. There might be guns pointed at them, and there was no guarantee they would make it out of this mess alive, but to Zane it was arguably the happiest moment of his life.

He'd found the One. And Sebastian loved him back. Deep urgency to get out of this mess safely and spend the rest of their lives together nipped at his heels, but he also felt an underlying peace unlike anything he'd ever experienced. It was strange as hell to be scared to death and deliriously happy all at the same time.

He understood now the concept of having found a person worth living for and fighting for.

As the wait stretched out, he had plenty of time to think back to all the times in his life when he'd been self-destructive and angry, had taken stupid risks and not cared if he lived or died. If only his younger self had known this extraordinary man was out there waiting for him, he would have done so much so differently.

He supposed he couldn't regret whatever path had finally led him to Sebastian and Sebastian to him. But as he sat there, facing death beside the man he loved, he felt that past version of himself falling away and passing into the ancient history of his life before Sebastian.

Claude declared himself hungry and left the room to head for the kitchen. The guards stirred, and there was discussion of who wanted what to eat among the thugs. Zane took advantage of the movement and noise to mutter under his breath to Sebastian, "I got a message to a friend to call Wild Cards."

Surprise and something fierce ignited in Sebastian's gaze. "This could work. While you were gone, Erebus agreed to interview me."

"Who all's coming?"

"No idea. Hopefully a chunk of their top brass."

"About the plate I brought—" Zane broke off as Claude came back into the room carrying glasses of water that he set down on the coffee table in front of the two of them.

Claude announced, "One of the men is making sandwiches for everyone. If you need to use the restroom, you two, the men will take you up one at a time."

Apparently Sebastian's request to become a member of Erebus had forced a temporary upgrade in their status and care by their captors.

The sandwiches were dry, the water was tepid, and they spent the afternoon forbidden from speaking to one another and entertained only by a few magazines. Zane read them all cover to cover. Twice.

He spent an uncomfortable night sleeping on the sofa. He leaned right and Sebastian leaned left, and they dozed fitfully, waking each other up every time the other one moved. And yet every time Zane woke and felt Sebastian's thigh pressed against his, a little frisson of happiness soothed him back to sleep. All in all, it was a terrible night's sleep and one of the best nights he'd ever had.

The next day passed in sheer boredom and discomfort. They had no cell phones, and he'd read all the magazines four or five times now. Etienne had to be losing his mind. Frankly, Zane was surprised the Frenchman hadn't stormed the house, or at least called the police to storm it. The good news was that Etienne knew where they were. He'd dropped them off.

Now that he thought about it, Zane suspected Etienne was outside, nearby, keeping an eye on this place to make sure they weren't moved to some other location.

He hoped desperately that the lack of a rescue by now meant that Janice had indeed gotten a hold of the guys at Wild Cards, and they and Etienne were planning some sort of major rescue operation.

He could use a shower and a shave, and he smelled himself getting a bit ripe. A change of clean clothes would have been nice too. But at least they weren't getting tortured or left tied to chairs in that nasty basement. As captivity went, he supposed this wasn't bad.

About suppertime, if the pinkening light coming in the front window was any indication, Claude came into the living room to announce, "Erebus will hear your petition, Mr. Gigoni."

"When?" Sebastian asked.

"A meeting place will have to be arranged, and one more person has to arrive in the city," Claude replied with markedly more respect in his voice than up to that point.

"I know the perfect place for a meeting," Sebastian offered. "I own the building. The room is ultraprivate and secure and can hold a hundred people easily, so the Erebus representatives can bring all the security they'd like, and the guards can stay with their principals the whole time. Totally private access. No one will see your people coming or going. The authorities don't even know it exists. Your guys can go ahead and vet it if they'd like. And besides that, it's the coolest place ever for a meeting like this."

Zane grinned. *The speakeasy.* It was indeed the perfect place for a secret meeting of crime lords plotting something big. The thugs were all nodding in approval at everything he was saying about the meeting site.

"Where is this place?" Claude asked. The man actually sounded reasonably civil. The prospect of Sebastian becoming an Erebus bigwig had done wonders for Claude's attitude.

"Lemme give one of your men the address. I'll write a note for the manager to let him go downstairs and check it out. It's underground."

The note was duly written, the address passed over, and instructions for how to open the secret bookshelf in the back office relayed to the security man Claude chose for the reconnaissance mission.

Sebastian looked well satisfied with himself as the guy left the room.

Zane risked whispering when the two remaining guards were distracted, chatting together. "Won't it be dangerous for us to be down there alone where they can just kill us?"

Sebastian's eyes twinkled. "Pere knows *all* the secrets of the room."

"Hey, you two! No talking!" one of the guards called out.

Zane sat back. *All the secrets?* What did that mean? Obviously Sebastian had something up his sleeve that depended on Wild Cards being at the meeting too. How were they going to get word to Pere and his reinforcements that the speakeasy was the site of the meeting? He thought about it for the next two hours but still hadn't come up with any ideas when the guard came back from his expedition.

"Well?" Claude asked.

"It's perfect," the guy said reluctantly. "And it's pretty cool too. It's one of them old clubs people went to way back when booze was illegal."

"Did you tell my manager to clean it up and lay in food and drinks for the meeting?" Sebastian asked.

"Yeah. Just like you said to. He said it would be up and running by ten o'clock tonight," the thug replied.

Claude looked undecided for a moment, then picked up his cell phone. "The meeting place is set and checked out. Whenever Mr. Elliott and the others are ready, we can hold the interview." He listened for a minute, then replied, "Yes, sir. We'll see you at midnight."

As Claude pocketed his phone, he said direly to Sebastian, "I hope you know what you're doing. Once you've seen their faces, if you don't get in, you'll be eliminated."

Sebastian nodded calmly. "I would expect no less." He looked over at Zane. "Do you trust me?"

"With my life."

"That's actually what's on the line tonight. But I swear, I will take care of you."

"Ditto, my dude. We're in this together, no matter what happens, right?"

"No matter what," Sebastian answered firmly. He leaned forward and Zane met him halfway. They sealed the promise with a kiss. It was nothing special, just a brief meeting of lips and exchanged breath. But even that small contact was enough to send Zane's pulse racing. Sebastian's pupils dilated hard as well, and he smiled ruefully at Zane.

"Soon," Zane murmured.

Funny, but Zane was okay with however this turned out. Good or bad, dead or alive, he and Sebastian would be together to the end.

CHAPTER TWENTY

SEBASTIAN WAS stunned by how cool Zane was under pressure. He was frankly humbled by Zane's absolute trust in him to save both of them from this mess.

Now he just had to pray that Pere had gotten the message from Zane's friend and brought a small army to rescue them. The subcutaneous tracker in his hip hadn't done anything weird to indicate that it had been activated, but he had to believe that, once Wild Cards had gotten the distress call, it had been located.

As soon as Pere saw where Sebastian had gone for the meeting, he would know what Sebastian wanted him to do. After all, no self-respecting speakeasy was without a few hidden escape routes for its more important customers to slip away from the inevitable police raids that happened from time to time. His was no exception.

Sebastian spent the next hour working through possible scenarios in his head of how Etienne and Pere's men would enter the club. Who they would see first. Who would shoot first. The best spots in the club to avoid being hit by stray bullets. He envisioned a half-dozen possible seating scenarios of where he and Zane would be put for this meeting and where they would have to dive for cover from each one. If he were Erebus's security team, how would he react to a sudden influx of armed attackers? How would he get his guys out?

His analysis was exhaustive, bordering on a bit obsessive, but Zane's life would depend on him reacting correctly to split-second changes in the situation. And he'd be damned if a single hair on Zane's head would get hurt tonight.

He looked over at Zane yet again. He never got tired of looking at him. Not only was he physically attractive, but his heart was just as beautiful, and once he'd gotten to know Zane, it shone in his eyes and on his face, clear as day.

"Okay, you two. Time to go. The boss wants you in place well before the big dogs get there."

Sebastian smiled. No indeed, it wouldn't do to keep the Erebus big dogs waiting. God, he hoped every last one of them was there tonight. Apparently Pere's inside man at Erebus's Greek headquarters had given them a complete list of names of the top operatives in the consortium. The key now was to get as many of them together at once as possible, arrest them all, and take down Erebus for good. Though it couldn't hurt getting more hard evidence on them for a prosecution here in the States, as well. Like catching them with a currency printing plate. On the assumption that Pere and company would be taking video of the meeting for future criminal prosecutions, he made a mental note to mention the currency plate aloud.

He was put into the back seat of an SUV, and Zane was shoved in beside him.

Indignant, he snapped, "That's my future husband you're pushing around. When I'm accepted into Erebus, I'm going to remember the faces of anyone who roughed him up."

"Future… what?" Zane gasped.

He stared at Zane, uncomprehending for a moment while he spooled back what he'd just said. *Oh. Oh! Holy hell.* "Umm, sorry. I probably shouldn't have just blurted that out like that."

"No," Zane said in obvious shock. "It's fine. We're under a little duress here. I get it."

"But I meant—"

"Save it back there," the driver said. "Claude said not to let you two talk to each other on the ride over."

Right. Because they were going to cook up some dastardly escape plan in the back of an SUV. At gunpoint. With no phones or other resources. Sesbastian probably ought to be flattered that Claude was so afraid of his capabilities. Little did the bastard know that it was Zane who'd gotten the word out and called in help. *Ha!*

The car pulled up in the alley behind his pizza parlor. Zane was helped out of the car a great deal more politely, and he stepped out as well. He didn't bother looking up at the rooflines for snipers. In the first place, there was no reason to tip off their guards to look up there, and in the second place, Pere's guys were way too good to be spotted so easily. But Sebastian had no doubt they were up there already. The manager said the joint would be ready at 10:00 p.m. Pere's guys had probably been up there a couple of hours before that, and it was closing in on midnight now.

"Where to?" Claude demanded from beside the SUV in front of theirs.

"Into the office. Your men should already have the staircase open," Sebastian replied.

They piled inside the kitchen and then into the tiny office in single file. He went down the familiar stairs into the speakeasy, which bustled with life. A bartender he didn't recognize stood behind the bar in an old-fashioned shirt with garters holding up his sleeves. He prayed the man was one of Pere's guys.

An ensemble of jazz musicians was playing in the orchestra pit. No way of telling if they were Wild Cards men or just a band. A pair of bouncers stood by the door—definitely Wild Cards operatives. In fact, Sebastian knew one of them from a visit to Wild Cards HQ last year.

Praise the Lord and pass the potatoes. Zane's message had gotten to the Wild Cards, and they were here in force. Suddenly he felt a whole lot better about his and Zane's chances of making it out of here alive tonight.

A waiter came out of the kitchen and laid a tray of canapés on a buffet table. No telling how many Wild Cards guys were in the kitchen acting like cooks and waiters. A woman came out from backstage, wearing a flapper dress, long beads, and an authentic 1920s hair bob. She, too, was a face he remembered from his last visit to the Wild Cards offices in London. Weren't the Erebus people going to be shocked when she pulled out a weapon and started firing at them? She started to sing, and damned if she didn't sound just like a performer straight out of the Roaring Twenties.

Even Claude seemed impressed by the joint as he gestured for Sebastian and Zane to be seated at a long table that had been set up in the center of the dance floor. Okay. This wasn't too bad a spot. A little open for Sebastian's taste, but a quick tumble and roll would bring him and Zane up against the bandstand, close to a secret trap door they could crawl through to get behind the heavy oak structure of the dais.

It took a few minutes of waiting, but finally Claude moved over to nibble at the buffet, and no guards were watching them. He was startled when Zane leaned in close to whisper, "I have something to tell you."

"Not now."

"It's important."

"What?" Sebastian said from behind unmoving lips.

"I had a set of fake plates made. The one I brought back is fake. It's made of magician's metal. It gets soft when it's warmed up and will break if they try to use it to print money."

Sebastian stared at him in blank shock. *The audacity of it. The sheer lunacy.* "My God, that's brilliant." He ought to be furious with Zane for keeping it from him all this time, but right now he could only summon gratitude. No matter what happened tonight, Zane's trickery would stop Erebus from counterfeiting millions or billions of dollars. Now he could only pray the Wild Cards and whatever law enforcement types they'd brought along would stop the entire Erebus Consortium tonight, once and for all.

Zane leaned back, smiling a little.

Sebastian's mind raced. How did that change the equation? They could let Claude and the briefcase escape if necessary. That made his job a great deal easier. All he had to worry about now was keeping Zane safe. "No matter what I say here, don't forget how I feel about you. Promise me you'll trust that."

Zane smiled at him. "Sebastian, no matter what happens tonight, I've had the extraordinary honor of loving you. If I don't live one more day, I've had that. And it's enough for me. I'm at peace, no matter what happens."

Sebastian was, in a word, staggered. No one, *no one*, had ever felt that way about him before. Not his father, who'd left him, not his mother, who'd chosen oblivion in a bottle over him, *nobody*.

He wanted nothing more than to gather Zane in his arms and tell him all the amazing ways Zane made him feel, but he spied Claude turning away from the buffet table and heading back in their direction. He murmured without moving his lips, "When it goes bad, topple your chair over backward, roll over to the band pit, and crawl behind it."

"Will you come too?" Zane muttered.

"Of course," he lied. "I'll be right behind you."

Claude plunked a plate of food down on the table beside him, and Sebastian was grateful for once that he could say no more.

They didn't have long to wait for Erebus members to start showing up. The first man arrived about ten minutes before midnight. Probably a newbie to the consortium, trying to make a good impression. A second man arrived a few minutes later, and then two more came in together. *Wow.* They might bag a whole bunch of the top Erebus people at this rate.

All in all, a dozen men arrived, all prosperous-looking and middle-aged or older. Finally one last man arrived. Sebastian recognized George Elliott. Pere had mentioned that he was one of the Erebus big dogs when they'd talked a few weeks ago. Elliott was a bit of a celebrity in his own right, simply because he was so damned rich. Allegedly, he was one of the wealthiest men in the world.

The pomposity in the room was tangible as the consortium members took their places around the table and a ring of security guards loomed around them. Which was fine with him. The goal was to arrest these criminals, not slaughter them.

"So, Mr. Gigoni. Mr. Vanderpohl tells us you think you have what it takes to contribute to our business enterprises. Why is that?"

"Because I'm better at what you do than you are," he replied.

Elliott smiled blandly, not rising to the bait. "And what is it you think we do?"

"It's obvious what you do. You've corporatized crime."

"And why do you think you've got something to offer us?"

Sebastian leaned back. "I assume you've done your homework on me in the past twenty-four hours. You know where I come from and where I've gotten to." He paused for effect. "Well, you know about my legitimate assets, at any rate."

Zane shot him a startled look. Which was fine with him. Secrecy was key to these men. Evidence that he hadn't told even his boyfriend of his supposed illegal activities would weigh in his favor.

Not that this was an actual job interview, of course. This was a game designed to get these men to admit to their criminal activities.

"You have other assets?" Elliott asked casually. Too casually. He was interested.

"Of course I do. I'm not a major slumlord for nothing," he joked. Put these men at ease. Make their security guards relax. "My off-book assets span several continents. As you have no doubt discovered, I spent a number of years in the British Special Forces and was stationed in a number of... interesting locations. While there, I took the opportunity to form any number of relationships with various local warlords and people of influence. I would venture to say my contacts are even more far-reaching than yours in certain places."

"Indeed?"

"How extensive are your operations in Southeast Asia, for example? My impression is that you don't have much reach into that area yet."

"I beg to differ," one of the other men piped up a shade irritably.

"Really?" Sebastian challenged. "Then why haven't I heard of you? I know you've heard of me." He named one of the most powerful crime rings in all of Asia. Of course, he had nothing to do with that outfit, but these jerks wouldn't know that.

There was an audible inhalation around the table.

Rapidly he fired off the names of crime rings in Africa, South America, and Eastern Europe. They were all groups his British military unit had gone after at one time or another. It was a calculated risk to name the gangs and hope that Erebus wasn't already in bed with any of them, but he couldn't expect Erebus to cough up information if he didn't do the same.

He stared around the table, making eye contact with each Erebus man in turn. "How much more reach, influence, and profit will you have when I merge my organization with yours, gentlemen? You have me at a disadvantage in answering that because I'm not aware of the full scope of your outfit, of course. But surely there will be synergies aplenty to exploit."

As he'd hoped, one of the men suggested how smuggling could be made more efficient if they could find a better source of South Pacific shipping to mesh with their opium operation. Another suggested that trafficking through South America would be cheaper than trying to bring in stock—as in human slaves—from Asia. Before long an animated conversation was in progress, with Sebastian making suggestions enthusiastically. Lord, this stuff was prosecutor's gold. They were confessing to crimes spanning the globe as they considered how to integrate all the crime syndicates he'd named into their corporate structure.

When they finally wound down, Sebastian asked casually, "By the way, I'm curious as to why you used Zane Stryker as the mule to move your currency plates. He obviously wasn't a random choice because the suit in the suitcase fit him perfectly. Was it a ploy to reach me?"

One of the men answered, "I confess, we were not aware of your relationship with Mr. Stryker. Had we known, we would have found another mule. Our apologies for encroaching on your... turf."

He nodded graciously. They didn't need to know he and Zane hadn't met before the suitcase switch.

The man continued with his explanation. "We've had a few... setbacks... recently, and we were concerned that one of our own people might be spotted coming into the country. Hence, we decided to employ the services of a courier completely unattached to our organization. It was a risk, but we chose somebody with a checkered enough past that if he were caught, the authorities would believe he was a smuggler and take him down for carrying the plates without digging too much deeper than him. Plus, we needed someone recognizable enough for our people to watch him from a safe distance. And you have to admit, Mr. Stryker stands out in a crowd."

Sebastian spared a fond glance for Zane. "He does, at that."

"It was easy enough to slip one of our people into a photo shoot and take a suit that had been tailored for him. We judged him to be someone who would take the money we offered and not go to the police. He's known to live a, shall we say, high-profile life. Of course, we had no idea he had access to your considerable financial resources. It does help explain his extravagant lifestyle."

Sebastian nodded as if these idiots had pegged the whole situation exactly correctly.

The man concluded with, "We mistakenly judged him to be desperate enough for cash that he would ultimately cooperate with us and not go to the authorities."

Another man leaned forward. "Given that you met Mr. Stryker directly at the luggage storage area and knew without having seen the contents of the suitcase to take evasive measures with the luggage and your boyfriend...."

Whoa. They'd had surveillance on him and Zane even at JFK that first day, had they? Yikes.

The man was still speaking, "...begs the question of how *you* found out about the plates arriving in the States, Mr. Gigoni."

He shrugged. "You didn't honestly think I would approach you like this to do business without doing my homework on Erebus, did you? Of course I have people inside your organization. I got a tip that the plates were coming to New York." He added, "I do have to wonder, though, if you have all the other necessary resources in place to print money."

The man waved a casual hand. "We've spent several years accessing paper, ink, even a fellow who worked at the Bureau of Engraving and Printing to run the operation. I assure you, we've taken care of all the details. The plates are the last piece in the puzzle."

Elliott raised a hand from the other end of the table. "Enough. We'll need the names of those moles you've placed inside Erebus. Indeed, we'll need proof of everything you've told us. Full access to your financial records. Names. Contact procedures. Everything."

Time to spring the trap. *C'mon, Pere. Don't fail me now.* Sebastian leaned back in his chair. "Why would I hand all of this over to you without any guarantees from you?"

"You'll just have to trust us, Mr. Gigoni. After all, we have you at a disadvantage."

"And how is that?"

"We have the currency plates we came for, and we have no need of your considerable assets to be a fully effective conglomerate. Not to mention, now that we know which... extralegal... organizations are yours, we can just as easily move in and take them over for ourselves."

"About those plates...." He let his words trail off.

"What about them?" Elliott asked quickly.

"Have you looked at them yet?" Sebastian asked leadingly. He allowed himself enough of a smirk that George Elliott couldn't fail to notice it.

"Bring them to me," Elliott snapped.

Claude produced the briefcase and opened it on the table. Everyone stared greedily at the shiny plates. They represented untold billions of dollars printed at their leisure, as much money as they could ever want or need, theirs for the printing. It was the mother lode for men like them.

"Has Matteus verified their authenticity?" Elliott snapped at Vanderpohl.

"Of course," Vanderpohl stammered.

Sebastian pursed his lips. "May I?" he asked, half standing from his seat.

"May you what?"

"May I show you something?"

Elliott gestured at the briefcase. "I suggest you consider your actions carefully. One wrong move will get your boyfriend killed."

Yeah, I got that memo the minute Claude locked us in the workroom. Pere had better be listening, because it was almost time to attack. In about thirty seconds, Sebastian was going to create the diversion the Wild Cards team needed to get the upper hand. It was now or never. All or nothing. Either the Wild Cards were here to save them, or he and Zane were about to die.

"Do you trust me?" he asked Zane under his breath for Zane's ears only.

"We've already been over this. I'm with you to the end."

To the end. God, he liked the sound of that.

Just once in his life, he was going to say the words aloud in case he never got another chance. He pushed back his chair, stood up, and looked Zane in the eye. "I love you."

CHAPTER TWENTY-ONE

ZANE SMILED up at Sebastian. Something was wrong. He couldn't tell what, but Sebastian was mentally bracing for something bad. He watched warily as Sebastian strolled the length of the table and leaned over the man at the end of the table's shoulder to pick up the back plate—the fake.

Crap. Sebastian wasn't going to reveal that the plate was fake, was he? They would all turn on him. He was the one who'd gone and gotten the second plate, after all! He started to push himself out of his seat, and he opened his mouth to tell Sebastian to put it down, to back away from the damned currency plate and let him take the fall for this.

But Sebastian speared him with an intense look and shook his head slightly, as if he'd guessed Zane's intent. Cursing, Zane subsided in his seat to watch helplessly as the disaster unfolded.

Sebastian picked up the plate. "Shiny, isn't it?" He rubbed it briskly on the sleeve of his coat, as if to polish it. Of course, he was warming up the plate.

"Feels real." Sebastian hefted it in the palm of his hand, then rubbed its back with his thumb.

He held it up to his face, incidentally breathing on it as he examined the fine engraving. "Sure as hell looks real."

"What's your point, Mr. Gigoni?"

Sebastian grasped the plate firmly in both hands, and before Zane even had time to wince, he snapped the plate in half.

Everyone at the table surged to their feet, shouting. The security guards lurched forward in knee-jerk reaction, and Sebastian threw the two halves of the plate down on the table.

In the middle of all the chaos, Zane's stare never left Sebastian. Hence, he saw the moment when Sebastian looked down the table at him and nodded sharply, as if now was the moment for Zane to do something specific. But what?

His mind went blank. He didn't understand!

Elliott shouted for order, and a couple of the security guards moved toward Sebastian, but then all of a sudden a dozen or more men streamed out of nowhere. They wore camouflage and bulky vests and carried guns at their shoulders. The security guards whirled, and their guns started to come out.

Holy crap. There was about to be an all-out gun battle in this room that suddenly seemed about the size of a tuna can.

And it dawned on Zane that *this* was what Sebastian had meant when he referred to "things getting bad." He threw himself backward, tipping his chair over. He leaned his head forward to keep it from hitting the ground along with the chair. He had just started to roll toward the bandstand when gunfire erupted over him.

Dear God, the noise was deafening. Bits of wood and glass flew everywhere, and he threw one arm over his head as he crawled grimly for cover. He dived behind the oak bandstand, joining the musicians already cowering there.

He looked around wildly. Where was Sebastian?

He poked his head out to look for Sebastian's tall form, but the room was full of smoke and flying debris and men wrestling other men to the floor. However, he knew Sebastian very well. He'd studied and obsessed over every line, every muscle, every nuance of movement of the man he loved, and he spotted Sebastian's silhouette diving through a doorway in pursuit of another man who'd gone through the opening ahead of him.

Zane jumped up and sprinted across the room, hurdling downed bodies, dodging two fights, and flinging himself into what looked like a coat closet. A dark tunnel opened up in the far wall. He raced into it and saw two men grappling ahead: Sebastian and a big bald guy.

"Get Elliott!" Sebastian grunted, jerking his head toward the tunnel. Then the other man had him in a throat lock.

Zane paused just long enough to haul back and slug Sebastian's captor in the nose as hard as he could. "Shit!" he cried as pain exploded in his knuckles and up his forearm.

Sebastian whirled and grabbed his attacker, shouting, "Go!"

Pain notwithstanding, Zane charged on down the tunnel, glad for his occasional runs when he got a wild hair to work on his fitness. In a few seconds, he spied a corpulent form ahead, jogging clumsily. He caught up with the fleeing man in a matter of seconds and tackled him from behind.

For a guy who'd never even seen a football game, he didn't tackle the fleeing Erebus man half badly, if he said so himself. Of course, it helped that the larger, softer man beneath him absorbed all the impact of the fall.

The man gasped for air, the breath obviously knocked out of him, but unsympathetically, Zane pushed upright and planted both knees on the man's shoulder blades. In under a minute, one of the camouflage-clothed commandos who'd burst in on the meeting, followed closely by Sebastian, came racing down the tunnel.

"Well done!" Sebastian cried.

Grinning, Zane let Sebastian hoist him to his feet. As the soldier took his place on top of the Erebus man and put zip cuffs on George Elliott's wrists, Sebastian wrapped Zane in a crushing embrace.

He returned the favor, hanging on for dear life. Sebastian's heartbeat pounded beneath his ear, gradually slowing to something resembling a human pulse. He listened to the sound in utter relief, for it signaled that they'd made it. They were safe.

At length, he lifted his head from Sebastian's muscular shoulder and asked, "What the hell just happened?"

"You saved the day. Wild Cards got your message and came to the meeting. They should have gotten enough on tape to put away just about everyone in the room."

"Are we safe?" Zane asked in a small voice.

"You and I may have to lie low for a few months while the rest of the members of the Erebus Consortium are rounded up, but tonight should pretty much have broken the consortium's back. This and the evidence Pere's inside guy has collected should be enough to put all those bastards in jail for a very long time."

Sebastian threw his arm across Zane's shoulder, and he looped his arm around Sebastian's lean, hard waist. They turned as one and started the long walk back through the tunnel to the speakeasy.

It was over. They'd survived the nightmare. His life could finally get back to normal. He could finish out his modeling career, and Sebastian could go back to his regularly scheduled life.

Now that the crisis was past, would he still want Zane in his life? Or had their torrid affair been purely a result of blowing off their mutual stress?

"What about the million dollars in my bank account?" Zane asked. "Who am I supposed to give it back to?"

"If Erebus is busted, there isn't anyone to give it back to. I'm fairly certain Uncle Sam will consider it a reasonable finder's fee for stopping a massive counterfeiting operation."

Zane gasped. "Are you serious?"

"I'll have my lawyers talk to the Department of Justice. I'm sure we can work something out."

Were his money worries finally over? Could he truly move on into a new life? Surely everything couldn't be working out this perfectly.

"About what you said earlier in the SUV and back in the club, Sebastian. We were under a ton of stress, and I know that stuff just slips out in the pressure of the moment. In the cold light of day tomorrow, when you wake up safe and sound, I don't want you to regret anything you said. This mess is over, and you can get back to your real life. I'm grateful for everything you've done for me."

Sebastian stopped, dragging him to a stop as well. "Are you blowing me off, Zane? Are you telling me you don't love me after all?" His voice was so raw, so sandpaper rough, it was barely intelligible.

"Me? Blow you off? Are you kidding? I'm crazy about you. I'm just saying I won't hold you to anything you said under the duress of staring down the barrel of a gun. What about you? Do you want to take back what you said, Sebastian?"

"No. Not one word of it. I didn't say anything I would take back."

He squinted at Sebastian in the near total darkness, unable to make out the expression in his shadowed eyes. "But… you proposed to me."

Sebastian's voice was low and fierce. "Yes. I did."

His mind went completely blank. "And you… you know… meant it?"

"Yes!" A note of exasperation joined the ferocity of that *yes*. "Look. You don't have to say yes or no right now. But promise me you'll at least think about it."

Zane snorted. "I don't have to think about it, you dolt. Of course I'll marry you! My God, I love you more than life."

It was Sebastian's turn to sound completely flummoxed. "You're sure?"

"Yes, I'm sure. Now kiss me and seal the deal."

And kiss him Sebastian did.

Of course, he kissed Sebastian back. Long and thoroughly. But eventually they broke apart, laughing at having forgotten where they were and that a major criminal bust was ongoing around them.

When they finally strolled back into the speakeasy, Zane gazed around at the carnage in dismay, but Sebastian shrugged. "We'll redecorate it together. It'll be fun. Speaking of which—"

Zane turned to face him, alarmed at the strange tone of voice from Sebastian, who continued ruefully, "I might have made a few phone calls to Parsons."

"As in the world-famous school of art, fashion, and design?"

"Yup. That one. Turns out they're willing to give you a place in this year's incoming class of students. They knew your work as a model, and I might have called a few designers too, who apparently gave the admissions people at Parsons stellar recommendations for you."

Zane's jaw dropped.

"You don't have to go. I just thought you might consider staying in New York and taking your career to the next level like you talked about."

"That's more than the next level, Sebastian. That's a whole new career. You shouldn't have done that for me."

"Hmm. I see I still have some work to do in teaching you to accept gifts. You'd better get used to it, though, because I'm showering you in beautiful things for the rest of your life, whether you like it or not."

"I'm still paying for my own school."

"That can be arranged. Do you remember that your grandfather owned a little piece of land near the East River, and the deed was in your safe deposit box? It wasn't worth a dime when he died, but it's worth more than enough to pay for your tuition now. If you won't sell it to me, I'll find you a buyer and get you a fair price for it. That and the money from Erebus should be plenty not only to pay for your schooling, but also to set you up in business as a designer if that's what you want. Assuming you won't just let me write a check for the whole thing."

Zane blinked at Sebastian, stunned. Finally he managed to choke out, "You're one step ahead of me, aren't you?"

"Ha! I'll never get ahead of you. I have a feeling you're going to keep me on my toes for a very long time to come, Mr. Stryker."

"That I will, Mr. Gigoni. That I will."

New York Times and *USA Today* best-selling author, CINDY DEES started flying airplanes while sitting in her dad's lap at the age of three and got a pilot's license before she got a driver's license. At age fifteen, she dropped out of high school and left the horse farm in Michigan where she grew up to attend the University of Michigan.

After earning a degree in Russian and East European Studies, she joined the US Air Force and became the youngest female pilot in its history. She flew supersonic jets, VIP airlift, and the C-5 Galaxy, one of the world's largest cargo airplanes.

She also worked part-time gathering intelligence. During her military career, she traveled to forty-two countries on five continents, was detained by the KGB and East German secret police, got shot at, flew in the first Gulf War, met her husband, and amassed a lifetime's worth of war stories. Cindy has turned many of her experiences into novels of military romance and suspense.

Cindy's hobbies include professional Middle Eastern dancing, Japanese gardening, and medieval reenacting. She can also be found often on various social media, hanging out with her friends and fellow readers.

Winner of a Golden Heart and Holt Medallion for writing, Cindy is a five-time finalist and two-time winner of the prestigious RITA Award for Romance Fiction, two-time winner of RT Book Review's Best Harlequin Romantic Suspense Novel of the Year, and is a Romantic Times Lifetime Career Achievement nominee.

STUD ♣ GAMES

POKER FACE

CINDY DEES

A Stud Games Novel

Surveillance, seduction, and extra-dirty politics.

Christian Chatsworth-Brandeis has a problem. A huge one. The US senator he works for has run away with his latest mistress on the eve of a make-or-break fundraising event, and it's up to him to cover his irresponsible boss's tracks.

Stone Jackson, Senator Lacey's new bodyguard, looks enough like him that, with some extensive grooming, he might pass for the senator. Christian and Stone hatch a plan to substitute Stone for the senator, but Miami madness and the incendiary heat between them are throwing obstacles in their way. It's a race to find the senator and pull off the con of the century before the attraction between them spins completely out of control.

Previously published by Dreamspinner Press as *Ace in the Hole* by Ava Drake, July 2016.

www.dreampsinnerpress.com

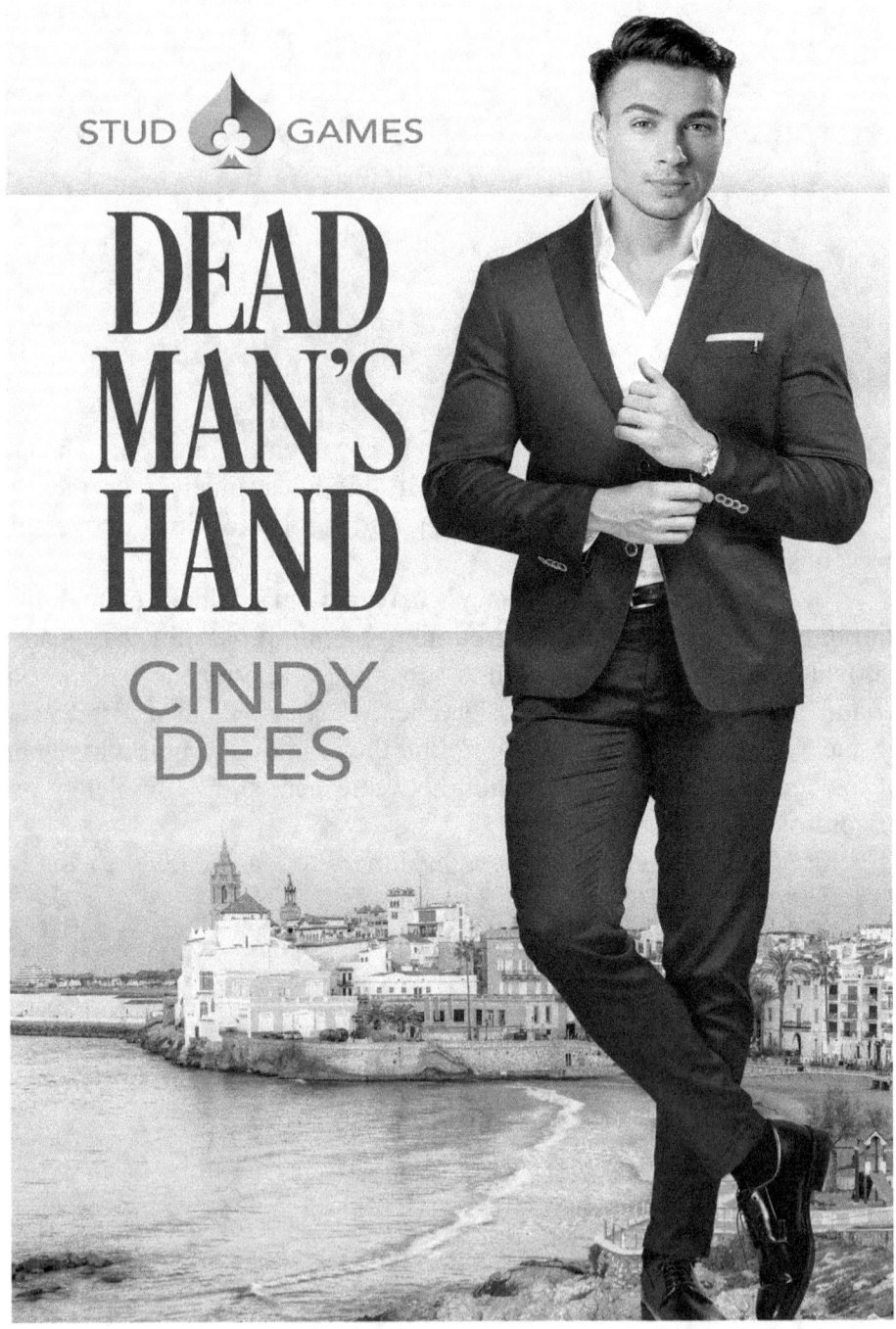

STUD ♠ GAMES

DEAD MAN'S HAND

CINDY DEES

A Stud Games Novel

Temptation, peril, and dirty poker.

Love is a high-stakes game.

When Collin Callahan, British secret agent, goes up against math genius turned surfer bum Oliver Elliot, the battle is epic—and so is the attraction. They're pitted against each other in an exclusive, ultra-secret—and ultra-illegal—poker match in Gibraltar. But when players start dying and they could be next, they find a common goal: catch the killer before it's too late.

Evenly matched at poker and romance, they each wrestle personal demons that threaten to consume them as the stakes climb. It's an all-or-nothing gamble with both life and love on the line as they fight to be the last seven-card studs standing.

Previously published by Dreamspinner Press as *Seven-Card Stud* by Ava Drake, November 2016.

www.dreamspinnerpress.com

Also from Dreamspinner Press

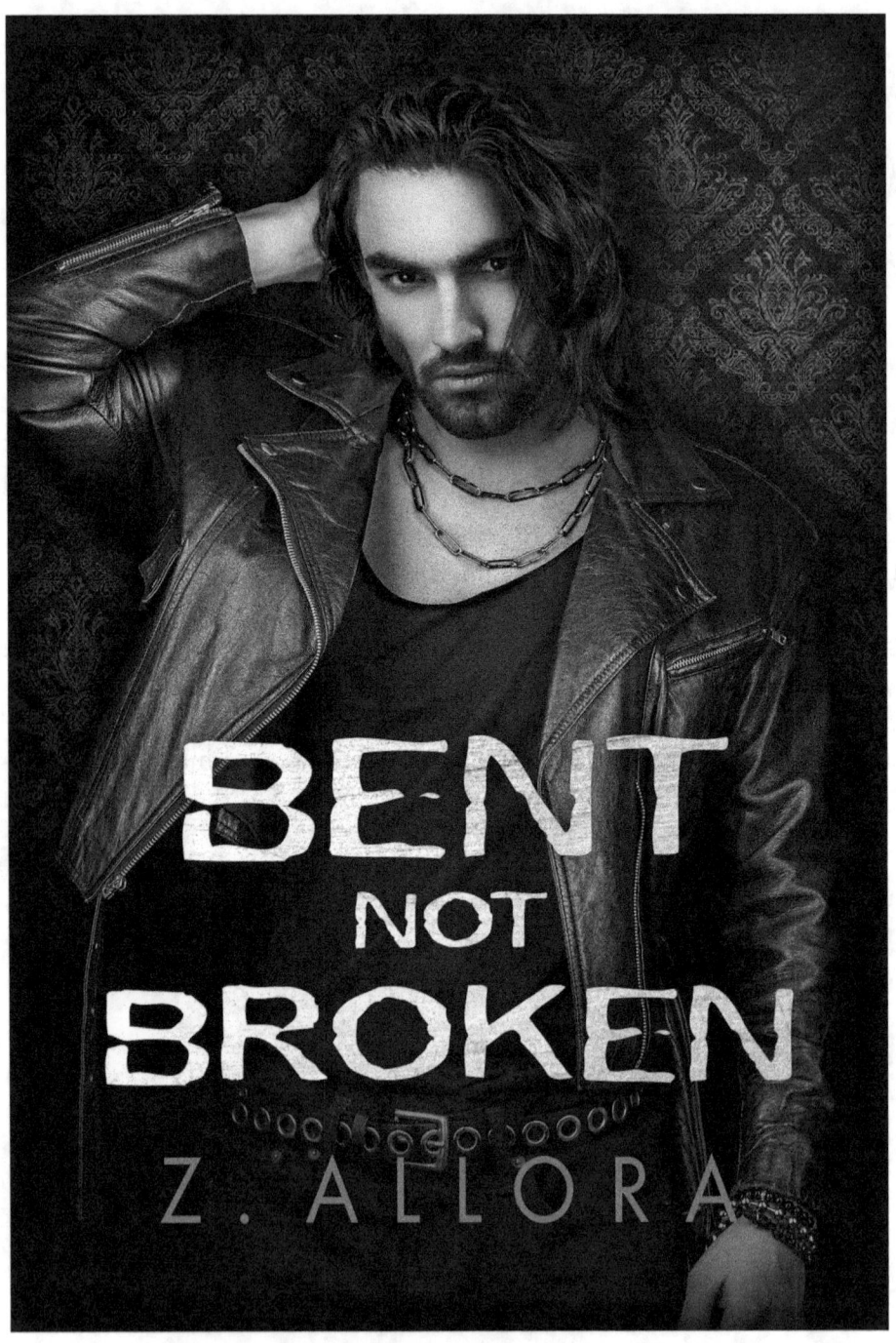

ROWAN MCALLISTER

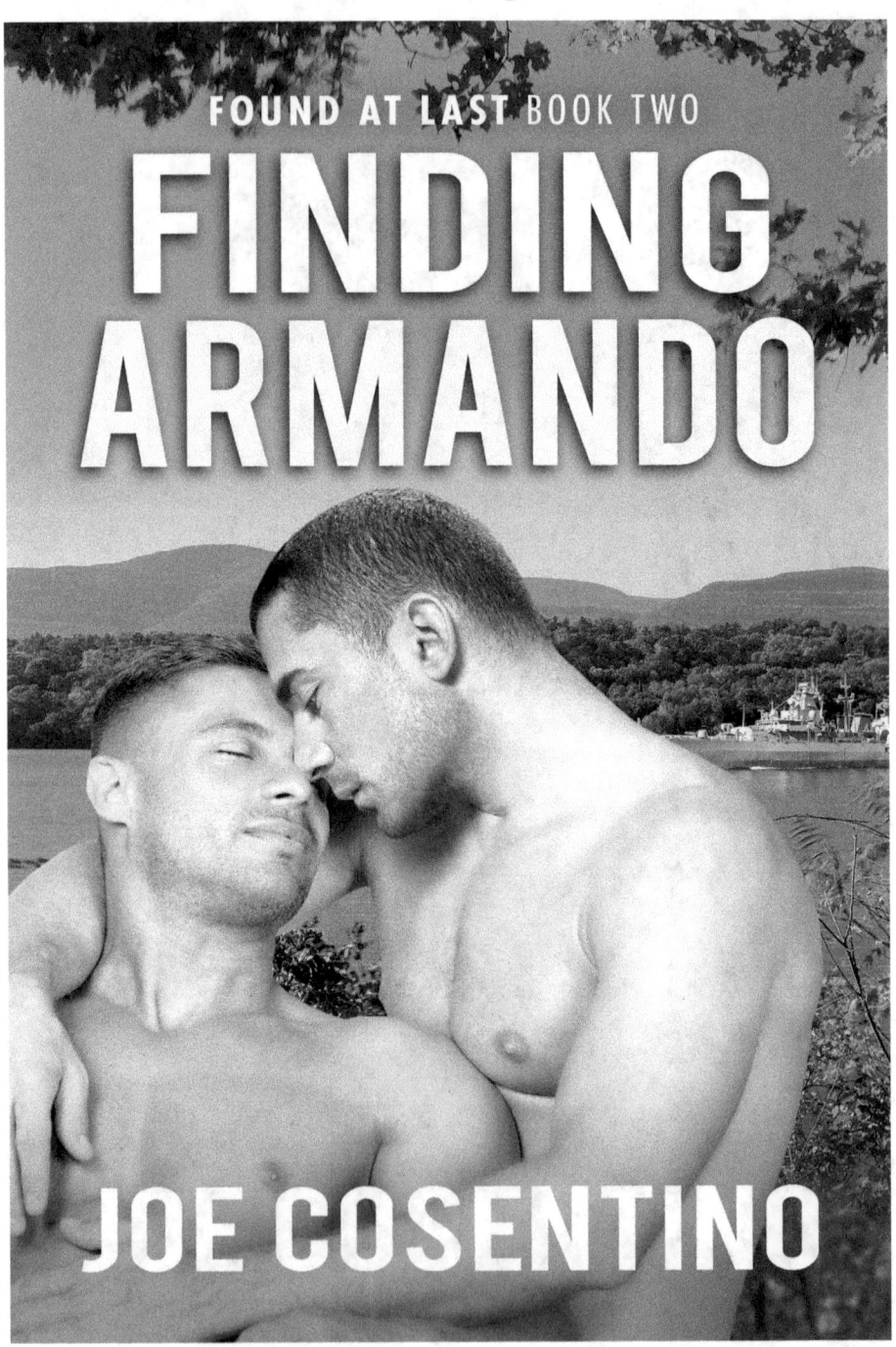

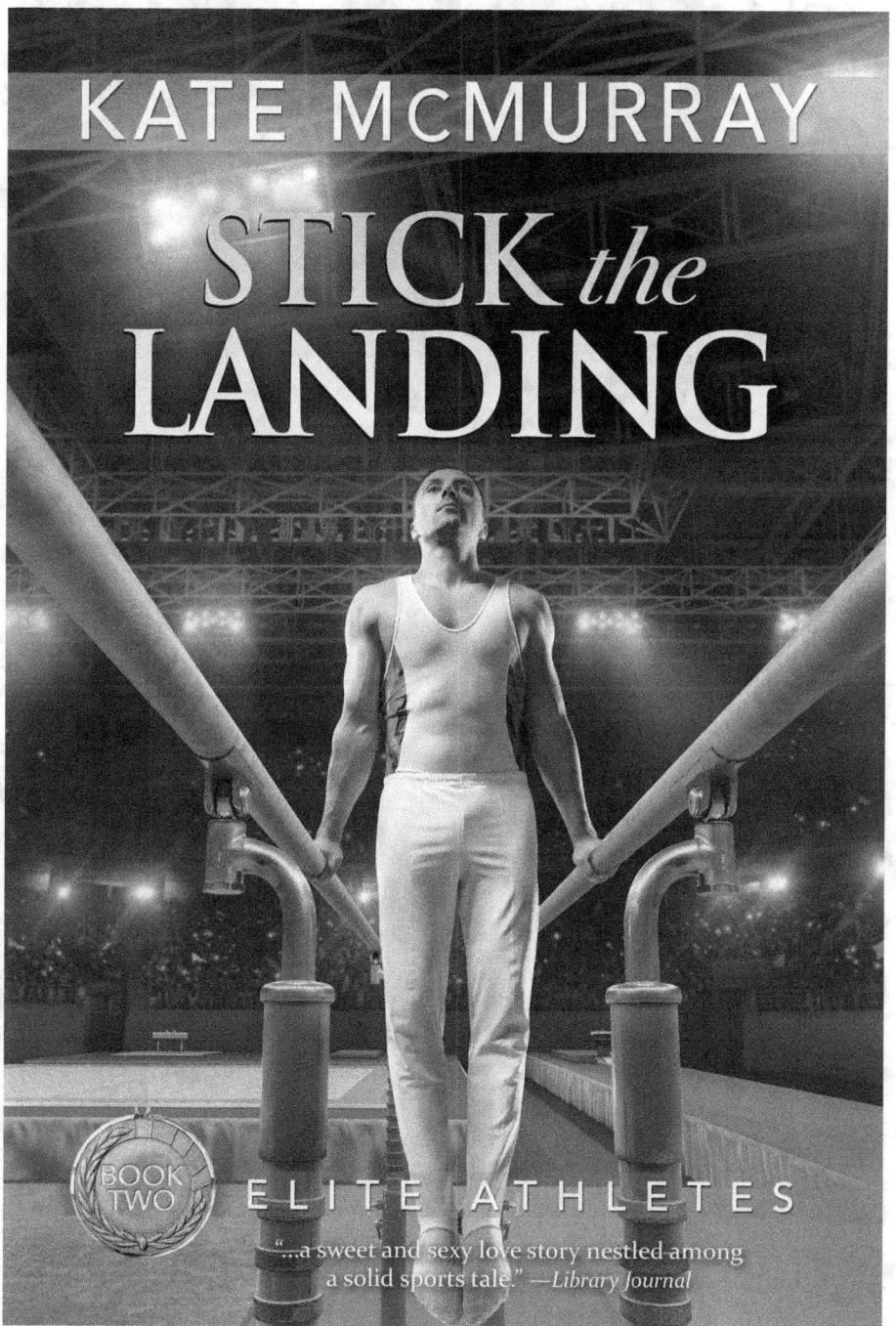

www.ingramcontent.com/pod-product-compliance
Lightning Source LLC
Chambersburg PA
CBHW070119260626
47160CB00004B/1543